LADY AT THE LODGE

The Wentworth Family Saga

Book Three

Graham Ley

SAPERE
BOOKS

LADY AT THE LODGE

Published by Sapere Books.

20 Windermere Drive, Leeds, England, LS17 7UZ,
United Kingdom

saperebooks.com

ISBN: 978-0-85495-147-5

CHAPTER I: AT HAZARD

Summer 1796, at sea off the Azores

Captain Richard Neville of the frigate HMS *Telamon* ducked into the master's cabin, approving of what he saw. It was bare and simple, with a quill and a pot of ink on a table. The master of the troopship, Nathaniel Beamish, was thickset and dark, and his face was devoid of expression, although Neville recalled him laughing easily enough back in Plymouth.

Beamish followed him into the cabin and pulled the door closed behind him. 'Nasty business, Captain,' he said in a low voice. 'Will you be wanting to see…?'

'No, thank you, that won't be necessary. He is guarded, you say?'

'There's a lock on the door, seeing as how it's the slop room, Captain. And I have the key here —' he tapped the side of his thick, black jacket — 'just to be sure.'

'Well, we should bring them in, Master Beamish. I am to be seated here, is that right?'

Beamish nodded and waved his hand towards what must have usually been his own chair, with the writing materials in front of it. He then swung back to the door and opened it. 'You may come in, gentlemen. The boys will stand,' he added sharply, as one who fitted that description came in with wide eyes.

Aside from his own men, there were two other officers in the mix, both of them in army red. Neville stood up to take the hand of infantry Major Stanton, whom Beamish had invited to come in a jolly boat from another of the transports to join the meeting. The major gave Neville a nod and sat down. A much younger man, also in a crimson coat but with less decoration to his shoulders, stood back, his face pale. Neville noted the lieutenant's nerves and wondered what lay behind them. Surely not his first death? The brigade had been elsewhere in Europe. In addition to the two army officers, Neville had William Craythorne, the sergeant of marines he had brought with him and his most reliable midshipman, Toby Fanshawe, who glanced at the wide-eyed ship's boy and then kept his eyes firmly on Neville. There was, finally, a balding man with wild hair and a loosely tied cravat, whom Neville took to be the surgeon.

'Well, gentlemen, we know why we are here,' Neville began. 'A most distressing circumstance so soon on our voyage out, and as yet unexplained.' Here he glanced instinctively at the army lieutenant, who kept his head bowed and his hands in front of him on the table. 'Mr Beamish has asked me to convene this meeting, and we shall try to keep it brief and to the purpose. Your account of it, Mr Beamish, if you please.'

'Yes, Captain. He was found this morning, I'm saddened to say, and of all places in the slop room. It was Will here who found him, and he came straight to me.'

'May we have his name, Mr Beamish?'

'Ay, sir. It is William Caws, although we all call him Will … or indeed Billy.'

Neville looked up from his pocket-book, in which he had scribbled a few details. 'The dead man's name, if you please, Mr Beamish.'

'Oh, yes, indeed. It is…'

'Thomas Thoresby, Tom. Ensign Thoresby,' said the army lieutenant, lifting his head up and looking first at Neville and then around the table. Now that the proceedings had started, he seemed more resolved.

'Thank you. And your name, sir?'

'Lieutenant Jack Harding, of the same company. A messmate.'

'Mr Beamish, who found Ensign Thoresby?'

'It was Will, Captain, William Caws — the ship's boy.'

Neville laid down his pen and sought the boy's eyes. 'Now tell us, Will, how you found the poor gentleman, if you would.'

Will, or Billy, as he preferred, pulled at the end of his sleeve with restless fingers. 'I was on lower, if you please, sir, not doing any harm, but...'

'Come on, now, out with it, Will. The captain can't have us all idling for too long...'

Beamish was not harsh, but his voice was firm. Will knew the tone too well, and so he plunged in.

'It was Tibby, sir. I've been looking for her. The other boy has too, but he would drown her kittens. So I wanted to get her first. Looked all over, too. But that's why I was on lower.'

Neville looked questioningly at Beamish, who spluttered, momentarily at a loss.

'The ship's cat, Tibby,' explained the ship's surgeon. 'She was carrying kittens and looking for a birthing pen.'

The midshipman looked disdainfully at the ship's boy, then returned to his former impassivity.

'I saw the door to the slops room was open, so I peeped in, but it wasn't Tibby,' Will went on.

Neville had started writing again. 'You will thank the boy, Mr Beamish. He may go for the moment, but he must stay just outside and be kept in your cabin after, if you do not mind. Surgeon, what is your name?'

'Oliver Cawden, Captain.'

'I believe you went down with Mr Beamish. Please could you describe what you saw?'

'Ensign Thoresby had a pistol wound in his left temple. There is no neat way of doing it.'

'When was this?'

'This morning, Captain,' said Beamish, 'forenoon watch, that is, say about five bells.'

'Very good, Mr Beamish. Mr Cawden, in your estimation, when did the ensign die?'

Cawden rubbed his chin. 'Not an hour or two earlier, I would judge. No, not long at all.'

'Thank you, Mr Cawden. That will be all that we require of you. You will keep mum, I trust, for the while, at least?'

The surgeon nodded, scraped back his chair, cleared his throat noisily, and left the room. Captain Neville laid down his pen and cracked his knuckles. The midshipman looked quickly to the other end of the room to hide his smile: Clicky Dicky, they called him in their berth, and in the officers' gunroom. The marine sergeant had caught his eye, but when they faced Neville, their faces were composed.

'Well, gentlemen, I believe I speak for the major as well as myself when I ask who may be able to shed light on this tragic incident?'

'Hear, hear,' said Major Stanton, who did not relish the drudgery of inquiry into incidents of this kind. Let the navy do what it could, and be done with it. But the silence continued, and so the major set his countenance and cleared his throat in order to follow his usual path, which was to look severe and turn matters over to a junior officer. The lieutenant read the signs, and decided to meet trouble halfway. His face went pale again.

'What is it that you have to tell us, Lieutenant Harding?' asked Captain Neville. He had no direct authority over the lieutenant, and no licence to reprimand or punish in the army; he simply wanted to know the truth.

'I fear it may be… That is to say, Tom had been distracted, sir, wandering off, rarely speaking…'

'Since when, Harding? Today, yesterday, a sennight ago? Bark it out, man!' The major did not appreciate Harding's failure to address him directly.

'Since … before we reached the Azores, Major.'

'Do you know why, Lieutenant?' asked Neville. 'Did he receive letters from home at the Azores? We are a slow convoy, by all measures, so there would be time for bad news to catch him up. Yet grief is one thing…'

'And money is another,' said Beamish. 'Come, Jack, if you don't tell, I shall.'

The major snorted, but he had begun to see how this might play out: it was looking ugly.

Lieutenant Harding looked at Captain Neville. 'There was gambling, sir. It's a long voyage, and the days are long too, cooped up as we are. Evenings are the same. It was nothing, but it got out of hand. Some of us dropped out, some were never in, but when the play got deep, we warned him — Tom, that is… He was only a lad. The ensigns are new in, and Tregothen — well, he drew them to him. We did our best to draw Tregothen off, too, but he was mad keen. He saw one or two of the younger men as gulls, which they were. Tom was the worst of them, poor lad.' The lieutenant fell silent, oblivious to the major's reddening face and the veins standing out in his neck.

Captain Neville was thoughtful. 'And then? Are we speaking of cards or dice, Lieutenant?'

'Cards at first, and then dice. We were all out by then, so we did not see it. They were on Hazard. Tom wanted to win it back, but he failed.'

The major could no longer contain himself. 'So where is Tregothen?'

'Lieutenant Tregothen disappeared at the Azores, did he not?' said Neville. 'So Ensign Thoresby would have been unable to play him again. I surmise that young Thoresby was ruined, and had perhaps deeply committed his father's income, too. Men have killed themselves for that before now.'

'I think you must be correct, sir!' Harding was impassioned now. 'Yes, Tregothen told us that he would be skipping transports, but only to the next port of call, to find others who liked a game and who were not such dull Jacks as we were.'

'Our next landfall is likely Antigua, Lieutenant, as any sailor would have informed you,' said Neville. 'It was a ruse; Tregothen never intended to change his berth. I presume that you will conduct a search, Major, but I doubt that we shall find him.'

'He is a scoundrel,' was all that the major had to add.

The scratching of Neville's pen could be heard for a minute or more. Then he looked up. 'Let me give you my verdict, gentlemen. We shall leave it to the army, of course, to notify Thoresby's family in the usual manner, and to pursue any matters of discipline. I take it that is proper, Major, in your judgment? Good. In the log I shall register a bare outline, by indicating "death by misadventure while in passage". This should satisfy the authorities, and prevent unnecessary upset to his family. But I must also emphasise that we gain nothing by letting the truth of this affair be known amongst the convoy. Should any ask, use the word apoplexy, and shrug your shoulders. Lieutenant Harding, seal the mouths of your fellow-officers. I hardly need to tell you how poorly incidents of this kind are taken, so soon into a voyage. Seamen are of a most superstitious disposition.'

None spoke, although feet scraped under the table, so Neville continued.

'The arrangements will be as follows: you and your marines, Sergeant Craythorne, will stay on this ship under the command of Midshipman Fanshawe, who will be acting strictly to my orders. Mr Fanshawe, you will have the body wrapped, trussed and laden with ballast. We cannot offer Thoresby a full service. Once troops and the day crew have retired this evening, you will follow Master Beamish to where he chooses and offer the body to the sea. Master Beamish, I shall provide you with a short prayer to read. Tomorrow, at first light, I shall send the cutter for my marines. I think that covers everything. We must be very discreet, gentlemen. The event itself is bad enough; we want no aftermath. Thank you, gentlemen, we have stayed long enough. The ship's master will accommodate you and your men, Sergeant. Keep out of the light as much as you can.'

Neville stood up, stretched, and closed his pocket-book. The men filed out, with Beamish quietly passing on some instructions.

'Mr Fanshawe?' said Neville.

The midshipman came back to the table.

'You are to see that they keep to it well, Toby — our marines, that is. The master will manage his side capably enough. Above all, you must wait until the swell comes up, and then order them to let go. I would rather seamen did it, but seamen talk amongst themselves, while marines have no words with them if they can avoid it.'

The midshipman left the cabin. Captain Neville took one more look round the room and stepped out after him.

Jowan Tregothen stood on the deck of the schooner with his face turned aft, relishing the wind. He could tell that this was a south-westerly, and it would have him home far faster than he had imagined. He could smell the scent of the oranges wafting up from the hold. It was strange and amusing to be in the company of a cargo of fruit rather than malodorous soldiers. Still, they had been fun, young and lively, unaware for the most part of what awaited them at the end of their voyage. He had made enquiries, and he knew what army service in the West Indies meant, and that was an early burial at the bottom of a pestilence pit. Troops were dying in their thousands, not from the enemy, Toussaint or the regular French, but from the assortment of diseases that abounded in those climes. He could not put a name to them, but he had been told of the fevers, and that was enough for him.

He breathed in deeply, then glanced over towards the steersman, who was not looking at him. What he really needed was a bottle of wine, but he only got a glass at the meagre dinner at the captain's table, and he chose not to linger there for fear of attracting too much curiosity. In Ponta Delgada, he had handed over his uniform to a shopkeeper in exchange for a decent set of clothing that would get him through the short voyage and ashore. He wanted to appear as a travelling Englishman.

He let his thoughts drift back to the excitement of the last week. Ensign Thoresby, the young fool, had played himself into a corner, coming back again and again, to Tregothen's astonishment as note after note was passed across to him. These were not the casual IOUs of a disappointing game, but what amounted to a whole inheritance. Tregothen suspected the debts could only be redeemed by the boy's family. Then it had to stop. The pleading was the worst of it: he had to strike the distraught ensign to make him see sense — that there was no calling back what had been done. After that, Thoresby had taken to wandering madly around the ship, and Tregothen had begun to fear that it might all go sour, despite the debts being matters of honour.

He shook his head. Usually he had the most abysmal luck: he had lost on horses, around the cockpit, on pugilists, and on two flies crawling up a wall in one case, admittedly in boyhood years. What had happened on the troopship had no precedent. He was therefore transfixed by what might even have been his skill, at least with cards. Yet the ensigns were young lads, after all, trapped below decks with nothing to do. The dice were another matter, and the play had made him sweat as it eventually came down to just the two of them. Why the bones had kept falling as they had, he did not know. It was devilish, there was no other word for it.

Tregothen had resigned his commission. The letter was even now in his pocket, and he would time its delivery before the news of his jumping ship returned from the West Indies. Then he was done with it. He had a handsome endowment here, stowed in his pocket, and that would be so even if old man Thoresby came up with some way to cast doubt on the debts. But pay them he would — out of shame if not for honour — just as Tregothen's own father had done in times past. The schooner was bound first for Salcombe, which would suit him well. He had business down in the west, and the banks in Tavistock would meet his needs for a start; then he would have to go to London. He had debts of his own to pay ashore, but they did not concern money. No, they were more what you might call tit for tat. The prospect made him smile.

CHAPTER II: THE DOWAGER REMEMBERS

Sempronie Wentworth wrinkled her nose in the mirror and pushed at one of the lines in her forehead. She was not usually given to gazing at her own image, but the forthcoming birth of her first grandchild was having a distinct effect on her, and her maid Betty had left the room to gather refreshments. The months had rushed by since the news that her son Justin and his wife, Arabella, were expecting a child, and life had been at sixes and sevens ever since. Yet oddly enough, the ailment from which Sempronie had suffered last autumn and winter had gradually diminished, and she felt well again.

She was now the dowager of the Chittesleigh estate, which had become the property of her son on his father's death. After Justin had married Arabella, Sempronie and her daughter Amelia had left the manor and moved into the dower house at Endacott. The distance was not great: there were only some ten miles between them. Both houses were in the heart of Devon, north of Dartmoor, and Hatherleigh was the closest town. Endacott had originally been purchased by Sempronie's late father-in-law, but had undergone improvements during the last year. Some of their acquaintance from Hatherleigh had already visited at Endacott, despite their short residence to date, the most assiduous being Thomas Darke, although the vicar Cradock Glasscott had also ridden out. Sempronie might have managed well with rather less of Thomas Darke, but he was an old friend of her husband's, and since his passing Darke had taken on a watchful role. Now she was out here, and more often on her own, there might be occasions when that attention would be more valued.

After moving out of Chittesleigh, which had been hard, she had had little time to get settled at Endacott. First she and Amelia had travelled down to Cornwall, to stay in the cottage that belonged to Colonel and Miss North of Polton Court, and then she had returned to Chittesleigh alone to visit Justin and Arabella. But she had found herself subject to restlessness, and had not stayed with them for long. There was that strange sentiment of being a little lost, of not quite belonging, and all the movement between residences had sharpened it into a longing to return to Brittany, her birthplace. She had known that whatever ailment she had could return at any time, and she might never be able to travel again.

The floorboard creaked in the passage outside, and Betty came in.

'Here we are, ma'am. You'll forgive me for pouring the cup, but I must get back on down for the hot water.'

'Thank you, Betty. There need be no haste this morning. We are idle, as far as I am aware.'

If Betty had any thoughts about idleness, she kept them to herself and pulled the door closed behind her.

Sempronie pushed the fine Worcester cup around on its saucer and mused. Despite his misgivings about the journey, Justin had arranged for her to cross the Channel with a discreet American sea captain named Harker. She had landed safely on the shores of Brittany and made her way to Kergohan, her old family estate. How it had all come back to her! Everything she saw there reminded her of her Breton childhood and her parents. Harker could come and go from France with impunity, and for the moment he was also released from any threat in England. The timing of Sempronie's journey was fortunate. But if anything, the visit increased her sense of detachment from the country she had adopted when she had married the Englishman, Wentworth. The beautiful Kergohan Manor was hers by right, as a de Guèrinec, even if she visited it now as an alien, almost in disguise. Since the revolution in France, lands had been confiscated, hers too, and the war between France and England, and the revolt of the Bretons against the new Republic, had set more than a physical distance between her and what had been hers.

Sempronie brushed away tears. At least her cousin, Laurent Guèvremont, son of her father's sister, had managed to acquire the manor and its estate, through various shady dealings with the Republican authorities. She had been able to negotiate with him in person, quite remarkably, about the boy Gilles, who still worked at Kergohan and was now about seventeen years of age. Gilles had foolishly entangled himself in the conflict with the Republic, but with Justin's help, he had extricated himself. Justin would not discuss how this had been achieved in any detail. Men could be so secretive, and Justin and his close friend Eugène Picaud were of that kind, prompted no doubt by activities that they had undertaken clandestinely, on behalf of the government and those in revolt against the French republic.

'Picaud' was an alias that Eugène used to obscure his aristocratic origins, and despite the risks he had been by Sempronie's side in Brittany. He knew of her negotiations with Guèvremont and had supported her when she had briefly returned to her beloved Kergohan. Le Guinec, Guèvremont's deceitful steward, was no longer in charge there. He had been replaced by a man named Daniel Galouane, who was reserved and polite. Daniel was from Saint-Domingue across the sea; Sempronie rather suspected he had been a slave but was now free. Her cousin had brought him there through some connection he had, and she had seen how he was beginning to restore the manor house and the estate. Daniel seemed to work well alongside Babette, a woman who had lived on the Kergohan estate since childhood. It might be that something would come of that friendship; even if Babette was no longer young, her looks were unimpaired.

Babette was the one who had taken on Gilles as a baby, and she had kept him with her all this time. They had made provision for her, but she had not wanted much. The steward of the manor and estate at that time, Mael Sarzou, and his wife had been desolated by the death of Gilles's mother, and Sempronie herself had been shocked, although the fact that the young woman was with child had in itself been disturbing news. The young mother had persisted in her refusal to declare who the father was, and if the priest *Père* Guillaume had heard it from her in confession, he would not speak.

As time went by, they had seen that Gilles had fair hair — a rarity in their community — and the suspicion had grown that Laurent Guèvremont was his father. Guèvremont had often visited Kergohan and had been seen with the young woman. Sempronie had even had occasion to speak to him herself about it, since she was the older of the two and destined to be *baronne* of the manor. Guèvremont's grandmother — his father's mother — had had the same hair as Gilles, and so did Guèvremont himself.

As Sempronie reflected on this, Betty knocked and carried in a jug and basin, and tutted at her mistress as only she could. 'Well, ma'am, you have not touched your drink. It will be cold by now. Let me fetch you another, and then I shall help you dress yourself.'

'Do not concern yourself, Betty. I am slow this morning. I shall wash myself contentedly enough, but I shall call on you to dress me. I am sure there are things you may do in the interval. I shall not keep you waiting long, I assure you.'

Betty smiled and bobbed to her mistress, and Sempronie returned to her musings.

Gilles's mother had a sister and parents. Mael Sarzou, the steward, had said that he thought they believed the young woman was godless in her sin, and would not accept her back into the family. The sister was called Jeanne, if Sempronie remembered rightly, and had been no kinder than her parents. How could people be so cruel? Still, she was relieved to have settled the matter. She had acted on an impulse when she met her cousin in Brittany, although she had discussed the possibilities with Justin before she left England. Kergohan was now lost to the Wentworths: they would never be able to take repossession of it. She had said her farewells to the ghosts and the empty rooms. But Guèvremont was a practical man, and something had drawn him already to acquire Kergohan, with some difficulty, no doubt: all Sempronie had wanted to do was offer him profitable enterprises which she possessed, in title at least, and to resign in perpetuity any claim to the manor. In return, she could hope that Guèvremont would agree to passing over the manor and lands of Kergohan to Gilles, whom she insisted was his son.

She sighed. It was probably the right decision. She knew from Babette and from her own son that as a boy Gilles had become warmly attached to Justin, and had even let himself believe that Justin was his father, though he accepted that Babette was not his real mother. Justin had a certain quality, which he took from his father: both men and women looked to him, becoming almost devoted. Thinking of his father, she found that compulsion all too easy to remember.

Sempronie picked up her facecloth and poured some water into the bowl. She dipped the cloth and wiped her face. The warmth was comforting. She glanced again in the mirror and resolved to give more time to her daughter. Amelia was visiting London with her friend Caroline North, who was of an age to be a chaperone for her. Sempronie hoped that this London visit proved to be more successful than Plymouth and the Dock had been for them.

What was it the poet Virgil had said? Those three words: *sunt lacrimae rerum*. Her husband had told her it meant that there was sadness in life, but she preferred the more literal translation he had given from the Latin, although he had doubted if it was accurate: *there are tears in things*.

CHAPTER III: TO BE A GENTLEMAN

Kergohan Manor, Brittany

Babette lay on her back on the pallet, putting her hands behind her head. She had been sleeping with her arm over her husband, Daniel Galouane, but he was peaceful now, and her shoulder was beginning to ache. It was dark, and there was no sound from the rest of the manor. But then she heard scratching under the floorboards — a mouse, for sure. One of the shutters was awry on its hinges, and some moonlight filtered through.

The other women had joked with Babette as the day of her wedding had come closer. They had told her all kinds of things that did not seem likely, laughing at her innocence. She had seen cattle coupling, but it was always over quickly, with the bull shaking his neck afterwards. She had been too young to ask questions about intimacy before her mother died, and she had never let a man get close to her.

Babette had been sure that lying with a man must hurt, because as a girl she had heard what she thought were groans and screams of pain when she had gone outside one night to relieve herself. Still, it was never going to be for her, while she was looking after Gilles as a baby and then a boy after his mother died.

But marriage to Daniel had changed all that, as Gilles grew more independent. Everything was now different, and she had even been able to laugh at the joy of it all. She had not expected the extraordinary ease and pleasure she had felt when her husband had first held her, and she now dreamed of conceiving a child of her own.

Next to her, Daniel moved in his sleep. Babette breathed in as the scent of his body came to her, and she sensed herself stirring. She turned towards him although it was late, reaching for his warm belly.

By the middle of the morning, Gilles of Kergohan — the boy whom Babette had brought up — was in the bakehouse. It had been attached to the side of the manor kitchen for as long as anyone could remember, and Daniel and Babette as stewards of the manor had been unsure whether they should renovate it and put it back into operation. Gilles was in favour, since he liked the idea of baking for the village as had been the case in the past, and so he took it on. The doorway was a mess, and some parts of the outer stone walls had opened up. Gilles had plugged those gaps, and he was now working with the cob mix on the inside of the upper walls. The hearth itself was in good condition, but the roof of the oven would need the same level of renovation that Daniel was undertaking for the side-oven inside the house. From time to time, Gilles went into the kitchen to see how it was done. However, he often ran into Héloïse Argoubet, Daniel's niece, who would tease him and distract him, and so he did not stay for long.

Daniel had his head and shoulders stuck in the smaller oven in the kitchen. Héloïse reached down into a basket of moist clay and handed up fistfuls to him. He slapped it into the holes and cracks that had formed. Over time Héloïse got bored and took to tickling his feet, since they stuck out as Daniel levered his upper body around in the small space. He then banged his head on the roof of the oven, and Héloïse had to stick her own head into it to apologise to him. As usual he forgave her

21

instantly. Babette had talked to him about that, saying it might not be good for her always to be let off. He had agreed, but he kept on doing it. In the end, Daniel told her to take a break and go and see what Babette was doing.

Héloïse found Babette up in the cider house, where she was soaking the barrels Daniel had made in preparation for the first batch for several years. Babette believed that if she kept them damp, they would not shrink during the later summer months before the apples were harvested. She brought the buckets of water up laboriously by herself, but when Héloïse appeared she asked her to take the handcart and maybe fetch Yannic to help her. Yannic came down to the manor from time to time, like other men and boys from the village, as much out of curiosity as anything else, although Babette was clear that in the case of the grown men, day-payment in eggs and cheese was not enough, and there would have to be something else when the autumn came. In Yannic's case, it had become obvious to Gilles that despite his nagging pursuit of Yaelle's younger sister up in the village, Yannic had his eye on Héloïse too. This made Gilles react very badly indeed, so Yannic took to whistling casually through his teeth while he worked if Gilles caught sight of him.

When Héloïse came to find him, Yannic brushed the hair from his eyes and put aside his rake to help her draw the water from the well. She was heaving on the rope because she wanted to take the lead, but while she was leaning over the well-top Yannic leaned across her to lend a hand. His expression was relaxed, his eyes innocent. She pushed him away, but not angrily, and then told him to draw the second bucket himself.

At that moment Gilles came out of the bakehouse, covered in clay and dust, and when he saw them together he dusted his hands, placed them on his hips, and glowered at them both. Nothing could have provoked Héloïse more, so she stood close to Yannic and made a show of placing her hands on his as they passed the bucket between them, all the while darting glances at Gilles. For his part, Yannic broke his own rules and grinned over at Gilles, who spun on his heel and walked into the kitchen. Héloïse's blood was up now. She pulled the handcart up the slope next to Yannic, bumping into him and not caring what anyone thought.

Babette was waiting at the top of the hill. She waved to them both, but by now the heat was on them, and they could hardly wait to get the buckets into the pressing house, close the door and go stealthily round the side. Héloïse did not resist as Yannic placed his hands on her, and though she avoided his mouth, she let him kiss her neck once, which made her draw in her breath sharply. Yet that was enough: she was beginning to get scared. Babette might come round the corner at any moment, and there was the priest to consider. She hurriedly put her hand on his shoulder, eased him back slightly, and tried to slip away.

Yannic breathed on her cheek. 'Not so fast, my lovely. Now's our chance,' he said in her ear.

Héloïse began to panic as he pressed her against the side of the barn. She could feel him hard against her now, and she was both shocked and terrified. She fought to keep his hands from her breasts, but she could not scream or shout, ashamed that Babette would know what they had been about.

Just then, the bell rang from down in the courtyard at the manor. It broke in on them, and Yannic released his tight hold on her in surprise. It was just enough for Héloïse to break free and run round to the door of the pressing-house for safety, then off down the slope. Babette came out of the shadows inside, drying her hands on her skirt. She looked shrewdly at Héloïse running down the hill, and heard Yannic's steps going up and away through the orchard. But the bell had her attention, and although she did not fear fire or a disaster, since Daniel, Gilles and one or two other men from the village were there in the manor, she wondered what it was that could not wait. She would speak to Héloïse afterwards; having a girl to look after as well as a boy was a new burden.

There were two good horses down in the yard, and Daniel, Gilles and a man wearing a cravat were standing around looking at them. One of the horses was brown, the other black. They were sleek, well-cared-for, and big. They would take some handling. Héloïse moved across to one of the animals, stroking its neck and whispering to it. The horse shook its head and stamped one hoof; but it then stood quietly while Héloïse continued stroking it. She kept her eyes away from everyone, which strengthened Babette's suspicions about what she had been up to. It was worrying. The man who had ridden in with the horses looked familiar, but he and Daniel went off round the stables and out into the fields. Gilles followed them. Babette decided to get into the kitchen and prepare some food. She had been there for a short while when there was a shuffle at the door, and she looked up to see Héloïse.

'Can I help?' asked Héloïse. 'I can fetch some eggs. There were some there this morning.'

Babette smiled and nodded; from the way she ran off, it was obvious that Héloïse was relieved. She came back some minutes later, put the eggs down on the table, and picked up the basket of clay by the oven, which she took outside. Nothing was said. Babette went quietly to the door and saw

Héloïse looking at the bakehouse, tracing the work that Gilles had been doing with her fingers. She then crossed to the horses, drew a bucket of water from the well, fetched a small trough from the stables, and poured the water into it.

The cock crowed out the back, and the hens came fussing through the yard. A tethered cow looked up from the field, and then went back to ripping grass. The horses drank, the brown one pushing the other aside and then allowing it to drink, before giving a final, sharp nip to show who was in charge. Daniel came across to her, and Gilles went over to the horses with the man who was somehow familiar to her. Suddenly, Héloïse was nowhere to be seen.

Daniel spoke to Babette. 'Gilles has been sent for by *Monsieur* Guèvremont. He will go to Auray. Do not be concerned. *Monsieur* Guèvremont wants him to learn accounting, and he will be taught. The man with the necktie is Guèvremont's steward. Guèvremont wants Gilles to be a gentleman. He will be taught to ride as well.'

Babette nodded. This was as she had expected, sooner or later. Gilles was already good with practical matters, and he was picking up the management of the estate, learning about buildings and crops from Daniel. 'For how long? I hope he will be home again for the harvesting. I shall get him a bag of clothes. We can send on more later, if he is staying. As it is, what he takes now will have to be slung on the back of the horse, I suppose. Do they know that he can hardly ride?'

Daniel laughed. 'Well, he hasn't said, but he will have to own up to that quite soon. He may need a leading rein, looking at that brute. It's a big one.'

Babette went up the stairs, and came down slightly out of breath with a bag of clothes. It was a hot summer; Gilles would not need much for the time being. And Guèvremont would probably furnish him with some decent clothing, to be presentable in the town. She passed the bag to Daniel. All of a sudden, she remembered the stranger's name: Le Guinec. He was the steward who had replaced poor old Mael Sarzou, who had vanished into the *landes* somewhere. She thought she knew something else about the man, but she could not remember what it was.

Le Guinec saw her looking, and waved at her in acknowledgement. He was holding the bridle of the black horse, and in a friendly way he motioned Gilles up into the saddle. Gilles mounted the horse with relative ease, so he smiled back at Babette. Out of the corner of her eye, Babette saw Héloïse, standing in the shadow of the stables. Daniel reached up and secured the clothes bag behind the saddle. It would have to do for now. Babette walked over to Gilles and gave him her hand. He bent down and kissed it. Le Guinec placed a hat on his black, wavy hair, then lifted it to bow slightly to Babette, who curtsied in response.

The brown horse with Le Guinec on it suddenly moved away. Gilles was caught unawares, and as his black mount started to follow its partner, he fell backwards towards its rump. It was undignified, and he rocked forwards quickly to grab the pommel of the saddle, gradually sitting upright again as the horse kept walking. Le Guinec looked over his shoulder to check that his charge was still in the saddle.

The riders passed Babette and Héloïse, who were now standing together at the end of the stables. Gilles had been blushing and prepared to stare out Héloïse's mockery, but to his astonishment she had not laughed at him. Her face was grave, and as he glanced back at her, he began to feel worried. He would have liked to say goodbye, and he wanted to see if he could sense what was wrong. But all of a sudden the two horses passed the end of the building and walked up the sloping track. The last he heard was the cockerel, and then there was only the sound of the creaking saddle, and the horses' hooves kicking the loose stones.

CHAPTER IV: THE ABSENCE OF HIGHWAYMEN

England

The post-chaise rumbled contentedly over the road, but Amelia Wentworth reached quickly for the handle as it lurched sharply to one side and then righted itself. She heard a curt reprimand to the horses from the postilion through the open side window. Her companion, Caroline North, awoke from what she would later assert was a brief slumber and exclaimed, 'Heavens!' She then readjusted the skirt of her gown, gazed out of her window, and then drifted back to sleep.

The journey to London out of Cornwall and Devon made Amelia muse on the subject of highwaymen, or the gentlemen of the road. Experience had taught her that 'gentleman' was a rather loose term, and that the manners and conduct of those so called were often even looser. Since the events in Plymouth, she was also no stranger to their abrupt and wilful violence. Amelia had been obliged to rescue her friend, an actress named Thirza Farley, from Lieutenant Tregothen — a brute who had assaulted Miss Farley in her own lodgings. Tregothen had subsequently been forced to accept a commission in the regular army, and shipped off to fight in the West Indies. Amelia, however, had succumbed to a fever, and her constitution was still weak.

Caroline stirred, cleared her throat and opened her eyes. She turned to Amelia and spoke kindly. 'You are quite well,

Amelia? Is something the matter, child? I heard you sigh, I believe.'

'No, nothing, thank you.'

'Well, m'dear, a penny for your thoughts, then. I had momentarily lapsed into being poor company, I fear, but I shall make it up to you now.'

'Oh, very little of any worth, Caroline. I was just wondering how many capes or collars a highwayman might have to his greatcoat.'

'A highwayman? I trust we shall see none of those.'

The carriage creaked noisily again. Amelia decided to tease her companion a little further. 'Yet I believe I overheard your brother the colonel saying that the heaths near London were a dangerous stage of the journey, and even that one notorious criminal had taken to riding postilion in order to draw his victims into a trap.'

Caroline was indignant at her brother Colonel North's indiscretion in allowing this vulnerable young woman to hear such a thing on the eve of a long journey. 'Well, George should know better than to set wild ideas flying! Wherever could he have heard such a thing? I'll wager it is from stable talk. I shall have stern words with him when I return. You must not be unsettled by such tattle, Amelia, after all you have been through. Why, there is Sam, up above, to accompany us, and...'

'And Sam has a heavy pistol at his feet.'

Caroline waved her hand in disbelief at this revelation, and Amelia laughed at her friend's discomfiture.

'Come, Caroline, the colonel should not be blamed for his precautions. No doubt Sam is happy to play the man, with Martha there beside him.'

'I shall have none of that, Melia, for you tell me she is a good girl. Besides, she will be lucky to get three words together out of Sam, with two of those three being on horseflesh.'

Though the journey was tedious, Amelia felt safe enough in the company of Sam Rigg, their coachman, and Martha Cox, Amelia's maid. The countryside rolled by, green and placid. For a while the road surface was surprisingly even, and the travellers found they did not have to raise their voices.

'So, come now, we must change our subject. You shall not miss Cornwall?'

Caroline's question was not quite as innocent as it seemed, and to her annoyance Amelia found herself blushing. She turned her face away to look into the haze of the landscape, and mustered what she hoped was a confident tone.

'Oh, no, not at all. That is, I have the best of it with me, barring the colonel, of course, and his good graces and boundless courtesy.'

Caroline considered that it was just as well that her brother had not heard this description of himself, so guilelessly given but hardly encouraging to the fond hopes he still nourished. 'We shall miss our dear Eugène, I know we shall. So attentive, too, not least to your mother...'

'Yes, Eugène is a good friend to our family,' Amelia answered reticently. She was still staring out of her window, now at a towering white cloud over the brow of some wooded hills.

Caroline reached out a gloved hand and placed it lightly on Amelia's. '*Monsieur* Eugène Picaud's duties summon him, Melia, and he will be back amongst us before we have concluded our stay in London, which will be full of diversion. Come, now, he took his leave of us with as much apology — as properly and as civilly — as might have been asked of him. That we do not know precisely where he is and what he is doing...'

'What we do know is that he will undoubtedly be sailing directly into danger, as my brothers did before him, and that there is none who can say he will return alive. It is in the nature of war. We also know —' and here Amelia could not quite restrain a smile, despite her evident distress — 'that he will be fearfully seasick on the voyage, as he always is by his own account.'

'So it is, Amelia, and we must make the best of it. The war, I mean, not his *mal de mer*. We have much to do in London, and many sympathisers to meet in the cause of abolition. What is more, we can rest assured that Eugène will be back to rescue you from some unforeseen hazard.'

Amelia went quiet, and looked closely at the cloud, which was now changing shape.

For some weeks before Eugène had unexpectedly announced his departure, Amelia had sensed that something was in the air, and she had experienced partly excitement and partly apprehension. Since her confrontation with Tregothen in Miss Farley's apartment, and her stark recognition of the injuries he had caused the actress, she had been far more prone to a flux of emotions — a presentiment of some disaster being the strongest. She had returned to Polton Court to resume her visit to Caroline and George North, residing once again at the cottage in the grounds. She had done her best to shake off anxious feelings as they arose, but she was rarely successful. On Colonel North's invitation, Eugène had come to stay at Polton for a week. Though Eugène and the colonel had visited Amelia and her mother at Polton cottage together in the first instance, they had chosen to make subsequent visits separately.

In the parlour, Eugène had chatted to Amelia about his schooldays, finding humour in everything, imitating speech and manners, even gently mocking her brother Justin, who had been like an elder brother to him. He mimicked his own family as well, including his mother with her scolding and the Touraine dialect that she used.

On the morning he had told Amelia he was leaving, Eugène had first regaled her with some anecdotes of the military life he had shared with Justin, suitably modified for her feminine ear. He then sprang on her the suggestion of their favoured walk down to the stream which ran through the colonel's estate. The sun was warm, the breeze light, and the path was dry and firm. Amelia took his arm while holding her parasol in her other hand. He was silent for a while, and she stole a look at his face, which seemed grave. This did not escape Eugène's notice; he lifted his head, grinned, and squeezed her hand, but soon reverted to his reverie.

Amelia felt the flutter of panic that had become her companion all too often recently, but she did not know what to say. Eugène stopped their walk for a moment.

'Miss Wentworth, this has been a most delightful week. I hope I have been some distraction to you. At times I have felt you to be languishing a little — pardon me for my boldness. Granted, what you have seen… I do hope you will forgive my foolishness as much as you have indulged it. Like many things for which some apology is due, it was meant well.'

Amelia took her arm from his and placed her parasol in the hand closest to him. She found that she did not know quite what to say to him, so she took a few steps forward. Her words came out stiffly, but she tried to lighten the tone as she progressed. 'How could you doubt that your presence at Polton and at the cottage has brought my mother and me entertainment, and in my case, some degree of comfort? Although I admit that I remain unsure whether I should call you Mr Picaud, or *Monsieur* Picaud, or even Picaud at all.'

'I… Yes, I confess that is very trying. But as exiles, we are under certain constraints still. Which brings me…'

It was evident that there was something that he needed to say, and that he was finding it difficult. Amelia wanted to make it easier for him, although her own pulse was hardly regular. Perhaps the calming effect of rippling water might come to their aid.

'Let us go to the bank of the stream. The path leads to it directly, and there is our little gravel beach that affords us a sound footing, before we return to avoid the heat of the day.'

'Yes, of course,' he said.

They walked on, and Amelia kept her eyes on the path, trying to conjure up the prospect of something unlooked-for and yet pleasant in what was to come. They reached the bank of the stream in silence, and with one hand he helped her down a slight slope onto the gravel. She folded her parasol and stood gazing at the black water.

Eugène coughed. 'I must take my leave. That is, not just leave Polton Court, which must be expected, since I cannot presume on the colonel's hospitality further. I … have to leave the country again, to embark from Plymouth. The rest…'

Amelia could not look at him. Her fear was profound. She knew he would die. The parasol hung down uselessly from her wrist. Eventually, she forced out some words. 'When will you leave? I cannot ask where you will go. Brittany, or perhaps America, Canada, even, where my mother says they speak French…'

In her agitation, Amelia turned quickly towards her companion, but the skirt of her gown was caught by the parasol, and her feet slipped on some wet clay that lay to the side of the gravel. Her body hit the soft, sloping bank and she slid into the water. Eugène leapt forwards, too late to catch her but immediately by her side, knee-deep in the stream, attempting to pull her gently upright. She slipped again, even deeper, and he quickly put his arms under her and lifted her clear of the water. There were strands of weed in her hair and across her face.

Amelia gave way to her feelings. She cried into his shoulder, great racking sobs, the water from her gown drenching them both. With just a moment's hesitation, he touched his lips gently on her forehead, and her hand gripped his arm compulsively.

She spoke softly, and in French. 'You may set me down.'

He did so, and stood back, but not very far.

She laughed a little. 'What a fool. It is just as well I left my bonnet. I must look a fright.'

'We must beware of a chill. With your permission…?'

He moved a little closer and detached some strands of the weed from her hair, then placed his frock coat around her shoulders. She was calmer. But in looking at her and touching her, he was a lost man.

'And now we have soaked your coat, thoroughly. Perhaps we may walk back.'

Which they had done. He came the next day to enquire after her, and to take his leave. There was some laughter. She was convinced that she would never see him alive again.

Brentford had been the last stop before London itself, with the final change of horses and the dirty inn. There were harsh accents here, an odd mixture of rudeness and almost abject servility, which left Martha wide-eyed, a country girl in the largest city in the world.

London presented a strange, shifting pattern. At one moment, the tall houses on either side seemed to create walls for the carriages that passed by, a world of stone laced with ironwork, with remote figures glimpsed fleetingly through the windows. But then, without any warning, there appeared a wide park, with rides along its outer edges and walks across it, and bonnets and hats in a bewildering parade of shapes and styles. This panorama was followed by streets of shops where high fashion was in evidence, both in the elaborate displays and on the people who strode or glided by, their parasols or canes at a jaunty angle.

Yet in other parts, where the streets lost their veneer of elegance, there was a different impression. The few shuttered shops were dingy, but in their place were all kinds of sellers, and far more women than Amelia had noticed before. They had hens in cages, a few flowers and vegetables on trays, glistening fish and shellfish, and piles of drab and worn clothes, like those in which the sellers were dressed. In narrower streets and in the warmth of the day, the smells became overpowering, not from rotting produce but probably from some factory. Then again there was a change, the sellers replaced by large stone buildings and hurrying men in dark clothes, high collars and cravats. There were tall doors pushed back, and more and more carriages, some finely painted, others tatty, jostling and blocking each other as the drivers gesticulated and shouted at each other.

The post-chaise swung from side to side, scraping perilously past the wheels of one box-like vehicle. It then rolled a little way down the street and, with some cries to the horses from the postilion, came to a halt. Caroline looked keenly out of the window, and called up to Sam to come down to the carriage door, and set the step for her.

'We are looking for a brass plate set on the stone, which announces the premises of Easton and Blunt, Bankers. That is, if the postilion knows his direction, and this is truly Lombard Street at last,' she said. 'Bear up, Amelia, we are nearly at the end of our journey.'

The door swung open, and Sam stood aside for Caroline to descend. She peered back into the compartment.

'Sam will hand Martha down, and she will sit with you now, Amelia,' she reassured her friend. 'I shall look for Easton and his clerk. The man's name is Joseph Claydon, as you will recall. It is with his aunt that we shall be staying. He will accompany us to Hampstead, which is a little out of town — with fresher air, I hope. Sam will stand by the horses, in case the postilion decides to head off to the stables before we have descended. Look to Martha first, Sam. Now, where is that brass plate?'

Amelia nodded. She had been told of the arrangements before, and was content to leave Caroline to make contact in the manner which her brother had settled with such care. Besides, her head was too full of lively impressions of the city, and she felt both numbed and astounded. Even here, in what she had been told was a discreet banking quarter of great respectability, there was an immense bustle. Just across the street stood a building which men entered and exited like bees in a hive. They all carried packets and sacks. She thought that this must be the general Post Office of which Colonel North had spoken, one of the busiest places in the country aside from the dock, he had said. Her eye was caught by a young woman by the door of the Post Office, without a bonnet and in a strange style of dress. It did not seem that what she was wearing was either new or *à la mode*, and her attitude seemed odd, standing still as she was alongside so many running men.

Amelia's concentration was broken by a series of cries, and the magnificent sight of a coach swinging into the road led by a team of four horses. There were shouts to the driver and into the building, and boys rushed out of it. The coachman called out to the passengers, while his guard handed down sacks and parcels. Around the straps of the harnesses Amelia could see lather on the horses, who had clearly been driven hard. A boy ran out with nosebags, while others scuttled down the side of the building and returned with pails of water.

Caroline was still delayed, and Amelia's attention drifted again to the young woman, who was now alert. Amelia sensed a romance and watched as the passengers dispersed, some from on high, and others from inside the coach. The young woman did not immediately see whom she wanted to see. But, at last, a young man jumped down from the mail-coach and stretched his limbs briefly. He was sporting a fantail hat, pulled down a little to one side, and a double-breasted waistcoat with fashionable wide lapels. Amelia watched as the young woman moved away from the wall and came over to him. He took a bag from the rear of the coach, then, hearing what the young woman said to him, he lifted his hat to her and smiled.

Amelia saw his face quite clearly, and with astonishment recognised it. The couple crossed the road, strolled down to a stand of hackney carriages, spoke to a driver and climbed into one. Amelia stepped down from the chaise, walked the short distance along the street, and looked over at the door of the mail-coach. Plainly written on it in gold lettering below the window, on a wine-red background above the royal coat of arms, were the words 'Plymouth London'.

Eugène Picaud had not sailed away from Plymouth as he had said he would.

The hackney coach set its two passengers down by one of the long, tree-lined walks in St James's Park, which bordered conveniently on the Horse Guards building. They strolled side by side, Eugène with his hat under his arm now that its identifying purpose had been fulfilled. The young woman had a firm step, and she had no difficulty in keeping pace with him. They talked very little, and each looked up from time to time at the clock on the top of the central tower. Their discipline was marked, because they timed their turn to bring them to the top of the walk as the hands approached four o'clock, moving back slowly towards the portal of the building. Then, without the slightest discussion, they headed at a moderate pace into the shaded entrance and quickly disappeared.

William Windham, Secretary at War, was securely installed behind a mahogany desk in his high-ceilinged room, but he came from behind it when the two young people were shown in. He smiled, his sharp chin projecting his face forward at a slight angle, before sweeping his coat tails aside and indicating the chairs set out for them in the middle of the room.

'Punctual, I see. Good. Much to be admired, punctuality. Would save us all much time in administration were it observed more strictly. Ah, John, do come in.'

This invitation proved to be redundant, since the recipient of it was already closing the door behind him. He stepped forwards, holding a ledger under one arm, acknowledged Windham, and held out his hand to Eugène and then to the young woman, who took it firmly.

'Mr John King, of the Alien Office, is joining us,' said Windham. 'I believe one of you at least may be familiar with him? Mr King spends much time with our unfortunate friends from France, who reside here in London and on our Channel Islands. We receive much help from them.'

Windham smiled again. Eugène decided that this was probably a habit, rather than a display of friendship.

'Well, let me be clear and brief. There is sound reason to fear for the situation in Ireland. Theobald Tone, agitator for the United Irishmen, has landed in France after returning from America; he is unlikely to be there to taste the fine wine. We have much information flowing from Paris, thanks to the good offices of Mr King and his agents. If the French sail against Britain and, as now seems possible, to the coast of Ireland, it will almost certainly be from Brest, supported from Lorient. Mr King, do I leave anything out?'

'A precise summary, Secretary. I defer to you.'

'Good. Mr Picaud and *Mademoiselle* Heaume, one of you is known to me and the other to Mr King, and neither of you to the other before this afternoon? Is this correct? Good. Now, Brittany is of the greatest interest to us, and Mr Picaud has placed himself in a most useful capacity in the centre of the region. He may be in a position to gain important and revealing information. He is about to return to France. Mr King, if you please.'

'Mr Picaud, your servant,' began King, and Eugène bent his head in acknowledgement. 'Let me inform you. We receive correspondence in some detail from Jersey. It is your charge to procure for the Crown whatever information you can that may have some bearing on a possible invasion of Ireland and from there of Britain as a whole. This information may take any form, but we have reason to believe that you have already come across a thread. In that case, you will be in need of an associate. So, we introduce *Mademoiselle* Heaume, whom you will know henceforth as Coline, and only as Coline. She will stay in Pontivy or in Auray according to circumstances, but close enough to one or the other of the Guèvremont houses in which you will be residing. She will have active lines of communication through to the Channel Islands, notably but not exclusively from Saint Malo.'

'Do you wish to speak, *Mademoiselle*?' Windham asked, with his quick smile.

'Thank you, sir.' Her voice was strong and deep, although she could be no more than twenty-three or four. 'In Pontivy, I can say with confidence that I may be found in the Rue du Fil, at the low door in the small court behind the baker. It has a man's head from earlier times carved in the lintel. Small, with a hood. The Rue du Fil runs down to the Place du Martray. For Auray, I am uncertain at present; but you may ask at the Lion d'Or.' She did not look at Eugène, but she did turn to the Secretary at War, as if to confirm that she had his approval too.

'We are settled, then?' It was Windham, fidgeting slightly, and John King gave a curt nod. They all stood up.

'You may leave — perhaps one of you out of the front and the other out of the back. You will also travel separately, of course, but you have already made your arrangements. We have some letters for Commander Philippe d'Auvergne of the Royal Navy; please pass them to him when you land in Jersey, *Mademoiselle*. Collect them from my office tomorrow morning, if you don't mind.'

The door closed behind them. The two Englishmen stood close to each other, Windham with his hands clasped behind his back.

'Shall anything come of it, do you think? Is d'Auvergne informed?'

'He shall be, Secretary,' said King. 'The correspondence for him is written. We shall have to wait. Jeanne Heaume is a Jersey lass. She is known to d'Auvergne, who remains in charge of our French agents, and she has already been of good service to him. The clandestine traffic between Jersey and Saint Malo is well established, and d'Auvergne has other routes to the French coast besides.'

Windham shrugged. 'Well, any scrap from Brittany may feed us. But if the French have a scent of Picaud, he may find it is a long way to the coast.'

'Indeed. And Philippe d'Auvergne has made it clear that he does not want Jeanne Heaume sacrificed, in any circumstances…'

'Be that as it may, I must speak to the Secretary of State, and then away to Cabinet.'

CHAPTER V: GILLES OF KERGOHAN

The house looked grand from the outside, with its pillars, courtyard, iron gates and steps up to the main door, but it was as dingy as a stable in the clerk's office, which was at the back of the building. Gilles thought he would rather spend his time with a horse munching through hay than with Gaspard Fourrier — a dried-up bean of a man who would rattle if you picked him up and shook him hard. He could not decide whether the clerk smelled more of the lavender on his linen or of the smoke from his foul pipe, which stained the tips of his moustache a faint yellow.

There were far too many annoying distractions from the task in hand, although it was not as bad as meeting the *mignonne* — Joséphine Guèvremont — in the hall. She was the daughter of the master of the house, Laurent Guèvremont. There could hardly be a greater contrast between her and the dingy clerk: she wore pinks and yellows, gloves and satin shoes, and had a scent that caught you and would not let you go. Not that she had any time for Gilles. He had received a stare at their first meeting, when her father had introduced him to her and she had held out her hand to him. He had not known what to do with it, and she had withdrawn it with a slight curl of her lip. After that, she had completely ignored him.

'Well, can you repeat to me the difference between the *laboureurs* and the *métayers*?' demanded Fourrier.

'What?' asked Gilles.

'*Laboureurs* and *métayers*, young man. The difference. Come along, now, young man. These are essentials.' While waiting for the answer, Fourrier picked his nose enthusiastically, and then pulled a hair from one nostril.

'Disgusting,' said Gilles under his breath.

'What was that? Speak up, my boy, you have to show confidence. Come, we were just discussing this. The *laboureur* is the peasant who can live from his own land, while the *métayer* rents more land, borrows what he needs to make it flourish, and then pays back both the owner of the land and the supplier of his needs — who is most probably a merchant, by the way. So there you have it.'

So I do, thought Gilles. *And it sounds as if the métayer has had it too, the poor devil, paying out both ways.* He rubbed his eyes and decided to concentrate. It was too long until lunchtime to drift, although he was sure he could detect the beguiling odour of soup drifting in from the kitchen. He could certainly smell the bread, and it was wheat bread here, too, not rye, although the butter at the manor was better, in his opinion. He pulled his chair up to the end of the clerk's desk and placed his elbows on it.

'So the people we have working with us now at the manor are neither of those, who look after themselves for the most part,' said Gilles.

Fourrier looked pleased with his tutoring. He leaned back in his chair and placed his hands on the ledger in front of him. 'Correct. Your people will expect to be paid, in money or in kind. At least, they will in due time.'

'But we do not have any money, or at least we have only a little.'

'That will come, my boy, that will come. *Monsieur* Guèvremont has it all in hand, and indeed you will find that the overseer Daniel…'

'You must not call him that.' Gilles was sharp, and forbidding. The clerk looked at him with surprise, and then looked down at his hands. Gilles was insistent. 'You must call him a steward, never an overseer. I will not have it.'

'Certainly, it shall be as you wish, as he wishes, if you prefer. His steward Daniel has at his disposal moneys he has received from *Monsieur* Guèvremont. Let us assume that at the moment these men and boys are working in the way that they are used to doing, which is in the service they owe to the baron and so to the manor. I know, I know, it is now abolished, but habit is strong. They will be content for a while.'

Gilles heard the clanging of pots in the scullery, and the smell of soup was persistent. It might be later than he thought. Who could tell in this dungeon? He heard what he thought was the maid, Gaëlle's voice, which brought a smile to his face. He was not supposed to chat with her, but he did, and she told him what went on at the back of the house and elsewhere too, although she was more cautious about that. She had a young man who worked for the baker — he was good for a laugh, although he would have had Gilles by the throat if he thought he was pursuing Gaëlle.

Which he was not. For the life of him, he could not get Héloïse out of his head, even though he knew she would be scornful if he said he was missing her. And as for Yannic, he would come to blows with him if he had been hanging around her, looking for a chance to catch her unawares. It was never enough with Yannic, and any fool could see why he was down at the manor, offering himself for work. At least Yaelle's sister would give him hell if she found his eyes or his hands straying: Erell was not as lucky as Yaelle in looks, but she was as hard as the grit in the buckwheat.

'Gilles! Gilles! Ah, so you are with me.' Fourrier sat back again and rubbed his hands together. 'Good. Now, tell me about the *domaines nationaux* confiscated by the Republic. Which are the lands of first origin, and which are the lands of second origin? And which is it that *Monsieur* Guèvremont has purchased at Kergohan? This is a most important...'

'Papa?'

Laurent Guèvremont put down the copy of *Le Moniteur* that he had been reading and allowed his glance to rise to the doorway, where his elegant daughter was standing. She had not knocked on the door before entering, but it was she alone who had that privilege even if — out of respect for her father — she rarely exercised it.

Joséphine was dressed in a pale violet muslin morning gown with epaulettes tied with purple ribbons. Her hair was uncovered and swept up, with ringlets gathered prettily on top by a larger ribbon of that same hue. The oak parquet floor was polished, and her gown and petticoat had no train, so she moved almost noiselessly across it to kiss her father on his cheek. The whole effect pleased Laurent mightily, and he folded his hands in his lap. Joséphine opened a fan that was dangling from her wrist on a cord.

'It is warm in here, Father. Do you not feel the heat? There are windows that might be opened for a draught of air, and you might close the shutters on the direct sunlight.' She came back to his side and put her hand on his arm. 'Shall I summon Bernard to bring you your coffee? You never know, I might take a cup myself.'

Laurent took out his pocket watch. Like most of his possessions, it had previously belonged to someone else. 'That will not be necessary, my dear. It is approaching eleven o'clock, and Bernard will bring the coffee without being called. Now, come and sit near me. To what do I owe this pleasure? Have you tired of your morning walks, and of the shops within reach of us? It may be admitted that Auray is no Rennes, and still less Nantes.'

Joséphine pouted. 'I have no taste for your creaky old leather chairs. I could wish you would humour me by placing a divan in this room, to lighten its practical purpose. In the meantime, I shall take this armchair, which at least has a cushion upon it. There, I am now quite settled.'

Laurent waited, but Joséphine did not state her purpose in visiting him. He coughed and decided he must take the initiative. 'Well, my dear...'

'Father, I have some concerns about that young man.'

This was not what Laurent had been expecting, and for a moment he found himself considering to which of the potential suitors his daughter must be referring. This was Auray; there were not that many. He cleared his throat again, to hide his embarrassment. 'I do not think I know who... Let me start again, my dear. If there should be any man, young or not so young, who has in any way caused you distress...'

'I mean the boy you call Gilles, father. It is he who is of concern to me, and it pains me to mention it to you.'

Laurent's cheeks flushed, and his voice tightened with anger. 'I may have misunderstood you, Joséphine Béatrice, but do you mean to say that the young man Gilles of Kergohan...'

'You have touched upon my concern precisely, dear Father. You call him "Gilles of Kergohan", but are we quite sure that is the case? In what sense is he "of Kergohan"?'

Laurent came to stand by her, looking down in what he hoped was a benevolent manner. He had evidently misunderstood his daughter's concerns. 'The boy is certainly from Kergohan. But as for the rest, my dear... This is a delicate matter. There are many things that happen in life. Before your mother and I were... Well, no, that is not quite...'

'Before my mother? But the boy Gilles is younger than me, father.' Joséphine looked up at her father's face and saw his discomfort. Was her father, ever so confident of the rightness of all his actions, revealing feelings of shame? For a moment, she was terrified, and he saw that and held her hand.

'You must not in any circumstances upset yourself on my behalf, Joséphine. Yes, we may have heard rumours of allegations, but...'

'And I trust will hear no more of them. You yourself, Father, have declared that your father's mother had fair hair, but so also did your aunt, your cousin Sempronie's mother. Fair hair, just as yours and ... and that boy's.'

Laurent let go of her hand, after patting it gently, and returned to his chair. 'Indeed, my dearest, and that is precisely why our family should take care of the boy. Your cousin and I have agreed on this, and it is left to me to look after his education.'

'But he is being given the manor. It is Gilles who is inheriting the baronetcy.'

Laurent steepled his fingers. 'My dear Joséphine, we must be careful how we speak. There is no baronetcy under our new Republic. There is, perhaps, a barony, if we wish to be pedantic, because the lands still remain, as does the manor itself.'

'But, but, I had been expecting...' Joséphine stood up, and her face was strained and white. 'I had been expecting, Father, that I might have Kergohan as my residence, perhaps ... when I was married, if that were to happen. You all but said it to me, in front of others.'

Laurent began to worry, because he was convinced that he saw her shaking. But his mind was working sharply, and he picked up on something she had said. 'Others? Which others? Do you mean Leroux? Good Lord, was that when it was? What is Leroux, for heaven's sake, my dear? It was a passing thought, no more. The manor is run down, not a fit place for you.'

Joséphine's cheeks reddened, and her voice was quiet. 'I thought it was a promise.'

Her father stood up again, smiled benignly at her, walked across and put his arm around her waist. 'I can do better than that for you. And so will your future husband. You will have everything you could wish for.' He swung her round gently and held both her hands. 'But now, my dear, Bernard will be in with the coffee cups, and I have a meeting in here, as the hour must now be approaching eleven o'clock. I can hear the shuffling of my guests outside in the hall. Will you forgive me?'

Joséphine stood mutely, her face expressionless, then flashed a smile at him. He followed her to the door, and stepped back as she passed through.

CHAPTER VI: AN ACCIDENT

Mrs Claydon — Amelia and Caroline's host — was a good sort of woman, amiable and attentive. She was, as she said, well used to opening her house to the gentry, whose better class of manners and good breeding brought nothing but advantage to the small village of Hampstead. Some, indeed, had taken to residing there permanently, not least Mr Fenton, who had acquired the Clock House from Mrs Martin only a year or two previously, and given notice that it would now be known as Fenton House. Amelia found that she could not conceive of such a practice in Devon: the idea of severing Chittesleigh Manor — her family's estate — from its history by means of an abrupt change of name was abhorrent to her. Still, the power of money brought all other considerations tumbling down before it.

Mrs Claydon's house was neatly positioned at New End, a tidy quarter out of sight of the high street, which Amelia found suited her best. Mr Claydon, God rest his soul, had been a glover, and as the village expanded he had done very well for himself and his family, by dint of hard work and deference to those who came from a more elevated position in society. In his later years, apparently, he had had something of a reputation that even brought the higher classes out from the city to look at his wares. Amelia began to wonder if there had ever been such a thing as a line of gentlefolk waiting eagerly outside the premises, but she kept the thought firmly to herself.

This house at New End, and another close by it, were the late Jacob Claydon's generous legacy to his wife and daughter.

Mrs Claydon attended to the duties of a housekeeper herself, living in and leaving her daughter to look after the other property. After driving Amelia and Caroline to the house, Sam had been sent home to the colonel by the Plymouth stagecoach, while Martha had an attic room, with which she professed herself quite happy. The cook and the housemaid, who also served in the kitchen, came in from the village. It was an orderly household, and quite sufficient for their needs.

On their second day, Amelia and Caroline went out to explore the centre of the village. Most interesting to Amelia was the costermonger, with her variety of vegetables for the table, although Martha volunteered that she found it a dirty place and preferred to look through the window of the jeweller. At this hour, there were several traders with rough handcarts displaying pies, fresh gingerbread and sweets and other small temptations in the main street. On the way home they passed the milkmaid, returning with empty pails, and she smiled at them charmingly. Martha responded with a sniff.

The following day was a Sunday, and both Caroline and Amelia felt enthusiastic about a journey into London to hear the admirable John Newton preach at Saint Mary Woolnoth, which was just along from the bankers Easton and Doughty and the Post Office in Lombard Street. For many years Mr Newton had been outspoken in the cause of abolition, and he and the poet William Cowper had authored the *Olney Hymns*, from which he quoted in his sermon.

Amelia had detailed these opening days of her stay in London in a letter to her sister-in-law and lifelong friend, Arabella, who now lived at Chittesleigh Manor with her husband — Justin Wentworth, Amelia's brother. Like Amelia, Arabella had been involved in the terrible events in Plymouth earlier in the summer attached to the name of Lieutenant Tregothen. While Arabella had confronted his scheming, Amelia had encountered his violence against women, which had shocked her. It seemed from the letter that the idea of a recuperative visit to London was proving to be a useful distraction.

Arabella laid the letter down, yawned, and popped a sweet in her mouth. When she had gone to meet Tregothen in Plymouth, in her attempt to inhibit his advances to Amelia, she had assumed an alias of 'Mrs Fitzhugh', and she recalled how that had seemed both enjoyable and daring at the time. Yet with a harsh sense of guilt she had to acknowledge that the actress Miss Farley, who had helped her in deceiving Tregothen, had suffered cruelly as a result. She knew now that she had been rash in thinking she could restrain a man of that sort. One could never assume that things would turn out as one hoped.

Still, Amelia was evidently pleased to be in London, and wrote with her habitual spirits; but Arabella did not feel inclined at present to follow her into the undoubtedly admirable verses of William Cowper. Arabella was concerned that many were so strongly against abolition that her friend might distress herself to no avail. Arabella could see little to be gained by writing letters when men were by nature so obstinate and grasping. She feared that there would have to be violence and revolts before there would be change. This worry then became mixed in her mind with the contesting arguments she had heard advanced for women as a sex, and her husband's deep frustration with the repressive measures imposed by Pitt on political change. It all felt profoundly impossible for those dearest to her. However, she reflected that this might be because she was now advanced a few months into her condition and could no longer think as clearly as she would wish.

On that thought her face flushed, and she stood up so quickly that she knocked over the small table on which her friend's letter had been placed, alongside an empty wine glass and the packet of sweets. It fell onto the wooden floor, and the sound immediately brought both Thomas Paddon — the butler — and her husband Justin into the room. Justin's face bore an expression that it might have carried had the ceiling just fallen in. Thomas quietly closed the door to the hall behind him as he moved across to retrieve the glass, the packet and the letter, and resurrect the fallen table.

'I assure you I am quite well, merely clumsy,' Arabella told her husband. She then turned to Thomas. 'I should not have troubled you for this little thing, Thomas, but as always you are too quick for me.'

Thomas looked pained. 'I must hope that the conduct of my duties brings no dissatisfaction, Mrs Wentworth.'

'Mrs Wentworth has no complaint to make, Thomas, and neither do I. Rather the contrary, although I shall not do you the disservice of flattery,' said Justin.

He came across and offered his wife his arm. She looked to decline him, but then relented and took it. Thomas withdrew, his pride satisfied.

'It is no good you pampering me,' said Arabella. 'I shall not be made into one of those insipid wives who hang on their husband's arms or suffer a decline on their sofa. Do you wish to read your sister's letter? It is full of amusement, and earnest in some part too.'

'Well, I shall leave you then to stand on your own feet, since you would have it so, and I will be the one to fall into your chair. Is this of Monday?' asked Justin.

'I had not got to that. She wrote of Sunday...'

'Hmm.' Justin had started reading.

Arabella rang the bell. Thomas appeared silently.

'Would you have someone ask my groom Andrew to saddle my horse, Thomas? I shall be ready in a quarter of an hour, and I would like my groom to accompany me. He may bring my chestnut round to the front of the house.' Then, as she heard Justin shifting in his seat, she went on, 'You will say nothing, sir, or you will encounter my resolute displeasure. I have told you, I shall not be pampered in any way, nor restricted.'

Justin did not answer. Arabella went across and kissed him on the head. He made to grasp her with his free arm, but she slipped away to change for her ride.

Justin turned his attention back to Amelia's letter:

After my brief digression on that strange echo in the church, I must bring you back to the subject of the Olney Hymns, *which I know will be close to your heart! You must forgive my teasing, but with all your reserve about religious devotion, my dearest Bella, you will have to admit that these lines contain a most powerful image:*

God moves in a mysterious way — His wonders to perform
He plants his footsteps in the sea — And rides upon the storm

It is a colossal vision, but strangely one of power rather than of love. I was moved by a passage in another of the Hymns, *which brought to mind our cause:*

Dear Saviour, for thy mercy's sake — My strong, my only plea

These gates and bars in pieces break — And set the prisoner free

Our congregation tried their best to sing these through, but it was evident that only a select number knew the tune, and so we contented ourselves with a kind of rather mournful chanting that might be adversely regarded as mumbling. Sadly Mr Newton had little in his preaching this week that spoke to the heart or recalled his own troubled past in the dreadful slave trade. I confess, I could not spend as much time with sin as Mr Newton does, nor indeed with the wiles of Satan, whom I gather may be found around any corner, notably by the unwary.

Yet the name of William Cowper, the poet with whom Mr Newton composed the Hymns, *drew me to purchase a volume of the former's works. I am enclosing a paper on which I have written out some of Mr Cowper's verses, along with the sweets I have found for you. You must keep them away from my brother, or you will not see the half of them.*

Mrs Anna Laetitia Barbauld, who lives just across the high street from us in Hampstead, accompanied us on our visit to Saint Mary Woolnoth, and she it was who suggested that in addition we visit the Meeting House in Gracechurch Street, which lies close to Mr Newton's church. We were kindly shown in by a good sort of woman, a Mrs Bevington, and her son Richard, a quiet lad with a mop of chestnut brown hair and a shy smile. Caroline and I were both moved to be standing in the same building in which the meeting had first welcomed Olaudah Equiano and given solemn promises to 'exert themselves on behalf of the oppressed Africans', as Mrs Bevington justly recalled from his memoir.

We left Lombard Street and returned to Hampstead, to take a late morning walk on the heath. Richard Bevington came with us, and there we were attended by Martha, who seems a little distracted since we came to London, although she confesses to like the city. Richard is alive to our cause, and his conversation is eager upon it, though I did wonder at times if he was perhaps too affected by my person to be a fully reliable companion. His shy demeanour is to a degree agreeable, but he inquires rather insistently after the state of my feelings, as if sentiment were the ruling deity of my disposition, and he is a little too forward in wishing to help me over stiles.

Caroline is insistent that I must take the waters for my health and recovery, and so we are bound in the next week for the wells and gardens to this side of the city. In the meantime, I may be 'watered' more locally since there are chalybeate springs in the village, and a set of buildings devoted to their exploitation along the aptly named Wells Walk, including a pump room, I am told. I dare say this will make you grimace, and you may expect me to bear in mind your famous observation that you would not give such waters to your horse — which may be short-sighted of you, for he might be all the stronger for it.

I shall break off on that note. My love to my brother; to my mother I shall write separately, to Endacott.

Yours affectionately,

Amelia

Justin put the letter to one side, and felt distractedly in the paper wrapping for a sweet. He decided that he liked what he tasted, and so reached for another. It was a relief to gather that his sister was at least restored in spirits after her fever. The letter certainly amused him, and he knew that it had been written to be passed on to him. It also made him chastise himself for his own slackness in recent months in corresponding on the cause of abolition. He folded the letter and replaced it on the table, resisting the impulse to take another sweet. There was a knock at the door, and Thomas appeared. He seemed to be lost for words.

'What is it, Thomas?'

'Mrs Wentworth, sir. She instructs me to inform you that she is not injured.'

Justin sprang to his feet and ran into the hall. He could hear some commotion towards the back of the house, and he ran past an alarmed cook and kitchen maid who had been peering out of a window, and who returned to their preparations with sheepish glances. There was a back door to the stable-yard, and he emerged into sunlight to see his wife sitting on the edge of a mounting block, holding a pad to her head. She nursed her other arm in her lap. The stable-boy, Jem and the groom Andrew came round the side and paused, placing the armchair that they were carrying on the ground and looking acutely uncomfortable.

Justin stood beside Arabella. 'May I look?' he asked gently.

'No, sir, you may not look.' Her face was flushed, and there was blood on her cheek. He had never before been frightened for her, but he was now.

'What has happened?'

She lifted her head and winced a little as she moved her arm. 'What has happened is nothing at all, nothing that merits your concern. I have met with a little accident, that is all. I would be most grateful if you would stand aside and let my woman come to me. I believe Thomas has sent for her. Ah, Grace, you will conduct me to my room and minister to me there. You must understand, sir, that I will not be paraded in front of you in this state. Come, Grace, I need only take your arm. There, you will see that I am uninjured in all that matters.'

Grace said nothing and understood completely. She lifted Arabella's weaker arm to hold the pad lightly, and linked her own arm delicately through that of her mistress. The two women went around the house to the proper back entrance to the manor. There was a short silence in the yard.

'We shan't be needing the chair, then, sir?' Jem asked in a low tone, in the hope that they could remove themselves conveniently.

'Right. Put that damn thing down, and tell me what happened,' said Justin. 'And make sure it is the full story. She has come off the horse, that much I may guess. What else?'

Andrew stepped forward. 'It was a coney, Mr Wentworth. It ran out right in front of her, and her chestnut shied. It's always been that way — good in all else, mind you. Mrs Wentworth rode it out wonderfully, sir, but the critter pulled up short. Then, all of a sudden... It were a pity, sir, a great shame...'

'What then? You were behind her on yours, Andrew. Come, man, what happened next?'

'It was like Mrs Wentworth slipped, sir, when the horse stopped so suddenly. She must have lost her seat when it shied, sir, and its stopping shook her out. She held on well, but ended up on the ground. I was off my horse in a trice, but Mrs Wentworth fell on her arm and ... a bit on her head, Mr Wentworth. I'm so sorry, sir.'

Justin set his mouth, and breathed in and out slowly. There was no purpose to be served in being angry with this man. Andrew would give his best for his mistress, but he had been riding behind as he should, and there had been nothing he could have done. Damn rabbits — maybe he should shoot some? Or get Thomas to bring in his brother from the village to do the same?

'That will do. Return the chair to wherever you took it from. I want no noise about this outside this yard. Do you understand me?'

Both men nodded. They knew well enough that any talk would put the blame on them in some way.

'The horse? The chestnut? He's back here?'

'Oh, he's to rights, sir!' If Jem thought his master was worried about the gelding's welfare, he was soon disabused of that fancy.

'I should send him to the knacker's. Shying at rabbits, indeed! You will knock that out of him, Andrew, do you hear, before your mistress comes near him again. I entrust that to you. Don't let me down, now. I will have it so. Let Jem jump out in front of him. Or find a dog. I don't care how it's done.'

'Mr Wentworth, sir,' said Andrew.

Justin nodded, and the two men took the chair back into the house. Once he was alone, Justin picked up the whip that his wife had dropped, flexed it in his hands, cracked it hard against his boot, and cursed. He was in uncharted territory with this young mother and the expected child, and he knew it.

CHAPTER VII: A CLOSE SHAVE

Captain Nicolas Leroux had believed he would be late, but fortune was with him this morning. When he arrived at Guèvremont's town-house in Auray and was ushered into the hallway, he saw the tray of coffee placed on a table by the door to the study. Bernard closed the front door and walked past him to stand next to the tray. There was no sign of Picaud, but Leroux was greeted by Guèvremont's steward, Le Guinec, who was wearing his customary dark, loose-fitting clothing topped off with a white neckerchief. The pale streak in his hair lent him what Leroux regarded as a devilish look. The two men spoke briefly to each other, and Leroux glanced across at a mirror in which he inspected his uniform, his carefully brushed hair, and his chin and cheeks, which he believed he had shaved with skill. There was only one person whom he wished to impress. He had hopes of seeing her afterwards, coincidentally to all appearances, even if she was fully aware of her father's intentions and knew the hour at which he intended to conclude his meeting. But she would notice that small cut on his face and would tease him about it. He put a finger in his mouth and surreptitiously wiped it across the dotted blood.

The door to the study opened behind him. As he swung round, he was looking straight into the hazel eyes of his beloved, whose strained face was pale. As always, he found his heart pounding, but he attempted a formal bow to her, which for once he carried off quite well. She waited for the group of men to part to let her through gracefully. Fourrier fussed and flapped, and that sly fox Le Guinec produced a deeper bow, while his eyes ranged over her figure as he drew elaborately back. Only Bernard knew where to stand, almost manoeuvring Fourrier out of the way while effortlessly manipulating a silver tray of coffee and cups.

The men filed through into the study, where Laurent was waiting for them. Leroux was profoundly unsettled, because he had seen the look in *Mademoiselle* Guèvremont's eyes and picked up the slight shake of her head before she had swept past them all. He had not seen the incipient grin on Le Guinec's face, nor Bernard's impassive observation of it before he followed the others in, placing the tray on the small table dedicated to that purpose. Without instruction, Bernard poured and delivered coffee to them all. He then bowed slightly to his master and left the room, shutting the door behind him.

Guèvremont sat behind his desk, picked up his watch, and slipped it back into his pocket. 'Good morning, gentlemen. We have no need of introductions, nor indeed of an announcement of our business, because it is perfectly familiar to us. But we do need reports, most probably from all here present. I myself shall start this morning by stating that those to whom I made approaches for finance — that is, loans put down at interest rather than in hope of profit from the transactions — have all confirmed their commitment with one exception. It is of no consequence; we have adequate funds. Fourrier?'

Guèvremont sat back and played with a ring. Leroux sipped his coffee lightly, careful not to bring rough military ways into a civil setting.

Fourrier waved his arms around briefly, and then began in a brusque and efficient tone. '*Monsieur* Guèvremont, gentlemen. You will be aware that we were looking at a property to the south of Pontivy near the village of Trenonin, close to the

River Blavet, but with its own watercourse and indeed some springs. The buildings are diverse in nature, with one formerly the farmhouse, along with some dilapidated outhouses suitable for lodgings for workers, and two very large barns. The site lies on a slope down to the river, providing adequate terracing for the drying racks, and a landing stage, which may be approached by barges in conditions where the flow of the river...'

Guèvremont tapped the small, alabaster lion on his desk that served as a paperweight. The clerk stopped speaking abruptly.

'A summary will do, Fourrier, if you would. Admirable detail can sometimes be too much of a good thing in meetings of this kind.'

It was a kindly intervention because Fourrier's attention to detail brought much profit to his employer, but Le Guinec chose to remove the need for the clerk to continue. He fixed his gaze on Guèvremont's diamond pin, which he envied, and came to the point.

'The dyeing vats have been delivered from a warehouse in Pontivy. They were purchased, as I am sure Fourrier will agree, at a good price and in good condition. Work has commenced on the storage of fuel at the site, and I have engaged some carpenters to construct the drying racks. So we now await our consignment.'

This was a cue to Leroux to make his contribution, which he had carefully prepared. 'The consignment will be delivered to the works, some by wagon from here in Auray, others from Pontivy, where they have been gathered together. This is all now approved by the *commissaire de subsistances*. I must inform you that these uniforms will be red — scarlet, if you prefer. They are those taken off the *émigré* and rebel prisoners at Quiberon, who felt no shame in wearing the coats supplied to them by the English.'

Guèvremont frowned and raised an eyebrow at Le Guinec, who shook his head.

'We had not anticipated red uniforms, Captain Leroux. Are we furnished with the means to fulfil our commitment? How might that be done? Your *commissaire* wants us to supply black. Black from red?'

'Let us recall that we have been assured by *Monsieur* Picaud of the black walnut, which avowedly has the properties of a very fine black dye. In the meantime, we shall have to rely on indigo, *monsieur*.' Le Guinec looked across the room at a bookcase as he spoke, and as he expected, there was no immediate reply.

Guèvremont slid his paperweight a little sideways and back again on his desk, picked up his coffee cup, drained the sweet contents slowly and with customary pleasure, and stood up behind his desk. 'Well, that will be all, gentlemen, for this morning. We shall convene again in two days' time, at the same hour. Captain Leroux, you will reassure the *commissaire* that we are fully prepared, and encourage him to direct the flow of uniforms into our warehouse in Pontivy for carriage onwards to the works. Le Guinec, a word.'

There was no sign of Joséphine in the hall, so Leroux had little choice but to walk towards the front door. The clerk made his way to the back of the building, and Bernard closed the door to the study softly.

'May I presume to answer your expected question, sir?' Le Guinec asked Guèvremont when they were alone. There was no interruption from his master, so he carried on. 'We have had no word of *Monsieur* Eugène Picaud. Not for some weeks, not, in fact, since he left to accompany the former *baronne* back to England. This is something of a mystery, but it may conceivably be explained by the usual difficulties affecting any crossing of the Channel at the present time.'

Guèvremont was still standing, because he did not wish his steward to sit down and make himself comfortable. 'You have enquired after him?'

'Well, it is true that I know where he embarked with the *baronne*. But I...' The steward faltered.

'You may go on. Do not disappoint me again, Le Guinec.'

The memory of the failure of his previous intrigue against the *baronne*'s son Wentworth was painful to Le Guinec, but he went on, 'No, *monsieur*, I shall certainly not do that. I have taken the precaution of pursuing enquiries about this Eugène Picaud, not on the coast but in the region of Tours. I have sent to someone I trust for information, *monsieur*, knowing that you had some doubts.'

Guèvremont opened his eyes wide and raised his brows. 'Did I? And you were sharp enough to perceive them, Le Guinec?'

His steward failed to note the irony, and instead bowed to his master at what he felt to be a compliment to his sagacity. 'I expect to hear back from this agent soon. But, in addition, *monsieur*, I have not neglected the matter of the shipment of the walnut dye by Captain Harker. This Harker is a true American, from what I hear, in that he is a practical man who faces both ways — as the wind blows, one might say. His aim is to ship out *émigrés* from the Channel Islands, where many of them are marooned, to America and to bring back the dried black walnut to us. It will be a clever trade, *monsieur*, one worthy of you.'

It was meant to be a compliment, but as with a number of the steward's glib comments, it was badly judged.

'Except that I do not face both ways, Le Guinec, and you would be well advised to remember that. What may be overlooked in an American would not be tolerated in one who must be, unequivocally, a patriot.'

'Of course, *Monsieur* Guèvremont.'

'So we are expecting our black dye on his return crossing. We may have to obscure the delay from Leroux and the *commissaire*. You have a man waiting at the likely port of landing?'

'I do.'

'You must inform me of anything you discover, if that is the right word, about *Monsieur* Picaud and his family in Tours. You do understand me? I will not tolerate any more scheming, Le Guinec. Harker may pull out if he senses trouble.'

'Certainly, *Monsieur* Guèvremont. I shall inform you immediately. Will that be all?'

'Yes. Send Bernard in, if you will. Tell Fourrier to let the boy Gilles out of his clutches, and to report to me on his progress before dinner this afternoon. Now, call Bernard to me, if you please, and promptly. You must make sure that you visit Kergohan, and see how they are getting on. It is not a sentimental project, you know; I have money invested there, and I shall hold you to account for how it is put to use. Good day, Le Guinec.'

'Good day, *monsieur*.'

There was rain on the way back. Thinking that there would be greater tolerance in religion now that peace had been agreed for the region, the villagers had tried holding the Mass less secretly, in a barn halfway between Kergohan and Pluguel. All had gone quietly until one of the republican patriots had come to stand outside as it was ending. First he shouted at those who came out of the barn, and then at *Père* Guillaume himself, scolding him for being a recusant and breaking up the congregation. He told him that he should leave his vestments behind for someone better than him and cross over to England like the rest of the renegade rabble. So it had gone from fingers pointing at chests to a push here and there, and then shouting and swearing, which *Père* Guillaume had tried to restrain by raising his hands. But blood was up, and Héloïse heard the words *foutu bougre* several times before she decided to slip off.

It was a relief to be away from all of that. There was a field of crops to cross, which was easy, and she saw the gap in the trees where the path from Kergohan came out. She remembered that it rambled up, along and around before it met another track at a patch of rocks. She would have to turn right there, since it had been left on the way out, and Babette had said at the time that the other track led off to the village. Once she reached that rock, she would be down at the manor in no time at all: it was easy.

Héloïse enjoyed the quiet behind the pattering of the rain on leaves — so different from Saint-Domingue, where it would drench your hair and clothes, sluicing mud into small rivers. The birds seemed to respect the silence too, always at a distance, unlike the raucous green parrots at home that would descend on fruit, and then wait in the trees until you had gone. She found herself reflecting on the homily delivered by *Père* Guillaume; it had been about charity, and the need for Christian love to embrace those both far and near.

She also thought about his repeated warnings about temptation, which burned in her ears. Perhaps it was safer to risk being tempted by that which was far away rather than that which was near, if temptation infected the blood? Carelessly, she stepped on a jagged branch on the path, which made her trip and scrape her knee. She swore mildly to relieve the pain, and then grinned as she tried out *'foutu bougre'*, enjoying the sound of it.

The rain pelted harder, so Héloïse hurried along. She knew that Daniel had wanted rain for the growing buckwheat, even if she still turned up her nose at what they called *yod*: boiled-up mush that they ate enthusiastically with wooden spoons. She wondered if Gilles had taken his wooden spoon with him, and if he was eating *yod* and thinking of her, maybe even dreaming, as she liked to imagine. She dreamed about the kiss he had given her once and never again, for all that he looked as if he would like to, which was impertinent of him. Yannic could see his desire, and he seemed to get more out of taunting Gilles than he did out of chasing her, although there had been that one time when he had gone too far. Babette had spoken to Héloïse about it, as if she did not know when to get away from him herself.

The rain eased and she reached the rocks, glistening between dripping trees and bracken. Her feet slipped slightly in the clogs she had adopted in order to fit in. A bird flew away with a shriek, and she heard the crack of a twig and a voice. There was no one in sight, and she turned round to look back down the path. Silence. There was nothing to fear here, with so many trudging through the woods on the morning of a Mass. Yet, without warning, there was suddenly a girl in front of her. She was standing at the junction of the two paths, and Héloïse instantly recognised her as someone from the village. The girl had a rather odd grin on her face, and in a moment she was joined by two others, slightly younger than Héloïse. They had stepped out from behind the group of rocks, and one of them was sucking her thumb in an insolent way, while the other whispered in her friend's ear.

'Hello,' said Héloïse, because it seemed like the right thing to do.

The girls said nothing, but their eyes drifted over her shoulder. The one who had whispered put her arm through that of the other.

'You on your own today, then?' a voice asked behind her. Héloïse recognised it as the voice of Erell, Yaelle's younger — and much nastier — sister.

'Not now, I'm not, thanks to you, and I'll be glad of the company. But you'll be on your way up to the village, while I'm going down to the manor, now I think about it. How are you keeping, Erell?' Héloïse was no fool, and while she had been talking she had shuffled her feet to place the largest rock at her back, so she had an eye on all of them. She had no stick, though, curse it, and there had been plenty along the way.

'Well, I've been better, to tell you the truth of it.' Erell took a few steps forward, and two more of the older girls from the village stepped out from the shadows behind her. How many of them were there, for the saints' sake?

'Sorry to hear that, Erell. You must be careful what you eat, you know.'

The one who was sucking her thumb laughed at this, and Erell glared at her, her face glowing red. It was well known that Erell liked her food, and anyone else's if she could get hold of it. That sharp comment was the spark that lit the tinder; Erell moved closer.

'At least I'm not scrawny. Men can't stand the scrawny type. Nothing to get hold of where it matters.'

The two behind Erell laughed at that, as if perhaps they felt that they should, to make things even. But it was a stone that missed the fox, because Héloïse had no doubt that young men knew what they liked about her, and they looked it over often enough — too often for her taste.

'Well, maybe you should ask Yannic about that. It's my guess that he'd like to have his hands follow where his eyes have gone before. But I must be getting back. It's been…'

It was worth a try, but Erell grabbed a handful of her hair as she tried to walk away, and pulled her head back. Héloïse stumbled and fell backwards onto the ground, just avoiding banging her head on a knotted root. The two older girls came up and put their feet on her arms. The thumb-sucker came and kicked her behind the knee with a heavy clog. Erell knelt down, and twisted her hand tightly in Héloïse's hair. She pressed the blade of a small, worn knife down flat on the end of Héloïse's nose.

'You touch Yannic again and I'll cut your face, and we'll see if your blood's red or black,' she hissed. 'If I smell you on him, I'll rip your hair from your head, do you hear me?'

Erell had no time to hear Héloïse's answer. A small but strong hand swung down and slapped the side of Erell's face with alarming force. She fell sideways from the blow, the knife flying out of her grasp as she reached out to keep herself from going over completely. The three younger girls, who had seen this menace coming with wide eyes and open mouths, ran off one after the other down the path to the village. Héloïse rubbed her wrists and sat up, staring into the face of Yaelle, who pulled her younger sister roughly to her feet. Behind her, the two older girls were struggling pointlessly with an impassive Babette, who stood between them, holding their wrists in an iron grip.

Yaelle seized her sister's arms and leaned forward. 'What do you think you are doing? Over a boy, is it? Never let me see you with a knife ever again, or I'll take you to the magistrate in

Auray myself! In my day, we'd sort out our quarrels by ourselves, not with a crowd at our back. Shame on you, on all of you!' She looked round at the older girls and then dropped Erell's arms. Her shoulders relaxed just a little.

Babette released the other two, who thought about complaining to her about the marks on their wrists until they saw the look on her face. Héloïse bent down and picked up the knife.

Yaelle refused to look at her sister. 'Now, go!'

Babette put her arm round Héloïse, who leant her head against Babette's shoulder, and found herself trembling. Yaelle came up to her and kissed her on the forehead.

'I am sorry, I am so sorry. I have not been looking after her enough, since I got married. I should have seen something like this coming, but I would never have guessed at...'

'It's my fault. I let Yannic make up to me,' Héloïse interrupted. 'I too should have seen it coming. I am sorry you had to fight with your sister.'

Yaelle laughed. 'Oh, there has been worse between us, Erell and me, don't you worry. But I am still stronger than her, thank the good Lord. One day, it will not be possible. But ... she should not abuse you like that. You are both Christians, equal before Christ.'

Héloïse pushed her fingers through her hair. 'I've heard worse. Far worse.'

Yaelle was not to be mollified. 'But the knife? What has come over her?'

Babette breathed in slowly. 'Jealousy, Yaelle, and the times. She has listened as men have been killed; she has seen others pick up such weapons to defend what they believe is theirs.' Babette was thinking of Grosjean, Yaelle's husband, and said nothing more.

Héloïse gave the knife to Babette, dusted down her dress and rubbed the end of her nose. 'My mother's people have been raped and beaten, and more that I cannot tell you. And now they have turned on those who did it to them. I have hidden underneath a house and heard it happen. This was nothing. Erell would not have hurt me — not yet, at least.' She came up to Yaelle and wrapped her arms around her, kissing her on her cheek. Yaelle embraced her, then Héloïse stood back. 'I must thank you for what you did, truly. But please make peace with your sister for me. She will have no cause to quarrel with me again. And you can tell her that my blood is red, just like hers. We women have no need of knives to know the colour of our own blood.'

CHAPTER VIII: MRS BARBAULD

Eugène stepped off the boat and onto the dock, feeling greatly relieved. Contrary to his expectation, he had not been as sick as a dog on this voyage. From Jersey to Le Légué, the port of Saint Brieuc, was a relatively short leg of the journey, and it was sheltered for the most part by the land, Brittany to the west and the Cherbourg peninsula to the East. Frustratingly, there had been no news of Captain Harker in Jersey; but in any case the American would probably put in directly here or further east at Saint Malo. Harker had been fully confident of getting hold of the dried walnut drupes for the dye in Savannah, and had told his cargo of *émigrés* at the start of the outward voyage that, like it or not, they would have to disembark there, and take ship again to go through the straits to reach New Orleans. That much was more or less certain, but beyond that it would be down to the weather and a good portion of luck for Harker's warehouse purchases in Savannah.

Eugène stretched, yawned, and smelt the air. It tasted of ripe corn and warm leaves, not of salt, bilge and stale clothing. He picked up his bag and strolled off to find a horse for the first part of the ride to Pontivy. He would take a *chaise de poste* from there on to Auray, which would give him time to plan what he would say to Guèvremont.

Amelia woke up feeling slightly giddy when she raised her head from the pillow. She put it down to her usual complaint, and determined to rise as normal and call Martha in to assist her. There was a great deal that lay ahead, and she should not be put off by a foolish weakness. She sat on the side of the bed and looked towards the window, where the sun shone brightly. The air was cool, however, which would suit her well. She stood up, fixing her gaze on the small mirror opposite. She noticed that its frame had a chip in the side, which began to look like a wolf's jaw, oddly mysterious and frightening.

Martha had been up and about for an hour or so, speaking to Mrs Claydon about the day ahead, or at least the provisions for it. She then stepped outside to take the air. She might wait for her admirer for a short while, standing innocently by the railings in front of the house; but he either came or he did not, morning or evening, and he never stayed long. It was sweet when he came, because he had a way with words, and he would bring her a flower or some such trifle, and whisper in her ear. He even gave her a small handkerchief once. It had the initial 'M' embroidered in green in one corner, but she had detected another woman's perfume on it. He said it was rose water from the old girl who sold it to him. She half believed him, for who would look a gift-horse in the mouth?

But he did not appear today. Martha went back into the house in an ill humour, and caught a glance from Mrs Claydon, which she tossed off with a pert smile. It was time to look to her lady. She ran lightly up the stairs, past the chamber door and up to her attic. On the second or third step, she stopped abruptly. There had been a dull thud from Miss Wentworth's room, no mistaking, as if she had dropped something heavy. She paused, one hand on the banister, and held her breath. No sound, nothing at all, except what came up from the scullery. She skipped down the two stairs and tapped on the door. There was no answer, so she tapped again and slipped in.

Mrs Claydon and Miss North both heard Martha cry out. Miss North came rushing out of her chamber and round to Amelia's side, who was being gently supported off the floor by

Martha, while Mrs Claydon wisely stood at the door for the moment, allowing those who knew Miss Wentworth better to minister to her. Martha and Caroline placed her on her bed, propping up her head with a pillow and wafting Caroline's salts in front of her until a sign of life came back into Amelia's pale face, to everyone's great relief.

Yet Caroline remained extremely concerned. She felt the responsibility for Amelia's welfare keenly, after the trials that Amelia had undergone in Plymouth in the spring. Indeed, she kept to this refrain during the first days of what proved to be an illness, which progressed from a headache and giddy spells to a low fever. Mrs Claydon suggested the attentions of an apothecary; she knew Mr Wilson and was confident of his abilities, especially with what she called women's maladies. Here she nodded forcefully, and Caroline gained the impression that this was a personal observation, and that Mr Wilson might be favoured for rather more than the efficacy of his medicinal remedies.

The patient herself proclaimed that she was feeling better with a regularity that her symptoms belied. Martha continued to flit round her, not venturing too much in the way of conversation. After a while, Amelia was allowed downstairs to the parlour, and from there — with great caution — out into the sunny streets of Hampstead. She smiled a little at how she was supported on either side by Martha and Caroline, who would offer her assistance at the slightest sign of fatigue.

One bright morning they made their way along Wells Walk to the Pump Room of the chalybeate springs, which at that early hour was relatively quiet, and through the room into the Wells Gardens, which were fresh and delightful around the pond. There were one or two gentlemen indulging in a game of bowls with others standing idly by as spectators, one of whom looked casually across for a moment in their direction. In this instance Martha blushed and secretly smiled to herself, although she made no habit of responding favourably to forwardness.

Amelia's strength gradually returned to her, and it was arranged that on Friday, she and Caroline should call on the poet and abolitionist signatory Mrs Anna Laetitia Barbauld in Church Row, a visit that had always been planned. It was a homely and comfortable situation, the house being equipped almost as a library throughout its living quarters. It was furnished accordingly, with chairs suited to reading and sets of steps to reach the higher shelves. Her servant Esther Tranter was unassuming but attentive, and Mrs Barbauld confirmed that when she grew tired, Esther become her amanuensis.

Mrs Barbauld continued on a personal note to her young guest, 'So, my dear Miss Wentworth, we see that you are now recovered from your indisposition. I am glad of it.'

'I thank you, Mrs Barbauld, and can only be ashamed of my weakness,' Amelia replied. 'It may be that it was an effect of the change of scene, since I am so used to the tranquillity, perhaps even the dullness, of our rural life.'

A door slammed elsewhere in the house, and a shadow passed momentarily across Mrs Barbauld's face. The fingers of her right hand picked distractedly at the embroidery on her Italian shawl.

Caroline wished to relieve Amelia of continued reference to invalidity, and so she responded herself with a deft change of subject. 'We have been to Mr Eliot in Cornwall, who has written a letter of introduction for us to none other than Mr Wilberforce at Clapham, whom we hope to visit.'

'I do so hope you do, Miss North. Poor William has been despondent about the defeats of his bill earlier in the year. It should hardly surprise us. But at least it has been given further readings, and there are many whose constant support will keep the cause alive.'

'His resolution is undaunted, I am sure. We shall write at greater length to him if we cannot visit him ourselves. I am certain he will have been much restored by the spirit of your poems.'

Amelia's eyes brightened, and she became a little animated. 'Assuredly so, Caroline, and who could fail to be reminded of that stirring phrase from your pen, Mrs Barbauld? "Yes, injured Woman! rise, assert thy right!" This is how we must be! We must learn to act and speak on our principles, and you have been our instructor. "The Rights of Women" you resolutely made the title of that poem: how apt that is! Yes, now I recall — how does that couplet run now? "Try all that wit and art suggest to bend..."'

Mrs Barbauld came to Amelia's assistance. '"...Of thy imperial foe the stubborn knee." How kind it is of you, Miss Wentworth, to bring to mind my poor lines. Yet I believe I was not always so implacable.'

Amelia smiled across at her enthusiastically and continued in the same spirit. 'I am foolish to have stumbled, but my memory is not altogether failing. Those are worthy sentiments, but your poem also offers us a precept, perhaps even a rallying cry, which I have by heart: "Make treacherous Man thy subject, not thy friend."'

Caroline began to fear that Amelia was becoming a little heated, and once again chose to change the topic of conversation. 'I had in mind, Mrs Barbauld, to take Amelia down to Bagnigge Wells, which is a short journey, and perhaps Saint Chad's too. It was always our intention to take the waters. We might even go further into town by carriage, should all be right, and pay a visit to Wedgwood's display rooms. Would you care to join us?'

'Josiah was an old acquaintance, alas. Sadly missed. Yes, indeed, let us exchange notes on it, and find the day. The waters at Bagnigge and Chad's are much praised, and the gardens and walks at Bagnigge are very pleasant.'

Caroline and Amelia rose to take their leave. As if by an unseen signal, Esther appeared to hold the parlour door for them. As they walked into the hallway, they heard a man's heavy voice from further back in the house.

'Anna, Anna, where are you? The devil if you are ever here when I need you. Annie, Annie, I say!'

Caroline and Amelia went out into the bright sunshine. The man's raised, angry voice came through the open door.

'Anna Laetitia, Anna, where are you? I want you here, do you hear me? I know you're there! You must attend to me when I call…'

The front door shut behind them, with a clack of the latch. There was no other sound apart from that of the jackdaws, and Amelia and Caroline walked slowly down the street together to the centre of the village.

Amelia found that she thoroughly enjoyed the tiny world of Hampstead, now that she was feeling restored after her illness. She delighted in strolling through the heart of the village, observing the minutiae of trading, and then to the edge of the heath. Martha was carefully instructed to come with her on these strolls, and they did on occasion share some small snatches of conversation. There was much to observe, with faces and figures that grew familiar doing the same thing at the same time most days. The hackney carriages came and went up the main street, the carter clattered in at the same hour of the morning, and the boy who worked at the forge came to fetch a jug of milk for his master and gawped at the fresh buns in a predictable, wide-eyed ceremony every morning. The milkmaid, Molly, passed out of the village with empty pails in the same daily routine, walking along the road by the heath. They had spoken briefly once or twice near there, Amelia entranced by her dimples and admiring her jacket and neckerchief.

'Yes, it's neat enough, Miss, ain't it? Mrs Giles won't let me step out in a smock. She says I must look neat and prim, but I won't wear the bonnet. Not like Rose.'

Amelia was amused. 'Why is that, Molly?'

'Makes me feel hot and bothered in the sun. I like my hair loose, begging your pardon, for yours is dressed nice.'

'Well, thank you for the compliment. You are walking back to the farm?'

'I am, Miss. Downhill, mostly.'

'But it must be heavy carrying the pails up in the morning, Molly?'

'Oh, Lord, I don't do that, Miss! No, Mr Giles brings us up in the cart each day first thing, me and Rose. Begging yours, I best be getting back or there'll be a ruckus.'

Amelia watched her as she trod lightly down the road, while Martha glanced out of the corner of her eye at a gentleman who had stood idly by during the conversation. He winked at her and went on his way.

CHAPTER IX: LE GUINEC HAS A PLAN

Captain Leroux left his hand on the heavy latch of Guèvremont's front door as the butler and Fourrier disappeared into the back of the house. He hesitated and stepped softly back up the hallway, aware of the voices that drifted out from the study. He inspected the clock and the curious objects on the table, stared at the picture that had so fascinated Gilles on a previous occasion, and scanned his own image in the mirror. The cut had sealed itself, but there was still a short line of congealed blood, and he wiped his finger across it again.

He was waiting for Joséphine, but he feared that she had gone. He had seen the fear in her eyes when she had passed him outside the study, and he began to experience a desperation that never came over him in his military roles. This sense of helplessness ate away at him, and conjoined itself with thoughts of humiliation and social disgrace. Lieutenant Vernier had already said to him that he was aiming too high and had laughed at his pretensions, urging him to submit to the mercenary embraces found in the plush rooms of *Madame* Vaillancourt — embraces that brought cost but no consequences. Thank God that cynic Vernier could not yet read his mind. What did such a man know of the delirium that he felt?

A sound from the study brought Captain Leroux out of his reverie. He moved silently down the hall to the front door, and this time he lifted the latch in a smooth movement and stepped outside. He decided that he might still risk waiting in the courtyard, in the hope that Joséphine might appear, but he could not think of any convincing reason why he should be found standing there. When the door did swing open, he turned round to see the steward Le Guinec standing in the porch, smiling at him. Bernard shut the door quietly behind Le Guinec, who came forward with his hand stretched out to greet Leroux warmly.

'I see you are waiting for someone. Perhaps it was for me? If so, we share a thought, because I wish to have a word with you. Will you take a glass with me? Come, Leroux, we must be friends. Where there is profit, there is friendship. I know a little place.'

Leroux found himself unable to resist, not least because he suspected that the steward was well aware of his motives in always leaving the house reluctantly. Le Guinec lived mostly in the Guèvremont house in Pontivy, but very few of the affairs of the Auray household escaped him — or that sleek Breton ermine, the butler Bernard. He put on a cheerful face.

'Yes, of course. Lead on.'

The way down through the town was relatively quiet. It was a market day, which had drawn the crowds away from their quartier, and Le Guinec put his hands in his coat pockets and hummed a tune. Leroux was left with his own anxieties, but the steward laughed and spoke to him.

'What do you think of our revolutionary songs, some years on now, Captain? Are they as fresh as they were? Do your men still belt them out loudly as they advance into battle?'

'My men, as you call them, would soon have their throats slit if they sang their way along the hedgerows here. I can hear that you have a preference for "La Carmagnole".'

'Ah, well, I can picture that poor Antoinette breaking her nose just as she does in the song. Besides, "La Carmagnole" is more tuneful than that crude "Ça Ira", don't you think? Yes, here we are.'

Le Guinec stood aside for Leroux to enter the hostelry, an old building with a low lintel, emitting the warm, sweet smells of alcohol. There was a young woman at the bar, and a square, clean-shaven landlord wearing a stained apron. Le Guinec walked straight through the low-ceilinged room to a doorway at the back, ignoring the stares from those who observed Leroux's uniform. There was a small yard outside, with a neat wooden table and two chairs, and Le Guinec motioned to Leroux to be seated. The landlord appeared in the doorway.

'*Eau de vie* for me, Roic, and for the captain…?'

'Do you have a *Nantais*?' asked Leroux.

'Yes. Red or white?'

'White, at this hour.'

'And keep the door pushed to, if you please, Roic,' added Le Guinec.

The door closed evenly enough, but then eased open again, settling on its hinges and leaving a gap through which conversations could be heard. The young woman brought the bottles and quite acceptable glasses, perhaps a tribute to the men's obvious status. She was not pretty, Le Guinec observed, but her figure was comfortable, and she did not smell, as some did. Leroux ignored her completely, and narrowed his eyes as he prepared to concentrate on what the steward had to offer.

'*Santé*,' said Le Guinec, raising his glass.

'*À la votre*,' returned Leroux.

Le Guinec took a sip. 'Not bad. Yours?'

'Passable. I am no expert. I drank beer in Paris.'

Le Guinec leaned forward. 'You would be at home in England, my friend. Perhaps you will be one day. That is where your uniforms are destined, after all, is it not?'

The door creaked slightly in the wind that twirled around in the yard, brushing a few old leaves here and there.

Leroux's eyes narrowed further. 'You will appreciate that the disclosure of any information pertaining to the armies of the Republic, whether accurate or not, is liable to lead to an examination by a tribunal. There has been no such declaration made in any of our discussions...'

'Come, come, Leroux. I know there has been no such disclosure. But any fool might guess that there is a clandestine purpose to this rigmarole of dyeing black, or indeed that after the Quiberon fiasco last year someone has had the bright idea of playing the same game of invasion back on the British. To better effect, one might hope. Where will it be, then, I wonder, and who will it be with? The restless Irish? Some of them would be up for a fight, I'll be bound.'

Captain Leroux pushed back his chair and placed his hands on the table, lowering his voice. 'I would advise you, citizen, to keep any thoughts you may have to yourself, for your own sake, and for the sake of the enterprise in which your master Citizen Guèvremont is involved. That is a warning. I will not continue this conversation...'

'Sit down, Captain, for God's sake, and don't sound your tocsin. What I may think is nothing to anyone else, and I would be a fool to let it loose, apart from in this safe company. It is no more than idle speculation, and neither one thing nor another to me. I have weightier things to share with you, which I believe are close to your heart. What do you think of this boy Gilles? Pour yourself a drink, Leroux, for heaven's sake.'

At the mention of Gilles, Leroux had opened his eyes wide, and Le Guinec had observed his astonishment with satisfaction.

'For myself,' the steward continued, 'I am not happy about it. That the boy should be trained in balancing columns of figures is of little consequence. But that he should exercise a claim on the manor at Kergohan by virtue of some nonsense story about the colour of his hair must not be allowed to continue unchallenged. I am most indignant, Captain, that *Mademoiselle* Guèvremont should find herself in this situation — indignant on her behalf because, after all, the implications are severe. It is not just a matter of Kergohan, but taken at its worst it might undermine her expectations to inherit...'

Leroux's response was muted, but his manner was intent. 'It is most considerate of you to take the part of *Mademoiselle* Guèvremont. From one or two things that she has said in passing, I gather that she now regrets drawing attention to this trivial subject of the boy's hair — to that superficial similarity to her father's. There might ... be other explanations. We took dancing lessons together for a while, you know, and she let one or two things slip in casual conversation. There is much that one may, unintentionally, confide in a dancing partner...'

Le Guinec sniffed at his *eau de vie*. 'Oh, I have no doubt, Captain, no doubt at all. Not that I have the same experience as you, of course. Of dancing, that is. I believe the floor of the salon at the house is very well suited to practising one's steps. Yet there is little hope of the ball, I hear — a great disappointment to you both, I am sure.'

'What more of Gilles do you have before we leave the subject?' Leroux's voice was dry, despite his drink, and tinged with hope.

'Well, I was only wondering if some solution might be found. Something that demonstrated that, shall we say, his engendering did not take the course that has been assumed. The affair has not yet been investigated to a satisfactory standard, in my view. There is nothing conclusive, and I think that…'

'Your kindness will be profoundly appreciated, of that I am sure. By *Mademoiselle* Guèvremont, I mean. She stands to lose…'

'Yes, I am aware of what she stands to lose. For myself, I would indeed be delighted to resume the stewardship of the manor at Kergohan, which I had briefly in my charge before the present regime was set in place. Perhaps *Mademoiselle* Guèvremont…'

'It is my impression that *Mademoiselle* Guèvremont had set her heart on possession of the manor. I am sure that were it to be restored to her, she would insist on making her own appointment…'

Le Guinec ceased sniffing his drink and downed it in one. 'Well, in that case I shall pursue my inquiries. There is one other matter that I believe concerns us both.'

Leroux was beginning to feel rather strained, but he kept up his attention. 'Which is?'

'This fellow Picaud. What is your impression?'

'I have none, none in particular. He is not a military man.'

'I am not sure that I trust him. He came to us in unusual circumstances…'

'I am unaware of them.'

'It was to do with the transfer of the Kergohan property, its alienation from the branch of the family in England.'

'And?'

'I am saying that I do not believe that we know enough to trust him with any details about your consignment of uniforms, and where they might be going, or for what purpose, even if his suggestion of the American black walnut and its remarkable qualities as a dye may prove to be to our advantage.'

'So, we cannot do without him, but we must be careful with him.'

'That is about it, Leroux. You catch at my meaning well. I have a feeling that he may need to be apprehended. That is all. I felt it was my duty to alert you: as a good citizen, that is, as well as a good partner in business.'

'I am due back at the barracks. I am obliged to you, Le Guinec, on both counts. You will keep me informed, I am certain. Impostors of any kind should be unmasked. You have my approval in what you are doing.'

Which Le Guinec did not really need, because as was his nature he already had things in motion, and he would never have involved someone he regarded as a stiff-necked *raisonneur* like Leroux in anything that required deviousness. Still, the military man was decisive in action when required, and suitably ruthless: there was that incident not long ago of the slave-driver's bully, shot on the road like a mad dog. Le Guinec wanted Eugène Picaud removed before he gained any more credit with Laurent Guèvremont, who was quite impressed with him so far; suspicion often proved sufficient for that kind of purpose, especially if some taint of treachery might be alleged too. As for the manor and its lands at Kergohan, he did not like the present arrangement at all and wanted the credit for restoring the property and the estate to be his alone.

Le Guinec slapped some coins down on the table, hesitated about taking the bottle, and decided against it. He and Leroux then pushed their way through the dark interior, and out into the bright daylight of the street. Roic nodded to them in parting, and watched idly as the young woman went through into the yard, and came back with the glasses and bottles and the money. Roic looked at the coins and seemed satisfied with what he saw.

'You can keep the smallest of them.'

The young woman said nothing. She was already content with the coin he had given her for cleaning the bedrooms, several of which had been occupied the night before by wealthier farmers wanting an early start at the market. One of the rooms gave out conveniently onto the yard, and she had heard much of what was said below by the Republican army officer and Le Guinec, whom she already recognised as a member of the Guèvremont household. She had spoken to him once before, and had told him when asked that she was called Coline. She could see that he did not consider her attractive, so she doubted if he would remember her name; it was obvious that he had many other things on his mind.

CHAPTER X: A WALK TO THE VILLAGE

The sky was overcast and the weather cool, which was a blessing since there was shade only for part of the way. Arabella and Grace were on good, fine gravel while they walked from the manor through the grounds to the south gate, and for a while on an even road, but the slope down towards the village was becoming more broken. At one corner Arabella stopped to look over to the outline of Dartmoor, with the farmland falling away attractively towards it, the moorland hills with their tors a darker green and grey in this muted light. Further along the western side of the moor would be her father's house, what had been her family home. Sir Francis Wollaston now lived in Alverscombe Hall by himself, and she had visited him only twice since her marriage, although he had driven up to see them after a month, but then refrained, muttering something about young couples. Arabella ground her foot briefly into the dry earth by the low wooden gate, impatient for the freedom to ride again. Grace waited placidly, the food basket tucked under her arm. There was lowing nearby, and the hedge rustled as a muzzle poked above it on the other side of the lane, and a cow's wide eyes stared out at them.

There had been two weeks of relative inaction after Arabella's fall. Her knee had suffered most, along with her left elbow, both with grazes, and her forehead had sustained a cut. She was more exhausted by the accident than she had ever imagined she would be. Her father had been minutely careful of her when she was small, but had gradually relaxed his hold as she grew more independent in spirit. But there were times when Justin treated her as if she were made of glass, or rather the kind of Sèvres porcelain that his mother had had brought over to Chittesleigh from Kergohan. His cosseting infuriated her, and it had worsened once she had declared that she was with child.

Finally, she had insisted that she would walk. She went around the grounds at first, taking rests from time to time at the seats and the arbour, with Grace closely in attendance — a welcome return to past habits, which had not always relied on her riding out with her groom. There had also been a visit from the good Mrs Darke of Fishley and her daughter, who was inclined to giggle at nothing at all, and both were all sympathy for her injury, with the daughter sneaking glances at Arabella's belly. It was evident that Justin had spoken to her husband, Thomas Darke, while in Hatherleigh, and given time she would no doubt be subject to a call from that unctuous man Glasscott, the vicar.

Arabella's loose gown was now annoying her, since it felt like walking in a sack, although it had been exquisitely sewn by Grace to accommodate her condition. Suddenly, she felt embarrassed: it was as if she could not now be pleased with anything, and was irritated with all.

The two women walked on. The hills disappeared from view as the lane bent round before sloping down again. To the right there were woods, which came right up to a shallow ditch. It was a charming place, with an old cob barn off to the left in a broad pasture, and as they turned away Arabella caught a glimpse of a woman standing in a clearing in the trees. Grace had seen her too. The woman was staring at them, and had a crimson scarf wrapped round her hair. They began to walk on, but they heard a voice and looked back to see her call to another, certainly a girl this time, who came to stand by her side. Grace ventured that they were perhaps a family on the tramp, looking for work here in the summer season.

The cottage they were seeking was across the square, and a short way along another lane. The village of Chittesleigh was small, set on a flat section of land rather like a terrace in rolling country that stretched to the edge of Dartmoor. What stone houses there were, and there were few, were set around ground laid aside for a small cattle and sheep market. The rest of the inhabitants lived in the squat cob cottages with their mossy and weather-beaten thatch, and there were signs of one or two trades, including Will Cholwick the carpenter, who had already been up to the manor to set a table to rights and work on seats in the grounds of the manor. As they crossed the square, he looked out from his shed and smiled a greeting. Will's youngest child appeared at the door of the house in the arms of his wife, Mary, and Arabella was suddenly possessed by the fear that they all knew her secret.

She and Grace soon reached their destination, the cottage of Robert and Jenny Mudge. News had come through to the manor that Jenny was expecting her second child, and Arabella had wanted to bring her food and good wishes. Jenny received them with a curtsey and a flurry of orders to the old dame who was asleep in the corner, and the young boy who was standing with his thumb in his mouth. The old lady sprang to life and dragged the boy out of sight, while Jenny brushed a bench and invited Arabella to sit. This she accepted gladly, because she was a little tired, and strangely her elbow ached although it had done nothing on the walk.

'Well, Jenny, I am glad to see you. I have good reports of you, and what I see bears that out. How do you get on?'

'Mrs Wentworth, ma'am, I've been doing fine, and am glad you have good reports of me. I wish I could bring you something, but we only have small beer, which is not fit for you, though Robert likes it well enough, working in the dust and straw all day as he does. But you don't want to hear about that. You've been more than kind to come to see us, and you'll pardon that we are just plain and ordinary here...'

'Jenny, I shall take a sip of Robert's small beer, because I have a dry throat from the walking. Grace will help you.'

Jenny said something under her breath, picked up a jug from the table and ran to the room into which the boy had been banished, emerging with two pots and the replenished jug. With a smile, Grace took the pots from Jenny and wiped them quickly with a napkin from her basket, handing one back to her to fill. Arabella sipped the beer and put it down on the bench beside her. It was not to her taste, but it was better than nothing.

'So, Jenny, how are you? You must be nearing your time now. You look ... fit to burst, Jenny!'

Jenny laughed loudly, putting her hands on her belly. 'I am that, ma'am, and I'll be happy to be the old Jenny again. They say that after your first, the baby comes right out like a bean from a pod. All I hope is that he doesn't fall right out on the earth like a bean would do!'

Arabella's face went a little pale at this announcement. 'I am sure that nothing of the sort will happen. Do you have...?'

'Why, Gammer Mudge here has seen many into the world, including our young Billy over there, and the first is worst, as they say. I was in pain with him for two days and nights, and Robert fair lost his wits for me. He was half-mad with fright. But Gammer swore at him, begging your pardon, ma'am, and he held my hand at the last. Billy was a fat, round baby boy.'

Arabella began to feel slightly sick. She must at all costs keep Justin away from her if it was to be anything like that.

'But here am I rattling on about myself and nary a word for you, Mrs Wentworth. I trust you are quite well yourself now?'

It was an innocent question, but it left Arabella in a flutter. Did Jenny know of her condition? 'That is kind of you, Jenny. I believe myself to be fully recovered from what was a painful fall from my horse, with some small cuts. We must all put up with our misfortunes as best we may, and mine was very slight.' She stood up easily and gestured towards the table. 'Grace has brought you some tea leaves — does Robert like tea? — and a custard. Does your boy like a custard? I do hope so. We thought he might. If we may take them from the basket, we can take the basket back with us, and not leave you to return it. Now, if you will forgive us, Jenny, I believe we should be walking back.'

Grace dutifully removed the small packet of tea and the bowl of custard from the basket.

Jenny curtsied again. 'I must thank you, ma'am. Billy, come here, and see what the lady has brought for you. It is a custard, and you know how you like those. Say thank you, Billy, to Mrs Wentworth.'

The boy Billy mumbled his thanks and retreated to the safety of the old woman's side. Grace pulled the door back. The rain was steady and the sky was dark.

'Lord, ma'am, you must stay here, and I'll send Billy down on through for his dad,' said Jenny. 'It isn't far. Robert will go up to the manor for you and fetch down the carriage.'

Arabella sat down and looked at Grace. 'That will not be necessary, Jenny. Mr Wentworth will have harnessed the horses himself at the first drop of rain, or indeed before that, and the carriage will be with us shortly. I am only surprised that it is not here already.' She patted the vacant part of the bench beside her resignedly. 'Come, Grace, you may as well sit by me. We shall not have long to wait, if my judgment is correct.'

CHAPTER XI: JOSÉPHINE AND LEROUX

With her father going to Pontivy to visit those tiresome works and be thoroughly practical, taking Le Guinec with him, Joséphine at last saw an opportunity to arrange a meeting with Captain Leroux, avoiding the scrutiny of both of them. Even so, this was by no means simple or without risks. If she walked out to meet Leroux apparently by chance, then a maid would have to go with her, and Marguerite was far too simple to be sufficiently discreet. Yet if Leroux called in to see her at the house, she would need the soundest of excuses to be left alone with him. She sat down suddenly on the small chair in her dressing-room. How might it be done?

Eventually, she hit upon a scheme that would appear to be quite proper, and would not be especially noticed by the servants. She announced that she would be holding yet another dancing lesson in the salon, which would be delivered as before by the eminently respectable *Monsieur* Duchesne. He was to teach her and her partner some new steps. Her partner on this occasion would once again be Captain Nicolas Leroux, who had been favoured with that role in the past, since he was by now known to the family and the household in general. It would be on a given morning, for a maximum of two hours, since it was fatiguing exercise. Joséphine reviewed this scheme carefully over breakfast the following morning and again the next day to see if it had any weaknesses.

Her father looked up from his journal and surveyed her with concern. 'Would there be anything troubling you, my dear?

You have not said a word this morning, which is not your way.' He put down the paper. 'I am sorry if I provide no incentive for conversation. A newspaper is the bad habit of a man of the world.' He cast a glance behind him. 'Bernard, you may leave us now. We are quite well served, thank you.'

'I am quite well, Papa. You will be departing on Thursday, I gather,' Joséphine replied. 'Not for long, I hope?'

'My dear, not for long at all. Do not be concerned on my behalf. The roads are quite safe now, and there is a substantial garrison at Pontivy. Why, I might even take refuge in the chateau, should the town come under sudden attack!'

This was Laurent's attempt to lighten the atmosphere with a joke, but it failed. His daughter looked up at him in alarm, and he was struck by how distraught she seemed.

'But, Papa, why should there be an attack on Pontivy? The officers and the mayor here have all been saying for weeks how the region is thoroughly pacified.'

'And so it is, so it is. You must not trouble yourself. All will be safe and secure. When I return, we shall stroll into the town and purchase those new gloves that I promised you. I insist on it. The pleasure will be all mine.'

So Joséphine arranged to have a dancing lesson on the Saturday morning, of which the household was duly informed late on Thursday, when the dust had settled behind the wheels of Guèvremont's coach on the road to the north. It had, at least, the appearance of an arrangement, but only one of the supposed parties was actually given notice of it. When the day arrived, Captain Leroux was welcomed at the appointed time at the front door by Bernard, and ushered into the salon after being announced to *Mademoiselle* Guèvremont. She allowed her hand to be taken by the officer in order for him to brush his lips across it in clear sight of the butler, who then withdrew as the young man and woman assumed a polite distance from each other.

Not quite knowing what to do, Leroux sat down on the sofa, which had been left to the side of the room, since the carpet had been rolled up in preparation for the lesson. Joséphine stood for a moment, waiting for the sound of steps to recede from the hall. She then startled Leroux by rushing over and sitting next to him, with both of her hands clasping one of his.

'My darling, what shall we do?'

Her scent, the heat of her body, and her enticing hazel eyes — now full of apprehension — left him bereft of any idea of what he should say or do. His impulses gave rise to burning shame, yet they were as ardent and insistent as ever, and he was almost appalled by the idea that even now she might yield to him again. Was restraint what was appropriate? Why was he so uncertain, so inept? At the thought of ineptitude, he became so utterly dejected that he could hardly do more than grasp her hands and quickly release them. This would not do for her. Joséphine seized his sweating palm again, and looked at him with wide, soulful eyes that were now full of tears.

'Nicolas, what shall we do?'

Leroux could no longer resist, and he took her face in his hands and kissed her passionately. She succumbed with a moan, and then placed her fingers on his chin and gently turned him away. He could scarcely breathe now, but he controlled himself, and whispered to her urgently, 'But where is Duchesne? Do we not have a dancing lesson with him?' Then it dawned on him. 'There is no lesson? Is your father here?'

Joséphine shook her head and then burst into tears and buried her face in his shoulder. 'Oh, Nicolas, I believe I am with child.'

His whole body tensed with the enormity of the declaration. '*Amour de ma vie*, that cannot be true.'

Joséphine was astonished. 'How can you say that? How can you…?'

Leroux swallowed. There was a dryness at the back of his throat that would not go away. Joséphine awaited his explanation.

He struggled to find the words. '*Mon amour*, I can hardly speak of the wonderful moments that passed between us when we were last alone together, and I will acknowledge that my passion … was unrestrained.' He held up his hand as she attempted to interrupt him. 'But in consideration of your honour … I … do not think that our embrace could lead to…'

Here Leroux looked at her directly for help, but her conviction remained absolute, her ignorance of a man's strange body so complete that she could only conclude that one thing could come from such intense and exhilarating impropriety. But Joséphine was a Guèvremont, and the inebriation of sentiment could be supplanted by cool and sober assessment.

She spoke calmly. 'I shall not wait long for your offer, Nicolas. You do understand me?'

He nodded, speechless. But she was now embarked on a train of thought, and scarcely noticed his state.

'We may not count upon Kergohan. It is as we feared. My father is unbending on it, and besides, he does not understand, since you have not declared. You must seek promotion. There is no other way, and I shall have to reconcile myself to being a soldier's wife.'

Leroux spoke softly. 'Yet there is, *mon coeur*, some possibility that the boy Gilles may be proved to be a foundling. I have been speaking to one who believes he may be able to find evidence, sufficient to dissuade your father…'

'Who is this "one"?'

'You must conquer your distaste for him.'

'Le Guinec. You have been talking to Le Guinec.'

'Not so, *mon amour*. He has been talking to me.'

'So, he will unmask the boy. And how does he intend to explain away that mop of blond hair? Still, it is no matter. Let him make the venture. And *tant pis* if he is broken by it, no matter how much I might wish it to be true.'

Joséphine had stood up, now far more composed than at any time for the last few days. Leroux came to stand by her and tentatively reached for her hand. Their fingers intertwined.

Her voice was soft and low. 'You must call me Joséphine. You must say it, sir. I command it of you.'

There was a sound out in the hall. Joséphine shook out her dress, looked in the mirror to check her composure along with her coiffure, allowed Leroux to walk over to the window, and pulled open the door. Outside in the hall, where she had been hesitating loudly enough, Gaëlle curtsied with relief.

'*Monsieur* Bernard wished me to inform you that *Monsieur* Duchesne is unaccountably absent,' she said. 'He intends to send to him, but he wished to have your consent before so doing.'

The speech had been rehearsed by the maid, and it left her a little out of breath.

'That will not be necessary, Gaëlle. Captain Leroux and I had concluded much the same ourselves. We have conversed admirably, but the captain must now be leaving to return to his responsibilities. You will please ask *Monsieur* Bernard to show him to the door. I will take a step into town to make some purchases. You will ask Marguerite to attend to me, immediately, if you please.'

Gaëlle curtsied again and tripped happily down the hallway. Joséphine left the door open and went across the room to stand in front of the mirror. The two lovers waited at a distance from each other, in complete propriety, for the household servants to do as they had been bid.

Eugène was tired and hungry. He had with difficulty reached Corlay by nightfall, and with even greater difficulty had found a room at a run-down establishment off the main square below the chateau, which was mostly in ruins. The room was shabby and grim, but there was a tolerable stable at the back, with one or two hacks that were an improvement on the beast that had carried him reluctantly from Saint Brieuc. The instruction from the landlord was to be sure to leave his horse at the Reine Margot in Pontivy, in the market square, the next day.

On the road from Mur to Pontivy on the following morning, he passed one small column of Republican *bleus*. They extended him the courtesy of letting him ride through with a greeting, unmolested, their sergeant regarding him closely but not seeing him as a farmyard rebel. One of the younger soldiers snatched a fistful of the longer grass by the roadside and offered it to the horse, which swung its head aside to consider it, and then walked on with what Eugène considered a remarkable degree of hauteur.

He felt that Pontivy posed no problems for him, since he was confident that Captain Harker would already be under sail back from America. It was a matter of keeping the Guèvremont household happy in the interim, which might be difficult; but he could use the time to find out more. To the best of his knowledge, the dyeing works were still being put together south of the town. He had it in mind that he might go down there, but before that he had to call in at the

Guèvremont residence. There would be a room set aside for him, that was part of the agreement, and he could take the old *charette* from the house and rattle on down beside the River Blavet to see what was going on. If he had time, he might also call at the address in the Rue du Fil that he had been given, and see if he could find Coline.

The late afternoon sun was getting in his eyes when he came into Pontivy by the Porte de Saint-Brieuc and rode down past the chateau, keeping close to the bank of the river, and into the Place du Martray. There he asked a limping boy for the Rue du Fil, declined to be led rather than just shown, and set his horse's head across a short distance into the market square. The Reine Margot was at the blunt end of the square, and the tired horse knew its way to the stables at the back. Eugène slung his bag over his shoulder and strolled off back up the street in the direction of the chateau, in front of which he could see a good number of *bleus* milling around aimlessly before heading off over the bridge. Guèvremont's house stood to the right, identifiable by its short flight of steps to the door, which he rapped on roundly with his knuckles. A man he did not recognise opened the door with a curt bow.

'Good evening,' said Eugène. 'Allow me to introduce myself as *Monsieur* Picaud. The household has, I believe, a room awaiting me.'

'You will be pleased to step inside, *monsieur*. I shall take your bag and have it conveyed to your room. You may perhaps like to wait in the salon here, while I inform *Monsieur* Guèvremont of your arrival.'

The butler reached out a bony arm and took the bag, shutting the front door behind Eugène and opening a door to the right. There were, in this salon, several chairs with gold-painted arms covered in a striped pink satin. The servant shut the door, leaving Eugène alone. He sat down on one of the armchairs, concentrating on what he had not expected, which was the presence of Laurent Guèvremont. It was disconcerting, but it demonstrated how one should not rely on assumptions: he had believed that Guèvremont would be still in Auray.

The door to the salon opened without warning. Eugène rose from his chair, his mind still on what he would say to Laurent Guèvremont, and how much displeasure he might encounter, either for his absence or for the delays in waiting for the arrival of Harker. He kept an accommodating smile fixed on his face as he found himself unexpectedly confronted by Guèvremont's steward, Le Guinec.

'A great pleasure, *Monsieur* Picaud. We had expected you, but then had also accustomed ourselves to patience. It is quite virtuous of us, I am sure you will agree. Perhaps our reward will be in heaven. But more seriously, I trust that you may be bringing us good news. You come from one of the Channel ports, I assume — Saint Brieuc? Is our cargo now with us?'

'Citizen Le Guinec, my pleasure. It is a great convenience to find you here. Why, you may have saved me the journey onwards to Auray. Is *Monsieur* Guèvremont well? Do I find you both in good health? The air here in Brittany is salubrious.'

Le Guinec became resigned to a prevarication. He sat on one of the pink chairs and placed his hands on the arms. 'Jersey is famous for its dairy produce, I believe. You have come down to us from Jersey, have you not?'

CHAPTER XII: 'AM I NOT A MAN AND A BROTHER?'

During Amelia's further convalescence at New End, Mrs Barbauld became a good companion. There was much talk of Mr Wilberforce, his energy and manner of speaking, and of others who were tireless in the cause of abolition. They spoke also of the opposition to it, those in the Society of West India Planters and Merchants known as anti-abolitionists, who could boast of having Members of Parliament from some of the largest cities such as Liverpool, Bristol and Glasgow in their ranks.

Amelia was also regularly visited by Richard Bevington, from the Meeting House in Gracechurch Street, who joined in their conversations with ardour and then fell into silent contemplation, sitting on a simple wooden chair by an empty hearth. Caroline felt he was an awkward young man, but Amelia more generously insisted that he must do as he wished. Nonetheless, she was irked by him springing up to open doors for her, and being assiduous in delivering her cup and taking it away again before her drink was truly finished.

They all arranged to visit Saint Chad's and Bagnigge Wells, which were not far from each other to the north of London. They also planned to call in at the Wedgwood showrooms in Greek Street, for which they would need tickets. This would require an extension to their journey, but Amelia was adamant that she was sufficiently restored by now, and Richard earnestly exclaimed that he would support her in any eventuality. To accomplish it all, they left early in the morning, and Mrs

Barbauld insisted on providing a carriage, inside which Amelia, Caroline and herself travelled, while Richard perched alongside the driver.

The Wedgwood Rooms contained a rout, albeit made up of those Mrs Claydon would have regarded as of good breeding, some notably of London fashion, but there were others who from their diction seemed to hail from different parts of the nation, or other nations. The principal disadvantage, apart from the heat of the throng in some quite tight spaces, was the necessity of climbing from one floor to another. Yet the party knew what it was searching for, and soon found a collection of different forms of the emblem of the Abolition Society, the moving picture of a kneeling African man in chains, inscribed with the motto 'Am I Not a Man and a Brother?' For Amelia and Caroline, it was an opportunity to purchase a variety of goods with this cameo which might be given to friends or relations: a snuff box for a man, or bracelets and pendants for women. They made their way back out to the place where the carriage was waiting, but not before Caroline had observed to Amelia that there was regrettably not a black face to be seen in the crowd around the showcases.

Stepping through the gate at Bagnigge Wells came as a welcome relief. The air even this far out of the town was much lighter and less foul. The gardens were set out for tea and other refreshments, but they passed through into the Pump Room for the waters, which Amelia duly drank and indeed felt better for it. The party then walked out of the Long Room and over the bridge across the little Fleet River into the gardens. Here they found a variety of pretty flowerbeds, arbours with trailing stems, and a delightful little pond with a curious figure of a child clutching a swan — a fountain, it seemed. The company was gay, with uniforms in evidence, and young women who bore the mark of actresses, for they were brightly attired and sported bonnets with lavish feathers. It was, at least, charitable to think of that profession, and the reflection brought Miss Farley to Amelia's mind. After the easing of her illness, Amelia had sent a note to what she hoped to be the actress's residence in London, but she had heard nothing back.

They passed back by the neat little bridge, reviewing the booths and bowers which seemed tidy enough, when the breeze and a sharp spatter of rain convinced them to look for shelter. Their delay had been an error, for the Long Room was now packed and boisterous, so they stood awkwardly by the door while Richard disappeared behind the bobbing hats, heads and bonnets in search of a table. There was a young woman standing close by with an older but elegant gentleman in a fawn waistcoat, long breeches and hessians. He chose to quiz their party, looking first at Amelia and Caroline, but then intently at Mrs Barbauld.

Caroline noticed this behaviour, broke off her exchange with Mrs Barbauld, and spoke tartly to Amelia. 'Well, I have to say the manners are rather raw in this room, but it is what one might expect of mixed company such as this. Would you sense as I do the presence of the theatre here?'

Caroline then saw Richard's head bobbing at a distance. She tapped Amelia on the arm and pointed a finger towards him. At that moment, he found an opening in the press before it closed in again, but rather to their alarm they saw him take a tumble. Amelia could just see that he had been passing a table with a pair of young officers, one of whom stood up and bent over as if to help him up, assistance which Richard stiffly refused. The officer then leaned across and said something in his ear, and as Richard stepped away the man put out a foot to trip him again. Richard stumbled but kept upright on this occasion, while the officer sat down, leaning across to slap the table and enjoy his rough joke with his companion.

There was little to be done except turn away, so with the sun shining again and the showers past, they walked out and found an attractive bower. The boy waiters were buzzing about, and they sat and gave their order. Richard was understandably silent, and out of consideration no one mentioned the incident. The conversation ran almost inevitably on Wilberforce and abolition, after they had reviewed their purchases from the Wedgwood showroom. The tea arrived suddenly on a large tray in the capable hands of a maid servant, rather than one of the boy waiters. She proceeded to serve it with great delicacy. They were about to taste it when a loud and confident voice hailed them from the walk.

'Why, Mrs Barbauld! How pleasant it is to see you once more. We have escaped the crush inside to stroll in the sunshine. You are most snug there.' The speaker was none other than the gentleman seen just now in the Long Room, escorting his fair companion. His eyes ran over them all, but he smiled down at Mrs Barbauld in particular, standing at ease just beyond the booth. 'You will introduce me, I am sure, Mrs Barbauld, to your fashionable companions.'

'Here we have Miss North, and Miss Wentworth,' Mrs Barbauld replied politely. 'Ladies, may I introduce to you Sir Banastre Tarleton and Miss Robinson? And indeed, Mr Bevington comes with us, of course.'

Richard stood and made a brief bow, then sat down nervously.

'Your servant, Miss North and Miss Wentworth, and yours, Mr Bevington. Forgive my impertinence, but am I not acquainted with the name of Wentworth, and indeed of North? Bevington, I am afraid, escapes me as yet.'

Both Caroline and Amelia looked blankly at each other.

Tarleton raised his finger to his mouth as if in profound thought, and then made an expansive gesture. 'Ah, yes, Captain Wentworth, surely, and just possibly a Captain North. A brother, perhaps? In our campaigns in America? Such a long time ago now.'

'My brother Colonel North served in the colonial wars, Mr Tarleton, and so did Mr Wentworth, brother to Miss Wentworth, so you are correct in recalling their names.'

'Something of a backwoodsman, Wentworth, as I remember. Did better in Canada later on, on the ground with the natives there. Infantryman by preference; he liked to be close to the ground. Forgive me, there is George Hibbert and Thomas.'

Amelia felt a flush on her face, and Caroline prepared to be indignant on her behalf, but the two men to whom Tarleton turned approached quickly. They were dressed in the gloomier clothes of men of business, merchants or bankers, and there was an almost untidy self-assurance about them that would come of affluence.

The portly man spoke first. 'Banastre, there you are. What the devil are you doing out here? Thomas and I expected you in the Long Room. Attracted by the ladies, I dare say. Your servant, Mrs Barbauld. You will, I trust, have been convinced finally by the resounding and repeated rejection of the bill for abolition? It is past time that preposterous fancy was laid to rest. Now, Banastre…'

Mrs Barbauld stood up. 'Mr Hibbert, so little is such a worthy cause laid to rest that these ladies are here expressly to visit Mr Wilberforce…'

'Wilberforce, madam, is a spent force. We have set out the arguments again and again, and I would call it unpatriotic to ignore them. Have you not read Beckford? The whole scheme is a madness. If we restrict our trade, then the French, the Spanish, the Dutch, and even the Danes will take it up. That is it in a nutshell. Forgive me, madam, we should take our leave before I become eloquent. Your servant, ladies.'

His peremptory and dismissive confidence was hard to bear. Amelia had risen to her feet, and she was holding her medallion out in a trembling hand. Caroline had no hesitation in standing too, alongside her. It was Amelia who spoke. 'Do you see this, sir? Do you see its inscription? Does it not say: "Am I not a man and a brother?" It is the emblem of our cause.'

Hibbert hesitated, and then thrust his hands into his pockets insolently. 'Yes, I have seen it. Paltry work it is too, and yet many a pretty penny it has earned for that moral mountebank Josiah Wedgwood, who would make anything to suit the tastes of those with money to spend on gewgaws.'

The young woman who had been introduced as Miss Robinson pulled slightly but urgently at her escort's arm. He was for the moment too amused by the spectacle in front of him to wish to depart, so he patted her hand and remained where he was. Hibbert stood his ground too, but it was the taller man with him who now spoke for the first time, in a heavy and sarcastic tone.

'Ay, and Wedgwood's another dead man too, like that hypocrite Ramsay what had a black man as a servant, no less, him that were a slaver himself in the past. It's all humbug, no doubting.'

Mrs Barbauld, with her cheeks slightly coloured, answered him assertively. 'And you, sir, to whom I have not been introduced and scarcely now wish to be so, should do us the honour of making sure of your facts. James Ramsay was a wonderful man, and a vicar in the parish of Baron Barham. So you are mistaken; you are thinking of John Newton, who preaches even now in London.'

'Thomas. Be with us, please.' George Hibbert was now impatient to be gone, and not a little irritated, but his companion would not be corrected by a woman.

'Ay, Newton is that fool who wrote the hymns with that weak bit of straw Cowper, or whatever his name was. He was mad, wasn't he?'

Caroline North now addressed this speaker, in what she hoped was a restrained and dignified voice. 'We shall not dispute with you, sir. If you would be good enough to leave us, we shall be able to continue with our refreshment and our polite conversation.'

'Come now, Thomas, George is stamping his feet, and my sweet is keen to be indoors. Come along now, I say, if you will.' Tarleton had now tired of this game and wished to be free of further wrangling. 'Your servant, Miss North, Miss Wentworth, Mrs Barbauld — and, ah yes, how does your husband do now, Mrs Barbauld?' He was determined to remain civil, but he could not resist a parting gibe. 'I trust his — what should one say — his malady is not still agitating him? Odd that we should be speaking of the poet Cowper, just now, so similarly disturbed. Your servant, madam, as I declared.'

Tarleton and Hibbert swung away in contented conversation, with Miss Robinson still attached decorously to Tarleton's arm. Thomas was not so easily satisfied. His eye fell on Richard, who had sat throughout in strained silence. He leaned forward and jabbed his finger in Richard's chest, who immediately stood up.

'And what's with you, mister mum, cat got your tongue? You dress like one of those paltry folk who makes their money right enough but will not worship with the rest of us. Not a patriot amongst them. Not enough blood in your veins to say your piece, have you?'

'Now, that is enough, sir,' said Mrs Barbauld. 'You will leave us before offering more insult to any of our party. Please be gone.'

Thomas inclined his head slowly to look down at her and stuck his thumbs in his waistcoat. He turned his back on Richard and took several steps away. Then he swung around abruptly and pointed at each of the women in turn. 'I'll tell you this, Mrs Barbauld and Misses whoever-you-are: it'll be the ruin of this great country if we ever bend our ears to you. And there are many who think like I do, however gentlemanly they may be.' He had raised his voice, and there was a grating violence behind it. 'You meddle in matters you do not understand, to the detriment of the nation's finances. Desist, do you hear? I would have the lot of you shut up at home, I would, so help me. A good afternoon to you, and to that puppy there.'

They watched as he strode off.

Mrs Barbauld sat down and picked up her cup. She tasted the tea and put it down with a remarkably steady hand. 'The tea is cold. It is time we left. The weather is unreliable, do you not think?'

CHAPTER XIII: COLINE'S TRICK

Eugène tripped down the steps of the Guèvremont house after bantering with Tudual the butler, who was a good fellow for a chat. The sun was still warm but lower in the sky, the stones of the tall houses giving out a steady heat. Eugène found the Rue du Fils with little trouble, and it gained his approval because it opened at each end into a very different part of the town. He passed the baker, crossed the street to stare aimlessly at limp greens and crisp radishes, looked casually around to the left and right, and then ducked straight into the alley. He found himself standing in front of the lintel with the carved head, which was just as Coline had said, right down to the hood.

He rapped quickly twice, and the door was opened by a grubby boy with a mop of hair and a rough smock. He wore a ring on a cord around his neck. Behind him stood an old woman in the dark of a short hallway, waving him in. That was a relief, yet it was too easy to relax into being foolishly trustful: a sack was suddenly pulled over his head, twisted tight, and his arms were held in a lock behind him. The door slammed shut and he was pushed along blindly, up a few stairs, along a passageway, and down a flight of steps. The short, pleasureless trip ended with a knock on a door. He was breathing heavily, and had stumbled more than once. The door opened without a bolt being drawn, he was led in, and the bag was lifted. He stared into the face of Coline, who was sitting on a truckle-bed.

'Good evening,' she said.

Eugène rubbed his neck, where the sacking had left it sore. 'You have a capable band, and extend a warm welcome. May I take a seat?'

'By all means.' Coline extended a forearm to indicate a low wooden chest with metal edges, set against the wall on one side of the small room. Her face remained expressionless.

'Well, let's be started, then. What do we know?' Eugène sat down and began to recite what had happened so far, since nothing would be committed to paper. 'For my part, I've been at Saint Brieuc, and I know that Harker has not arrived. I found the steward and Guèvremont here rather than in Auray. You?'

Coline stared at the floor. She was wearing a dull blue dress with sleeves that seemed to have been cut short, and her hair was braided and gathered up. On her feet were good, strong shoes.

'I myself have been in Auray, at the place that I told you about. I've been working and overhearing. The steward talks too much, and quite loudly, when he thinks he is secure. I found out that he and his master were coming here, which suited me.'

'Anything helpful from your time there?'

Coline placed her hands almost demurely on her lap. 'Le Guinec believes that the unforms are destined for an attack on the British, across the Channel. The army captain — Leroux is his name, I think — will not confirm that.'

Eugène tapped his foot. 'They talked to me just now, Guèvremont and Le Guinec, about the dyeing works. They more or less failed on a first attempt this last week with indigo dye. They'll try again. They have procured a mordant, but indigo will never do it, because the uniforms are red — they were taken from the British at Quiberon. When Harker comes, it will speed everything up. It's a matter of time, a waiting game. I'll go downriver to the works they have at Trenonin, and see if I can pick up anything more.'

'I think they suspect you.'

'In what way? What makes you say that? They seemed…'

'The steward. He is suspicious, probably by nature. Perhaps he is covetous of his privileges, irritated by you making yourself indispensable to Guèvremont.'

'You heard that in Auray? Or should I say, overheard?'

'He was suspicious of another boy in the house too. I have forgotten his name.'

Eugène grinned at her. 'Another boy, eh? *Touché, mademoiselle.* That must be Gilles. I wonder what he has against him.' He stood up and stretched. 'Well, I must be off. Maybe next time we can meet in the Reine Margot. I can manage well enough without a sack stuck on my head and mouldy flour up my nostrils. Shall we say in three days, about the time of day that the diligence pulls in from Rennes? I'll do you the honour of giving a rap on your front door before I go down there.'

Coline looked impassively at him. 'Take care, *Monsieur* Picaud. That steward with the loud mouth is sly — with everyone, I suspect. You need to keep your eyes open.'

Eugène grinned at her again, and put his finger to his cheek as if in thought. 'Well, there's something new to try. Keeping my eyes open. Like I…'

'Like you did when you came in at the door here.' She was unimpressed by his flippancy. It was as if she viewed him as someone who might let it all slip out of their grasp with his casual confidence. It was not her style, and she had scant respect for it.

Eugène's grin faded. 'In three days, then.'

'They are asking around the town for more people at the works. I shall put myself forward. At least, that is my intention at the moment. The boy will let you out.'

Eugène's footsteps disappeared into the building. Coline stood by the narrow casement and stared out at a blank wall, tracing a flower in the dust on the window ledge. Then she walked over to the door, pulled it open, and called for the boy. He came promptly.

'I want you to go over the bridge. Can you run up the Carhaix road as far as Stival? The Guéhennec mill? Little Yann is the miller there. Tell him to have his horse ready, for the next week at least, or I'll put a spell on his wheel. Say that. The horse won't be gone long, if at all. I'll get it back for him anyway, by Saint Meriadec. There'll be something in it for him. Tell him, and come back here. Quickly now — bare feet are best for speed.'

For the first time, she sighed. That should be enough; she would need to look after this Eugène, a great deal more than she wanted.

The *charette* was everything you might wish for on a rural drive. It creaked and groaned, and was slightly battered, yet it pulled along well enough. It reminded Eugène of his childhood, sitting up high with Joseph, his favourite tenant-farmer on the estate, eating an onion and regretting it later, scattering the hens and riding high on the piled hay, looking out for the deer. Now he was older, he would probably prefer to drive with a woman beside him, one arm around her waist and the other holding the reins.

A young woman like Amelia, in fact, who had haunted him for a long time, and whom he had first met when he was not much more than a boy himself. Clasping her to him down by the stream at Polton Court, soaking wet and sobbing, had wrenched him so much that he was not in doubt about his feelings. Perhaps it was just as well that he had had to leave.

He could not be sure that those feelings were reciprocated, and he had no income and no prospects.

There was a flash of blue in the distance, at ground level, as the rough road turned a corner. It seemed a little out of place. Eugène grasped the reins firmly with both hands and guided the mare's head to the right of the lane. Jumping down, he led the mare gently around to face the other way, tucked her and the *charette* behind a tree, and left her to crop the grass contentedly. He slipped to the edge of the wood. Not far short of the buildings, crossing over from one side to the other, there was a detachment of blues. He had been with Le Guinec this morning, and nothing had been said about soldiers on duty at the works. The steward had confirmed the route with him; he had particularly instructed him not to go inland but to keep along the river road, which was where he was now — and where the soldiers were.

The pleasure had gone out of the afternoon for him. On the way back, the *chaumières* of the hamlet of Saint Michel looked poor and broken down. During the slow plod up through the suburb to the west of the town, Eugène made up his mind to call in at a forge on the road, and have the farrier take a look at the horse's shoes. There was nothing wrong with them as far as he knew, but an easy walk into town across the bridge was a great deal more inconspicuous than the cart grinding along. He was wearing a loose frock coat, and his shoes were practical: he would be better on foot, come what may.

Le Guinec had in his possession an introduction to the commander of the garrison at Pontivy written for him by Leroux, indicating in the barest terms his suspicions about a man named Picaud, supposedly from Tours. It was enough to gain some attention: the garrison commander held it loosely in his hand and led Le Guinec out into an empty court in the chateau, where they could be alone.

What Le Guinec could now tell the commander was that investigations by a reliable agent had revealed that the name Picaud could not be connected with anyone of the man's description in Tours itself. But something very interesting had been found on a list of *émigrés* from the Touraine. Careful scrutiny of the list had revealed that one *Vicomte* de Biel-Santonge had some twenty-five years back married the daughter of a bourgeois, with the maiden-name of Jeanne Marie-Elisabeth Picaud. It was evident that this young aristocrat had taken as an alias his mother's name, mixing truth with half-truth — the chosen region being a truth, and the surname a half-truth.

The officer asked what the citizen wished him to do. Le Guinec had no hesitation in replying: this was a dangerous criminal, a threat to the Republic, and should be apprehended. The suspect was this very morning preparing to leave the stables behind the Guèvremont house just down from the chateau to drive an old *charette* to Trenonin, which was downstream on the River Blavet, to visit works that were of vital significance for the affairs of the Republic. Le Guinec had carefully advised this man called Picaud to follow the road by the river, if that might prove to be of any help in arresting him.

The officer agreed at first that the best solution might well be to apprehend Picaud while he was at Trenonin. He knew of those works on the River Blavet, and indeed knew far more of why they were there and what they were for than he was prepared to reveal to the informer sitting next to him. He also knew that there was a small detachment of foot-soldiers detailed to stay in the Trenonin area, and that one of the few mounted men he currently had available at the barracks might be sent down to them promptly, with a description of the *charette* and the suspect.

But as the officer talked, Le Guinec's own deviousness suggested to him that Picaud might be clever enough to smell a rat before he stepped conveniently into the arms of a detachment of *bleus* standing in the road down at Trenonin. Therefore, he wondered if the commander — given the gravity of the situation — might consider placing guards unobtrusively at various locations in the town as well as the day went forward? After all, the suspect might just decide to pull back and return to the Guèvremont house without notice, so to speak. Were those precautions taken, the suspect could be seized without drawing attention to his accidental association with Citizen Guèvremont, which the officer would understand was only too likely to occasion harmful gossip.

The commander looked again at Le Guinec, declined to commit himself to anything further, and stood up. This informant was obnoxious, ingratiating, and plainly devious; but what he had found out might well have some substance to it. The Republican army's intention to foster an Irish rebellion against British rule had to remain secret, so spies from England needed to be flushed out. The army's commander *Général* Hoche would undoubtedly not want any hint of his plans to reach the damp and dreary shores of the stolid *rosbifs*.

Eugène began to experience the mixture of fear and excitement that came over him whenever he believed that he was close to being discovered. Once over the bridge into Pontivy, he decided on impulse to go to the left, around the chateau. The smell of cooking mingled with woodsmoke drifted out to him over its walls. He walked around the moat to the top of the street that ran down to the stable-yard gates at the back of the Guèvremont house, passing the entrance into Talmont Court. Everything was quiet. There was a notary coming out of a door, a maid bustling about, and a beggar sitting in a broken archway. He strolled down to the bottom of the street, glancing back up to where he had just been. Quickly he pulled his frock coat tightly around himself as he stepped out smartly down the final part of the hill, burying his chin in its collar. Two idling blue uniforms, with slung muskets, had appeared around the corner at the top, and they came to a halt. But he had gone before they looked down the street.

He cursed himself for walking straight into this. It was a bad time of day for concealment, with too few people about in the town. An empty lane stood opposite. He went down it. There was just a cat and oddly a sleeping dog lying next to it, the flies and smells oppressive in the heat. He was a lucky man, because round the corner to the right was the baker, the alley that he recognised, and the cobbled court and the lintel with the face and the hood. The door was opened by the boy, who had tied up his hair and was wearing a waistcoat and breeches. This time, he had a ring in his ear, instead of one on a cord around his neck. He was holding a cap, scrunched up in his fingers.

'She says to get out of town, to go to Stival,' said the boy. 'Little Yann the miller has a horse for you.'

'Does he? My *charette*…'

'The blues are all over your *charette*. Forget that. You should have stayed away.'

Eugène began to grow angry. 'What do you mean, "you should have stayed away"?'

The boy shrugged, and made to close the door. 'It is what she says.'

Eugène stuck his foot in the gap, his anger getting the better of him. 'And who is she to say that? Where the devil is Stival, anyway? How am I supposed to get there? What use is a horse if I...'

The boy stepped outside and shut the door. 'I'll show you. Come on.'

'Thanks,' Eugène muttered grudgingly.

The boy led him down a back way that was shady and cool, and then behind the west end of the church. It was easy progress as the light deepened and the shadows lengthened. The boy pointed to the other side of the square, whispered, 'Saint Ivy,' and crossed himself. Eugène saw a chapel basking in the golden glow. They ambled towards it. The market square was almost emptied of people and produce, with men and women and a few children scattered here and there, one or two with mules.

Suddenly a shout echoed in the square, followed quickly by another, and four soldiers came rushing in from different directions at the top, grabbing one of the younger men, while three more ran in around the west end of the church and slowed to a halt. The boy edged up against the front of the chapel and disappeared inside the porch. Eugène followed behind him into the cool interior, and the boy pointed to a flight of stairs leading up to a gallery above. Heavy feet ran across the bottom of the square, and two of the soldiers poked their heads inside.

'You should come out into the light, my friend,' said one. 'We need to get a look at you.'

They came in. One of them took the boy's arm, while the other grasped his shirt collar tightly. They took him into the light at the doorway, where they hauled him up against the jamb.

'What's your name, boy?' The one who had grasped the boy's collar was hot and irritable.

The other soldier clicked his tongue. 'Citizen, Henri, citizen. Remember to be civil.'

'Well, either way, you have a name, citizen. What is it?' Henri let go of his collar.

The boy removed the other man's hand from his arm slowly. 'Loic.'

The two soldiers looked at each other with weary faces. 'Loic, Loic, even the dogs here are called Loic. Still, you can't be our man — you're too damn young. There's no one with you, is there? You wouldn't be hiding anyone in there, would you?'

They shoved him aside and strode into the chapel, the one called Henri taking his musket from his shoulder, the other trailing along behind him. The boy moved silently to the bottom of the steps into the gallery, and clicked his fingers crisply, just once. Eugène crept down the steps like a cat, and they both slipped out into the square. A yell came from the base of the church wall, and one of the *bleus* began to walk across towards them. Another shout, and three more of the soldiers took up the cry, one breaking into a run.

Old Françoise had been stationed at the crossroads just short of the bridge. She had hung around there for much of the afternoon, shambling about distractedly, using the little Rue de la Cendre to get from one side to the other. Françoise heard the fracas up in the market square long before Eugène and the boy came running down the curving Rue Saint-Ivy. She caught a glimpse of their faces as they hurtled round the corner. At a signal from her, another young man, dressed in a coat and wearing a round hat with a shining hatband, came careering out of the Rue du Pont, heading straight for the bridge. He was clearly desperate, because he almost slipped as he pulled up sharply, staring wildly at the three guards standing in the middle of the bridge. Then he shouted, '*Sacré bleu!*' and threw up his hands theatrically. He charged off along the quay, swinging to the right up a small street leading to the town.

The soldiers on the bridge grabbed their weapons, shouted, '*Arrêter!*' — more for the sound of it than in any real hope — and ran off in pursuit. The last of them was already straggling when the first of the soldiers from market square came tumbling down the Rue Saint-Ivy to be greeted vigorously by '*Allez! Allez!*' The straggler led them off towards the quay, where the young man in the hat had disappeared. Some of the other blues coming down from the market square slowed to a walk not far beyond the corner of the Rue Saint-Ivy, and turned back up towards the church.

Françoise looked around, and then opened the shabby door of one of the houses through which she had hustled Eugène and the boy. She urged them out and the two walked briskly but casually across the empty bridge, and skirted round behind the hospital on the far side. They were soon lost from sight.

The hat was easily discarded. Coline shook down her hair and pulled the petticoat on over her breeches, lacing the bodice tightly up to the neck. She had already thrown the coat over a wall, with some regret, because it was of not bad stuff, but it was too dangerous to keep. She was pleased with how it had gone. The street she had chosen for the chase was a good one, because it forked not far up, and she had lost a good half of them that way. The rest was easy. Straight on led into the centre of town, and they had gone pounding up there like a pack of overfed dogs, while she had ducked down right and doubled back, down the Rue du Pont. The bridge was still empty of soldiers, and she had found Françoise, who had given her the petticoat and elbowed her into a dark alley, standing in front of it while Coline changed. They walked back together. Loic would be fine: he would be safe enough coming back into town rather than out of it, and in the deepening dusk.

She was relieved to be rid of Picaud. Today had been a sack of trouble, with far too much at stake. Maybe she would see what she could find out at the works on the Blavet, where there might be a risk of being recognised by that steward; or maybe she would go to Brest and take Loic with her. She could sew, and he could find work as a runner on the quays. There would be plenty of sails to sew in Brest, and plenty more loose talk to listen to at the docks. But that was another day.

CHAPTER XIV: GROSJEAN IS WOUNDED

The Chouan captain Jean Rohu surveyed his depleted forces in the dim light and cramped corners of the cellar. With Georges Cadoudal — the leader of the Breton rebels — at Quiberon only a year ago, he had had ten thousand men, and here now were just ten. Thankfully, the good Lord had mostly preserved them but what did they have in the way of weapons? Mostly nothing at all, since strong arms and fists were usually enough for the *bougres* appointed by the godless in Paris. One had a billhook, another a sickle lashed to the end of a stick, and he himself had the sabre he had taken from an injured Republican officer. Yet the English ships had brought muskets and ammunition to Quiberon last year with the *émigré* army, and two of his men had kept theirs safe. One did not have his primed, but the other had let fly, and miraculously by Sainte Anne had winged one of the Republican troopers, the blood spreading quickly over his blue jacket, his cries louder than a stuck pig.

His men had run; there had been nothing else for it. He thought at first of heading for the chateau at Grand Champ, but since the disaster and the death of the *comte* the rebel Chouans no longer had much support there. As always, the *landes* and the *forêt* offered them a refuge, and there they could lose the Republican blues easily enough. The man called Grosjean had insisted on cracking one of their skulls against a tree, or at least stunning the soldier who was getting on their tail. For his pains they had heard several muskets crackle at a distance, too far for any real danger to life, but the big fellow had taken a shot in his buttock, which was bleeding and would be giving him hell. Grosjean was from Kergohan and was built like a barn-door, but he was also quick. He was grinning across at Rohu now from under his black beard, but something would have to be done. The rest were uninjured, and not much out of breath.

Jean Rohu got up from the crate on which he had been sitting, climbed up the broken stairs, and looked out through a gap in the wall of the ruin. There was no sign or sound of any pursuit. His lieutenant, Tomaz Michel, scrambled up after him. There was no point in waiting.

'We can't look after Grosjean. Get one of the lads to take him west, and hide him somewhere. If he goes home, the blues will capture him; it's happened before.'

Tomaz looked at his leader. Rohu went on through thick and thin, when the others had given up, and the men liked him. 'We could leave him with the charcoal burners, if we can find them. They'll look after him. Maybe they'll get someone to come out from a village and tend to him. They will have to get that lead shot out of him.'

'Yes, that works. Get hold of him, and someone who knows the woods over to the west there.'

'Erwan.'

'He'll do. He can rejoin us later. Get going now. And tell those two it's an order.'

Rohu waited while Tomaz went and got all the men out, Erwan already by Grosjean, whose face was now rigidly set. There was a broad track that led up to the ruin, and a small clearing in front of it, but only paths off and away from it. The party began to trail up one of these, with Rohu and the injured man bringing up the rear. One of the men in front suddenly turned round, shouted, and waved his arm, and Rohu heard the horse thundering up the track towards them. The *chasseur* reined in, his horse rearing and knocking Erwan to one side, and he lifted his sabre to strike down on Rohu, who had been slow to draw his own. The *chasseur* felt his ankle gripped with immense strength, and his leg was torn out of the stirrup. He grabbed the pommel of his saddle in desperation and struck out wildly. He saw Rohu's sabre raised to slash his thigh, and so leant forward, kicking his mount and wheeling away, thundering back down the track. The others came running back, but Tomaz had wisely pushed up one of the muskets aimed at the fleeing *chasseur*.

Rohu looked concerned. Grosjean had saved him from a tight spot, but the slash on his right shoulder was a nasty one, and he could hardly move his arm. They bound it up as best they could, and then Erwan and Grosjean struggled off to the west, while the rest of the party struck up north.

Le Guinec walked at an easy pace along the quay at Le Légué. It was a neat little port, good for certain kinds of local trading, and other small vessels. There were so few boats you could see the brig or *goélette* or whatever it was almost as if it had a sign painted on it saying 'American'. It was of no matter. The Republic's representative close by at Saint Brieuc was fully informed; he had been instructed to waive duties and facilitate passage. The odd little man whom Le Guinec had just met who was the Republic's agent had done well in providing good waggons with sound horses to draw them, and a letter for the post-houses along the way to Pontivy.

Le Guinec walked straight into the *auberge* on the quay, known as Le Cormoran. He spoke to the landlord, patted him on the back, and walked on to sit next to the man at the table in the corner. A bronzed and weather-beaten face greeted him, and the man stretched out his hand. One finger was missing its tip.

'*Monsieur* Le Guinec, pleased to make your acquaintance, sir. Will you be seated?'

The hand the man offered was shaken heartily: if there was something you wanted, never be half-hearted, Le Guinec's father had told him. He also took care to speak impeccably in English. 'And I yours, Captain Harker. You will take a cognac with me?' As he spoke, the landlord appeared at his elbow. 'A cognac, Thierry, and the same for the gentleman here.'

'That's mighty civil of you. You had a good journey?'

Le Guinec laughed. 'You ask me that? My dear man, I must be asking you.'

Harker considered this. What did landsmen know of sailing? 'Rough at times, wind set contrary, easterly, midway through the passage. A touch lumpy in the western approaches. Nothing out of the ordinary.'

The cognac arrived, but it remained for the while on the table.

'It is all set, Captain Harker. We have all possible cooperation from the authorities. The waggons are along there, in place. We even have men for unloading. Your crew can sit back, although you will of course supervise. It is all very satisfactory, and we are very grateful to you.'

Harker looked down at the table and the cognac, and drummed his fingers. 'And what form will that gratitude that you mention take, *monsieur*? Your man informed me when I made landfall that Mr Eugène would not be with us, but that you would be attending yourself, on behalf of *Monsieur* Guèvremont. I have that right, do I not?'

'You do, sir. *Monsieur* Picaud has had to leave France suddenly, as so many, alas, find that they do.'

'So how will I be paid?'

Le Guinec placed his hands flat on the table. 'I have given thought to that. Part of my thinking was that an American such as yourself might have little use for *assignats*, since you are not resident in France.'

'True,' said Harker.

'So, I have a different proposal. They say that in good trading, a ship should never sail empty. Where there is demand, there may be profit, over and above the principal. My thoughts came out, sir, on the side of liquor and lace.'

'What kind of liquor?'

'Brandy, Mr Harker. And Breton lace. There is a good demand in England for both. We provide you with goods to the price of your cargo of walnut, and then you will be at liberty to make a settlement to your advantage somewhere obscure on the southern English coast.'

Harker leaned back. 'Let us say that this arrangement was satisfactory to me — just say, mind you. Where do I load, and where do you suggest that I should unload, if you take my meaning?'

Le Guinec smiled. 'The agent of the Republic will depart with the waggons.' He paused. 'I have kegs in the warehouse of a friend, just up from here, at Pordic. There is a small beach near there.'

'You speak as one who has engaged in this trade before, *monsieur*?'

Le Guinec did not answer but continued to smile.

'And so do you have somewhere you might recommend, a *rendezvous*, so to speak? A lucky landfall?'

Le Guinec pursed his lips. 'You might try Cuckmere Haven, Captain. On the south coast, just along from the old port of

Seaford. But take care: they'll stick a knife in your back there as soon as look at you.'

'I think a man from Maine like me can take care of that. I'll see the goods first.'

Le Guinec looked the American in the eye. 'I would expect no less of you, Captain Harker. Shall we raise our glasses?'

CHAPTER XV: AN URGENT MESSAGE

As Amelia and Martha were leaving the house at New End on what promised to be a fine morning, Martha complained that her bonnet was crumpled and that one of the ribbons was becoming detached, and then that her shoe was pinching her foot. They paused at the bottom of the steps, to enable Martha to adjust her shoe and to allow Amelia to confirm that the sewing on the ribbon would hold well enough until it might be mended in the afternoon. They then set out, taking the lane towards the heath; this was by now their customary walk. They were going past the Pump Room on Wells Walk when Martha tripped on a tree root. Her tears were soon dried, but it was concluded that she should return to the house while Miss Amelia would continue her walk.

In indulging her discomposure and discontent, Martha had been finding occasion for a grievance against the man she regarded as her admirer, whose flattery had been persistent but whose attendance on her not always reliable. On this very morning she had hoped for better. But a slow walk to the shops, and a slow walk back again with a quart of milk, with the inclusion of some dawdling at corners, had sadly confirmed his absence. His attentions had been tailing off, and she had hoped to find him falling in at her shoulder as she made her sorry way home, but he did not appear. She trailed into the house with a mumbled explanation to Mrs Claydon, and hobbled upstairs to her room.

Meanwhile, Amelia felt light-hearted. The sun was shining, the air was clean and fresh, and the paths were peaceful and relatively quiet. It was almost exhilarating to be on her own for once, although she was careful: the heath had its reputation, even if she believed that nothing adverse could affect her at this respectable hour. So, with good sense, she decided to stroll a little into the heather but to keep the path within sight. She laughed as she gave a small jump to clear one obtruding stem and congratulated herself on not catching the skirts of her gown on any thorns. It was all delightful, but she chose to walk round in a semi-circle, to emerge back safely onto the lane. In achieving this, she found that she might finally push aside the light branches of a small tree with silver bark and delicate leaves in order to get back onto the path by the lane. Taken by her delight in that manoeuvre, she burst out suddenly in front of a young woman.

Molly stepped back indignantly, clutching the yoke that hung on her shoulder with a protest on her lips, the bang of the empty pails in her other hand speaking for her. She then widened her eyes in a mixture of astonishment and amusement.

'Lord, miss, you don't half give a body a fright, popping up like that!'

Amelia was flustered, excited by her walk and the freedom of it. Molly's face was enlivened by the shock, and Amelia could smell the milk on her. She bit her lip. 'Yes, I know, I am so sorry, it was inconsiderate to be so sudden. I had not thought … to meet … to bump into…'

Here they both laughed.

'Ay, bump it were, by a whisker, as we say! Begging your pardon, but your pumps are mucky, miss. Here, let me brush them.'

Without waiting for an answer, Molly put down her pails and bent down to brush Amelia's shoes with the edge of her apron. Amelia had been looking down, astonished, at the top of the milkmaid's head. Without thinking, she let her hand touch her hair, stroking it gently with a finger. Molly looked up and then down again, rubbed the second shoe vigorously. She stood up.

'There, that'll do it.'

Amelia began to adjust the spotted handkerchief that Molly wore above her old-fashioned jacket bodice. She arranged it around Molly's neck, and settled it on her shoulders. Molly submitted to this mildly, but as Amelia's hands lingered on her upper arms, she turned back to pick up her pails, brushing down her apron.

'Right as rain, ain't we now? All prim and proper, as the missus says.'

Amelia took a tentative step forward. 'Molly...'

'Well, I must be getting on now, miss, or there'll be a ruckus.' She looked past Amelia and began to move smartly. 'Look, here's a gentleman coming on to see you, miss, and he isn't after my empty pans, that's for certain. I'll be a bidding you good day, miss.'

Amelia felt light-headed. For a moment dizziness took her, and she reached out an arm for Molly, but the milkmaid had moved out of reach. She put her hand to her face instead, and stared at the ground to steady herself. A voice came to her from only a short distance behind.

'Miss Wentworth? Miss Amelia Wentworth?'

'I... Yes.' Amelia stood still, and the man waited patiently.

The leaves of the silver birch rustled in a light breeze, which lifted wisps of her hair. She turned round, more in possession of herself.

'Pray, sir, what is your business? I am Miss Wentworth, but what can you want with me?'

The man was respectably dressed and someone with skill had paid attention to his hair, which was cut almost in the fashion, although a little grown out. His boots also left a little to be desired, but his coat and breeches were of a fine brown cloth. It was reassuring. 'Indeed, madam, you will accept my apologies for accosting you in this manner, but I am relieved to have found you. I am the trusted bearer of a message.'

Amelia frowned slightly, but the man bowed and handed her a piece of paper. 'With your permission.'

The letter yielded a mild but distinctive fragrance, and was indeed addressed to her. Amelia opened it and read:

My dear Miss Wentworth, you must forgive me for disturbing your enviable life in retreat at Hampstead. But I am aghast to inform you that my situation is nigh on calamitous, and our previous acquaintance leads me to believe you would wish to relieve me from further distress. The man who bears this letter is to be trusted, and he will convey you immediately to the side of one who hopes most sincerely that she may safely call herself your dear, dear friend, Thirza Farley.

Amelia's hand trembled as she read the letter again, and for the first time she looked at the face of the man opposite, whose expression was pained. Her voice was a little high when she spoke.

'What is the calamity of which Miss Farley writes?'

The gentleman moved his weight onto one leg and placed one hand inside his lapel. He shook his head slightly. 'Madam, I was not entrusted with that information, or, more precisely, I was instructed not to speak myself but to convey you with the greatest urgency to the writer of this letter. Those were my strictest instructions. I was to accompany you. That was the limit of my duties.' With this solemn communication, the gentleman bowed.

'How? How might you accompany me?' Amelia tried to concentrate, and found herself looking fixedly at the row of buttons on his coat. Her fingers still clutched the letter, her arm hanging weakly down by her side.

'Well, the means is here at hand, madam, courtesy of Miss Farley, that is. The carriage is at our disposal. Miss Farley thought to send a lady's maid too.'

He smiled reassuringly and gestured to a coach and pair standing a short way down the lane. The driver was at the head of the horses, and a woman of middle years in a plain bonnet was holding the door open, with a modest and patient air about her.

Amelia made her decision in an instant. She placed the folded letter in her pocket and walked steadily to the carriage, greeting the woman quietly, who curtsied and climbed in behind her. The coachman folded the steps and clambered up onto the box, where he was joined by the gentleman in the brown suit. No words passed between them. The horses shook their harness and pulled off down the lane towards the London road.

Amelia fell silent as the coach ran down beside the heath and then turned onto the main road. She had no impression of the journey, but an image of Miss Farley kept flashing up in front of her. Again and again she tried to assess the word 'calamitous' from the note she had read, but short of imagining horrors, she could make no sense of it. This was London, after all — perhaps it was simply pecuniary embarrassment. Thirza Farley was generous-hearted, and it was easy to believe that she might have loaned money to someone in need, and that it had now brought her into danger.

The woman who sat opposite her did not interrupt her train of thought, but stared expressionlessly out of the window. The wheels ground on, and the bustle outside alternately grew louder or diminished as they passed through different parts of the city, all of them unknown to Amelia. She now wished she had previously called upon Miss Farley, but recollected once more that she had received no reply to the note she had previously sent. Nor was there any address supplied on the letter she now had in her pocket.

They were eventually in a busy thoroughfare, and the coachman slowed his horses to an ambling pace, weaving from left to right to avoid carts and other coaches. Amelia thought at one instant that she had a view of the river and of masts, but the coach veered sharply to the left and drew to a halt at the entrance to a court. The door was pulled open, and the gentleman in brown gave a short bow as he offered her his arm to help her descend. It was a dull quarter, penetrated by noise from the busier street, which was just visible at the end of the lane. They walked into the recesses of the court and towards a staircase; young women and girls stared out from windows as they climbed the stairs. Amelia was now excited to see her friend, but the room that she was shown into on an upper floor of the building was empty. It had a small bed in it, a respectable ewer and basin, and some clothing hung over a simple rail.

'Miss Farley will come to you here, Miss, if you would be so good as to wait.'

There was a small, upholstered chair with a conventional striped pattern, in good condition. It seemed likely that there was a closet behind a plain, panelled door. Amelia sat down on the chair and became lost in thought.

A man crowned with a non-descript and tatty bicorne hat emerged from the shadows of an alley leading on to Narrow

Street on the north bank of the Pool of London. He was wearing a greatcoat with several capes over a dark, possibly brown suit, and a pair of scuffed boots. He looked impatient but remained inconspicuous amongst the bustle of lads and porters. A gang of them pushed past him with little ceremony, carrying sacks of coal from the colliers moored just off the stairs below. He had been in and out of the top of the alley for some time, standing back half-obscured in a recess that took him out of the way, but which allowed him to scan the street opposite. Carriages passed, and carts were laden and unladen, the coal coming off the boats to be stored up for the autumn and winter.

'Enough horses here to feed a cellar of mushrooms,' he muttered to himself, looking at the spattered wheels of the carts.

'Thinking of taking up an honest trade, are you, Jencks? My, my, that would be the day. Come now, out with it.' The speaker had come up behind him in that nasty way he had, no matter how much you looked out for him. 'You keep facing right ahead and tell me what I want to hear.'

Jencks swallowed. 'It's as you wanted. Easy as pie when it came to it. Safely stowed, just where we said. Sal has her tight.'

'What about the maid?'

'Oh, you don't want to worry about her. I had her all fixed up, eating out of my hand for the past couple of weeks. Silly little cow.'

'No, you fool, did you take her up too?'

For the first time, Jencks felt relaxed under this scrutiny. He laughed. 'We were going to take them both up willy-nilly, since you said it was past time, but blow me down — that fool of a maid bangs her foot and flaps back to the house. So the young miss was on her own. No struggle, easy as pie. Just talk, smooth talk, and that scribble you gave to us. Worked a treat. Mind you, I do have a way with them…'

'Safely stowed? On her own? Your woman can keep her trap shut?'

'Sal? Mum's the word with Sal, when she wants to. Sal'll burn her wrists for her if she gets uppity. Don't you worry.'

The other man hissed in his ear. 'Less of that. And you keep away from her, do you hear? Move her again if you have to, but you will let me know. Or rather, let Captain Teuling know. He'll be still in the Pool here, even if he's loading. But she's safer kept away from him.'

'Ay, the Dutch bastard.' Jencks swallowed again, and his voice trembled slightly. 'I'll have my money now, as we said. That's all fair.' There was a moment of silence, and then he heard a movement. Instinctively, he flinched, but a hand gripped his forearm, and next he felt a sudden weight in the pocket of his greatcoat.

'Half of it, as we said. Coin. The balance when she goes on board, and you take yourself off with that woman of yours. You know me: I keep my word. But I don't go easy on those who don't keep theirs, who let me down. You understand me, I take it?'

Jencks nodded vigorously.

'You have done well, Jencks. I reward those who do well. Keep that in mind. I shall be back in London tomorrow evening by seven, no later. Time and tide, Jencks, you'll have heard the saying.'

'Ay, sir, it's one of my own. It's said they wait for no man.'

'Not even dead men, Jencks. They pull them out of the river, just down there by the lime kilns before they get carried too far. It's a good trade, I hear, better than mushrooms. You go your way, now.'

Jencks needed no second command and crossed the street, one hand firmly in his greatcoat pocket, clasping the purse of coins. He had no intention of looking behind him. The other man watched him for a moment, then walked briskly up Narrow Street to the west, where a hackney carriage was standing by the side of the road. He put his hand on the door and spoke to the driver, who was sitting on the box under his black hat.

'Lombard Street. In good time for the Plymouth coach.'

He stepped in and shut the door, and the driver turned his horse's nose into the bright light of the setting sun.

CHAPTER XVI: JEANNE PLAYS A PART

Le Guinec travelled by diligence to Pontivy. Leroux had made sure there was an escort for the waggons loaded with the black walnut dye, even if he himself was off chasing rebels in the *landes*, rounding up the last of the resistance. Le Guinec wondered idly what would happen to the captain when it was all over, and his presence here was no longer required. Like all conquered provinces, over time Brittany would succumb to civilian administrators, and the soldiers would be sent to fight elsewhere, as they always were. So much for Leroux's ambitions for the lovely Joséphine. Le Guinec wondered how far that dalliance had got.

Since he had made the decision not to travel on with the waggons, he did not wait for their arrival either. It was enough to report on their safe departure from the coast, and confirm the arrangements for their reception. He had other things in mind, and found an excuse to take his own horse from the stable-yard at the Guèvremont house in Pontivy. Auray would be his ultimate destination, but he took his time. He stopped in at Kergohan without prior arrangement to check on how they were doing, and to be able to report with a lack of enthusiasm on what he found there.

He then rode on to Brandivy and out through the small village until he came to a cottage perched on the intersection of a lane and a rutted track. There he dismounted and found himself confronted by a woman of middling years, who wore a faded gown and shoes rather than clogs. She eyed him with suspicion, but her body was relaxed. Since her husband Henri Cariou had died, Le Guinec liked to think that he provided for her. He had always known that Gilles's mother had a sister, and in the intrigues surrounding the manor at Kergohan he had felt it might be advantageous to track her down. It had not been difficult; she lived where she had always lived, in a village close to Kergohan. They had now what he liked to call an understanding, which meant that he visited her from time to time when he felt the inclination, making sure that she and the villagers around her knew who was the *patron*.

'*Kenavo*, Jeanne,' Le Guinec greeted her. 'I shall want water for this beast, and some decent grass at least.'

Jeanne pointed to the well. There was a wooden bucket standing by it. Le Guinec grimaced and gave her the reins, while he pulled the water.

'Your horse can go over there,' said Jeanne. 'The grass is long enough to interest him. Stick the bucket by him.'

She went into the cottage, and Le Guinec followed her.

'So, do you still have any of the wine I left you?' he asked.

'I am no drunkard,' Jeanne replied. 'Pull the cork yourself.'

Le Guinec did so and took one of the two plain glasses that she had, and which he had given her. There was a box bed on the far side, and a bench and a stool. He took the stool. She leant on the wall by the hearth. There was a ham hanging from a hook, herbs tied and pinned to the wall, and a small *armoire* across from the bed.

'What do you want?'

Le Guinec looked up and grinned at her. 'I sometimes wonder about that myself. You do well enough here.'

She shifted her weight. 'Drink up and tell me what you want.'

'Jeanne, Jeanne, shall we say I am perhaps calling in a debt? Or maybe that is too coarse an expression. I am asking a favour.'

She scowled at him. 'You've had your favours from me, often enough. As and when you've chosen. This is different, I can smell it. Out with it.'

'I need you to talk about your sister.'

Her face became expressionless. 'What about my sister?'

'Oh, just what you have told me.' He poured a little more into his glass. 'This is really not bad at all.' He drank it. 'Who was the father of her child?'

Jeanne's voice was very low. 'I've told you, I don't know. She never told me.'

Le Guinec put down his glass, which he had held suspended. 'Jeanne, Jeanne.' He gestured round the room. 'Where does all this come from? Eh? I look after you, keep you warm, don't I? Do you have to dig and struggle?'

'No. What do you want?'

'Very, very little, Jeanne. Just for you to tell one man in a comfortable room that your sister said the boy's father lived at the manor. That's all.'

She stared at him in disbelief. 'Everyone knows that, you donkey! What's the point of saying that? Where else would she have … got with child?'

Le Guinec fingered his glass. 'Now, don't make me angry, Jeanne. All you have to do is to tell this man in his comfortable room that you are her sister, and that the father of her son was the young Wentworth, at Kergohan. Justin Wentworth.' He poured another small glass. 'I can speak the name for you if you have trouble with the English.'

'Who is this man in his comfortable room? Why does he want to know, after all this time? The poor girl…'

'You need not worry about that. He will be very pleased with what you say. And so will others be.' He drank the wine. 'Not least myself. And pleasing me is a good idea, is it not?' He got up from the bench. 'I must press on. I shall send for you, perhaps even come for you, when the time is right. You will just say that, no more, and say that she told you before she died. That's all. And I shall be very grateful.' He went towards the door and the sunlight. It was very dark in the room, despite the season. He stood with his face in the bright light, then turned towards her and sighed. 'And Jeanne, don't call me a donkey.'

A week or so later, Le Guinec took the small chaise from the house at Auray to bring Jeanne from Brandivy for the meeting with his master. Guèvremont had returned from Pontivy after a short stay in order not to leave his daughter on her own for too long in Auray. He had detected that she was out of sorts, and he did not know why, but it worried him. The expected cargo from America had now arrived at the dyeing works on the Blavet, and there were skilled men to supervise its use. Time alone would tell if it was successful.

Jeanne sat up alongside Le Guinec, who handled the reins competently. She hardly spoke on the journey, merely replying to one or two observations that he made about the places that they were passing, or the people, some of whom he viewed as comic figures, which irritated her. He drove through the gates of the house, left the horse to look after itself, and brought Jeanne up to the door. It was answered by Bernard, whom Le Guinec greeted curtly before marching into the hall. Bernard bowed to Jeanne, and when their eyes met, hers widened in astonishment. Bernard closed the door and, seeking her permission, preceded her towards the study door, where Le

Guinec was standing. Bernard tapped lightly on the study door and waited. Jeanne stared down the hall, and then back towards the front door, but not at Bernard. She was holding a bonnet in her hands. The door opened and Guèvremont ushered them in. The door was closed behind them.

'*Madame*, it is my pleasure. May I introduce myself as Laurent Guèvremont, of this town and also of Pontivy? You will be pleased to be seated. I believe that chair will prove to be the most comfortable.'

Jeanne sat down. She considered putting her bonnet on the small table to one side of the chair, but thought better of it. It remained on her lap. Le Guinec crossed his legs, which annoyed Laurent disproportionately. He himself sat at his desk and moved his paperweight to one side, and then back again.

'*Madame*...'

'Jeanne, *monsieur*, if you please.'

'Yes, of course. Jeanne, it is.' He cleared his throat. 'You will be aware just how sensitive this matter is. It concerns your dearly departed sister, and confidences you may have received from her nearly twenty years ago. You yourself were then a young woman...'

'I remember my sister, sir,' she said. Le Guinec shifted uncomfortably and tried to catch her eye, but failed to do so. She was looking resolutely at the floor a little distance in front of her.

'I'm sure you do. We... All of us here are aware that there was a child, joyously, just before her tragic demise — a son. In that we may rejoice...'

'I have never seen him. Not since he was a babe in arms. I can tell you nothing about him.'

Here Le Guinec sat forward, but Guèvremont motioned him back.

'You live near the village of Brandivy,' he said.

'I do. I have done since that time — since before then, in fact. My husband Henri…'

Guèvremont folded his hands. He did not want to hear about her husband, but he did wish to keep her talking.

'He died. That is all.'

Le Guinec showed signs of impatience, and Guèvremont now raised a finger in his direction.

'My sincere commiserations, *madame*. I too have lost a life partner.'

For the first time Jeanne looked up at him, to see a face that betrayed no emotion. She lowered her eyes again.

'Jeanne, it is difficult, I am sure, no doubt distressing, but we are here today because I have been informed that your sister spoke to you before she died.'

Jeanne looked at him again. 'We spoke several times, sir, when I could come to see her — when she was with child, and when it was born, sir. We weren't close, for all that.'

Le Guinec re-crossed his legs, ran his fingers through his hair, and rested his chin on his fist, facing away from her.

Guèvremont now unfolded his hands and took up a pen, holding it over the blank sheet of paper in front of him. 'And what did she tell you, Jeanne?'

'What do you mean, sir? She said much that women say when they are with child. She was afeared of pain, of death, even, God rest her soul…'

Guèvremont paused. 'Was there anything else?'

There was complete silence in the room.

'No, sir.'

Le Guinec pushed his chair back and stood up abruptly, his face bright with anger.

Guèvremont's tone was absolute. 'You will sit down, sir, and not interrupt me. I hope I make myself plain?'

Le Guinec concurred, but with a face like thunder.

Guèvremont turned back to Jeanne. 'You are sure, Jeanne, that she spoke of nothing else? You understand to what I am referring?'

'No, sir.' It was a prompt reply, almost pert.

Guèvremont now became exasperated. 'I was given to understand that you might have information about the boy's father, *madame*. Have I misunderstood? Please enlighten me promptly.'

Jeanne kept her eyes on the floor. 'I do not know who he was. My sister never said. It is my belief she was too ashamed.'

Le Guinec was speechless. He gripped the arms of his chair and stared at the back of her head menacingly.

Guèvremont ignored him and rose to his feet. 'I must thank you for your time, *madame*. It is most kind of you to come all this way. Now, if you would be good enough to step outside, Bernard will make sure that the housekeeper provides you with some suitable refreshment before your journey home.'

Guèvremont smiled and stretched out his arm to indicate the door. Le Guinec made to follow her.

'No, not you, Le Guinec. A word with you alone, if you please.'

Jeanne made her own way to the door, stepping around Le Guinec, who stood stiffly in her way. She let herself out.

Bernard was standing close to the door. She faced him, and he spoke with feeling. 'It's been a long time, Jeanne.'

He led the way along the corridor and down into the kitchen. It was some hours before the preparation of dinner, and the room was empty. He sat Jeanne down on a bench and went to look in the pantry. She gazed at the coppers and at the leafy parsley lying on the top, freshly cut.

Bernard came back out. '*Madame* Durand, our housekeeper, is out buying produce in the town. We have lemonade, if that is of interest.'

'Lemonade? Why, there's a thing. I'll take a glass of lemonade, thank you. Before that brute comes down here looking for me.'

Bernard went into the pantry and came back with the glass. 'Some like to stir more sugar into it.'

She laughed and sipped. 'Tastes sweet enough to me.' And then, without looking at him, she asked, 'How is your life, Bernard? Is it sweet?'

He sat down opposite her. She noticed that his eyes were lined, and his cheeks had sagged a little. He still had that same cleft in his chin. She had turned him away, because her parents had insisted on it, but she had hurt herself as much him.

'Why are you here, Jeanne? What do they want with you?' His voice tightened, and he looked away. 'What happened to your husband, Henri?'

She fingered her glass and wondered how much to tell him. 'He broke his leg. The wound went bad. Years ago now.' She drank from her glass. 'I think I should go. Le Guinec will be coming down for me.'

'What is this with Le Guinec?'

Jeanne put the glass on the table, and got to her feet. 'He … has looked after me.' She raised her hand to silence Bernard. 'Do not ask me how. I should go.'

Bernard stood up, and his eyes narrowed. 'Yes, go, but not with him, Jeanne. Not now. There's a door at the back there. You remember my sister Anne, from when you and I… She lives in the town now, Rue des Tonneaux, next to the one cooper who's left. Her name is Machaud, and she has a husband named Edouard and a small daughter. Stay with her; talk about old times. Tell her I shall visit tonight.'

Jeanne picked up her glass again, and he saw that her hand was trembling. She put it down. 'What will you tell Le Guinec?'

Bernard fixed his stare on a small crack in the wall opposite. 'I shall tell him that you had some refreshment with me in the kitchen, and then left the house. What else is there to say?'

Jeanne understood that this was a crossroads in her life. She stood up and walked out towards the heavy, bolted back-door of the house, which was down a short passage at the far end of the kitchen.

CHAPTER XVII: EUGÈNE IN LONDON

The dawn was grey, and the brig creaked and eased its way along with a slight breeze behind it. Eugène Picaud was on the deck, marking the ship's progress. The tide was master of all movements now. The rising sun lay behind the vessel, and its sharp light ran across the calm water, blocked by the sea-mist.

Suddenly, the mist lifted slightly and the massive, black bulk of a ship was revealed. It was pinned down like Gulliver, its hawsers groaning as the tide began to pull on them. The brig slipped smoothly between three of the grim prison hulks, one or two grey souls on the decks staring down as they passed.

The brig ran on, patches of mist still clinging to the land, and other sails could be seen in the waters to the north of them, mostly merchantmen, carrying the marvels of produce into the Pool of London. From the shore the clang of metal rang out across the water. And there, in the distance, was the source of it all, a chain-gang down on the strand with a longboat beached beside them, another two further along. The tricorn hats and coats moved among the bent figures, none looking out to sea.

The brig creaked as the slack sail caught a gasp of wind and then bellied, steering itself easily around Sheerness out of the broader estuary of the Thames and sharply into the Medway, the flow faster and stronger. More people were now on deck: a lad who touched his cap to Eugène before slipping below, a bearded man holding a cage with a cockerel in it, grasping the rail, an old sailor knocking out a clay pipe.

The dockyard at Chatham was like a ship on land, each part of it separated from the other, laid out in workshops until it all came together in the docks themselves. Picaud made his way quickly away from the quay, walking briskly to the south. All he had with him was a creased leather bag of clothing, which he had purchased in Jersey after the humiliating interview with Philippe d'Auvergne, who had asked warmly after Coline, but who had scorned the little that Eugène had to tell him. Still, it was no more humiliating than running from the streets of Pontivy, saved by an old woman, a boy with a ring in his ear, and an inscrutable and able young spy who plainly considered him no better than a nuisance.

The Royal Marine barracks was a new building, set back from the water. The guards on duty outside the main door made no attempt to obstruct Picaud's entry, but once inside he paused to ask his way. Down a corridor to the left, he knocked on a door, after glancing at a small nameplate on it, and did not wait to be called in. He slid his bag across the smooth wooden flooring, where it bumped against the ankles of a tall man in a red uniform who was standing by a window that looked out on a yard.

Major Francis Houghton looked round in surprise, staring coolly at the individual who had invaded his private space, and then at the offending bag. He prodded it distastefully with one boot, and then deftly kicked it into the far corner of the room. His face broke into a broad smile.

'Clowning again, *Monsieur* Picaud, or whatever you now call yourself! I see that you let yourself in as you always do, no matter what a man might be up to in his own rooms. I'll be damned if you don't ask me in half a tick if you might doss down on my floor. Come, take my hand and shake it like a soldier.' With that, Houghton stepped forward and took

145

Eugène's hand. 'Come now, a drink. First footing onshore, I'll be bound. James, where are you, man?'

A door into an adjoining room opened to reveal a young face.

'Claret, James, and two glasses on a tray. Make sure they're clean, James, do you hear? And scrub your hands, James.' Houghton turned to Picaud. 'Sit down, Eugène. I'll stand, if you don't mind. Leg gets stiff with too much desk-work. Well, let's have a look at you, then.'

Eugène showed what he hoped was a pleasant and relaxed manner under scrutiny as the young man came back into the room, holding a cheap tray with glasses and a bottle in reddened hands.

'Set them down,' said Houghton. 'Let me see those hands. They'll do. Better, James, better. Damned boys. Have to drill it into them.'

The young man left and closed the door, without being told.

'I'll wager you do, Francis,' said Eugène. 'And the lad is not shaving yet, I see. Ensign, I presume?'

Houghton looked a little sharp at that. 'He'll be signing soon. Very soon, we hope. We're short as things stand, very short right now. His father sent him down to see how he likes it, just for a week or so. James goes out at night from the barracks to lodgings. Ned takes him through the boot-room and shows him things. But enough of him. So, you're done with whatever your assignment was. From what I hear, you've been doing what I'm not supposed to hear about, if you catch my drift. You found me, then? I said I'd be here, and here I am.'

'Major Houghton, no less. It's a grand sound, Francis. I like it. Bottom of your glass, old man.'

Houghton drank only half of his, then looked shrewdly at Picaud. 'By my reckoning, it's what comes next that is puzzling you. One foot ashore, the other who knows where. You're a rootless man, Eugène.'

Eugène turned his glass upside down, swinging it gently between two fingers. 'The Régiment Loyal-Émigrant had its appeal. But Quiberon was not good, not good at all, nor indeed has … has my recent service been what I or others might have hoped. I find myself at what you *rosbifs* might call a snipped end.'

'A what? No such damned thing. Why, it's a loose end, I'll have you know, and I'll hear no more of your roast-beefs either, or I'll take you for a Jacobin.'

Eugène put the glass down and swivelled in his seat to look up the major. 'Would you take me for a marine, Francis? Get me away. There are fleets for Australia, service in India, even Canada. I might be useful in Canada. Justin Wentworth could be my sponsor, perhaps?'

Houghton, for all his apparently casual manner, was a good judge of morale if of nothing else. He pulled the other chair over to sit down opposite Picaud. He then drew his long legs up as he sat forward, putting both hands under his left knee to lift it into a comfortable position. 'It is my belief that you would make a good officer,' he said at last. 'Cool head under fire, no doubt, no doubt at all. But … give it a while, Eugène — that's my best advice. There might be difficulties, of course, what with … parentage — no, that's come out wrong — with the fact that you're French, dammit. I know, I know, and the Enlistment Act may cover it, or might be persuaded to cover it. Now, look, don't get me wrong, you're as English as a cup of tea in the rector's drawing room on a rainy Sunday in June, but there is caution, and there are rules.'

Picaud got up.

'Now, don't take on, for mutton's sake…' Houghton feared that he may have judged it badly.

'I'm not taking on, as you say it,' said Eugène. 'I must get to Rochester, and on to Gravesend for the London ferry. Let me shake your hand again, Francis. You've been a good friend.'

Houghton was now standing, and he clapped his hand on Picaud's shoulder. 'Best not to forget your bag, old man.'

Eugène did not. He paused at the door. 'I should be in London for a while. Perhaps drop down again sometime?'

'Good thinking. I'll be here, but you could let me know. Not always unoccupied like this morning. Bit of luck there.'

'Yes, it was good luck. I'll bid you good morning.'

Eugène left. Some voices were raised along the corridor, so Houghton strode across and poked his head out of the door. It was just orders being given. He closed the door and reflected on Picaud's request. He could hardly see him as a marine. No sea legs at all — he had no doubt his friend would be sick as a dog on the flat-bottomed ferry to London. But the man was at a loss, that much was plain to see.

Eugène ran up the stairs at Billingsgate and on to the quay. The market was long over. Sodden sacks and baskets stood stacked away to the right, some with seagulls squabbling over the few remaining tit-bits or raucously proclaiming their rights from a temporary perch. Eugène had with him his old leather bag, because he could not think where to stow it in his haste to fulfil his mission — perhaps the only mission now left to him. He was conscious that his face was flushed, like a schoolboy, he thought, and perhaps he was no more than that.

He disappeared up one of the alleys leading to Thames Street and crossed the main thoroughfare that led from the bridge. He then passed the approach to the imposing façade of the

Fishmonger's Hall and broke into a run back down to the riverside at Old Swan stairs.

The waterman ran the boat through the slack water close to the shore, watching out for the gradual turn of the tide. Eugène opened his bag and pulled out a much-folded paper, spreading it on his knee and tracing the relevant passage with his finger. He knew the direction he was heading in, and the name of Mrs Claydon — the landlady of the residence he was looking for — but would he know the house itself when it came to it? There had been mention of an identifying feature, an old carriage lamp that had been placed outside the door. He looked again at the letter from Amelia. Why was it that everything she wrote affected him so, and set him searching for signs of regard? No, there was nothing else there except what Amelia had been told herself, just that carriage lamp. He folded the letter again and stowed it away as the waterman barked out, 'Temple stairs!'

It was a short step then through the Temple itself, with its clerical bustle and buckled shoes, and along Chancery Lane to the hackney stands in Holborn. He was certain that the right road out of town ran up from near there, and it took very little time to secure a coach. They rolled up a street he had never travelled before. Gray's Inn and its fields to the left were attractive enough, the smells strong and sweet. A light breeze came through the window as the carriage began to creak, the horses hauling the weight up the long hill to Hampstead.

He decided to start his search with the post booth, so he swung into the inn that was attached to it. A thin, balding server informed him that the post was to be found at the counter down the hall, run by a man named Elias. Elias did know of two ladies by the name of Claydon, mother and daughter, and two separate houses, one at New End. Mrs

Claydon came in for the post herself, but she asked for a post-boy to carry bigger parcels for her, so yes, he believed there was a lamp of some kind by that house, and it was only a step away.

Eugène avoided the barrels rolling from the dray and dropping into the cellar, caught the eye of a maid who blushed as he smiled at her, and asked the direction again of an old gaffer, who set him right, waving with his stick. The sun had been flickering, but now it came out strongly, and a child with his thumb in his mouth held his mother back to wonder at the pace Eugène was setting. There were some railings, an array of perfectly respectable doors, and mercifully just one carriage lamp. Eugène ran up the steps from the street. He gave himself a minute before he knocked and stood back slightly, holding the bag awkwardly behind him.

He could hear voices and the sound of footsteps. Then there was a loud reprimand: 'Out of my way, girl!' He braced himself as the door was pulled open. A comely woman of some stature stood in the frame, and behind her two anxious faces, one more matronly, the other surely a maid. The woman in front of him seemed astonished.

'Your servant, madam,' said Eugène. 'Please forgive me for arriving on your doorstep unannounced. I was, however, led to believe…'

The woman's face had passed from astonishment to recognition in an instant, but her words were strangely distant. 'You, sir, unless I am mistaken, are Mr Picaud, Mr Eugène Picaud. Oh, my Lord.' She abruptly turned her back on Picaud and walked unsteadily down the hallway, as the maid came forward to take her arm and guide her onwards.

Eugène began to realise his mistake and cursed himself for his lack of manners. It must be a rare thing that Miss Caroline

North should answer the door herself, and in that moment he had failed to recognise her, for he had been searching for another, dearer face behind hers. The thoroughly respectable, matronly figure, who must surely be Mrs Claydon, now came forward, but he was still not ushered in from the step.

'You must forgive me, but I was invited to call here in New End by Miss Amelia Wentworth. I am a friend of her and her brother, Captain Justin Wentworth. My most abject apologies must be due to Miss North for unforgivably…' He broke off as he scanned Mrs Claydon's face, which was pale and expressive of shock, and felt a tightening in his chest.

Mrs Claydon looked over his shoulder and brought him in. She shut the door and held him by his forearm as she leaned in to speak in his ear. 'Miss Amelia has gone missing, sir. Miss North is distraught. She does not know what is to be done.'

Eugène breathed in deeply, handed his bag to the landlady without a word, and walked down the hall.

CHAPTER XVIII: GILLES AT THE MANOR

Grosjean did not complain once on the long journey through the forest. He made a great effort to shift for himself successfully, since he knew that his size would make it difficult for anyone to support him beyond a certain point. Erwan was not a thin man, and was of a fair height, so between them they were able to lean together and propel themselves forwards. Their greatest advantage was that they both knew the woods and the *landes* almost by instinct and could tread without noise on the forest floor. They were helped over the last stretch by the sudden appearance of Maelig, the woodsman who was the spirit of the *landes* above Kergohan. He stood expressionless, as if he almost expected them. They shook hands, and he observed the wounds without speaking, leading them immediately off the track they were following and by tortuous paths past outcrops of stone. They moved towards the smell of turf smoke, and then the muffled sound of voices.

The charcoal-burners led a good life, exchanging their charcoal and the timber that they had cut for all kinds of necessities. Their shelter was sound, the woods themselves well out of reach of the pastures that were home to the flies. They had remedies they had used for cuts and even for broken bones, but they knew that Grosjean would need fine iron-working pincers to lay hold of the shot that was in him, and brandy to help him as he gritted his teeth on the stub of thick green hazel they would give him. Maelig went on with Erwan, to take him down to the village and bring him back again.

When they told Yaelle what had happened to her husband, she was frantic. Babette had never seen her like that, and she had to hold Yaelle tight to stop her accidentally injuring herself. Maybe Erwan could have told it better, but he had a countryman's bluntness and a soldier's eye for brutal detail. Yaelle was down at the manor, and that was a lucky chance, because the blues would be looking for Grosjean and the fewer who knew of his injury in the village, the better. Maelig just stood by the well and helped himself to a pail of water, impassive as ever, but Daniel wasted no time in looking for a suitable implement. He had no metal-working tools, but he did have pincers that he used on the nails in hooves, and others that were smaller but narrow-nosed. He took wine, vinegar and garlic from the kitchen, and a strip of new linen from the store. Daniel and Babette comforted Yaelle, and she agreed that she would help them do anything.

They were with Grosjean before the sun had begun to decline. He was in a fitful sleep, lying on sacks of dried leaves that were in the shade of the charcoal-burners' shelter. Daniel placed his pincers in the fire they had made, and watched the burners blow it red and then almost white. Babette sat with Yaelle, who had not touched Grosjean and whose face was pale and drawn. They both waited to wake him for what was to come.

Gilles set about inveigling Fourrier into letting him visit Kergohan. He guessed it would be a long struggle, but he considered that Fourrier would be much easier to win round than the *bourgeois* Guèvremont, or the steward, Le Guinec. Gaëlle pretended to spit on the floor whenever Le Guinec's name came up. He liked to catch her in corners, she said, *le salaud*, or coming up or down the stairs. He would stand in her way until she had to push past him, and she knew what that was all about.

Gilles whined a bit to Fourrier about missing people at Kergohan, and when that did no good, he hit on the idea of saying that he ought to see how the crops were getting on, to start to calculate what they might fetch. Fourrier looked a bit more interested then, but what finally swayed him was a whisper from Gilles that he really wanted to celebrate Mass with the priest in the woods, and to go to confession there.

Fourrier was as religious as the Pope's kneecaps, something that he kept out of sight but which Gilles had discovered over time. That did it; from then on, all was agreed between them, and Gilles would go out to Kergohan to further his education on the land and stay there for two days or so. Fourrier would take leave at the same time to visit his great-aunt, who was sickly in Vannes, and from whom — as Gilles well knew — the clerk was expecting an inheritance. This period of leave would be cleared with the master, and not with Le Guinec, who was now in Pontivy, with rumours circulating in the house that he might be there for quite some time.

In the event, Gilles rode out on Sunday morning, since Fourrier had left to see his great-aunt the day before, and because Mass in the woods and confession with *Père* Guillaume was not as attractive to him as it was to the clerk. Confession was certainly not the right thing for him at the moment, since he would not want anyone else to know what was visiting him in the way of desires.

He took his time on the way out there, and that prevented the horse from getting excited or just plain overheated, since it was as hot as it might be. The ride up from Auray went smoothly, because the beast he had been given had got used to him, except when it was in the mood to prance around or break into a gallop. He passed some on the road who, he guessed, had been to Mass and who greeted him as he rode by, one or two even lifting caps. There were some lads sitting and laughing on the steps of a cross in a small hamlet, who broke off to stare at him with hostility. He even heard a stone skid by and a crack against the roots of a tree when he was a short way past them. He found himself looking out over the fields and the crops, considering what had been a good choice and what was misjudged. He assessed the health of the livestock, which surprised him by varying a great deal. Not much had been harvested as yet, but it was the Lord's day, so all would be quiet. The scythes might be standing against the walls in the cool barns.

He began to get sentimental, picturing the manor, the well, the yard and the stables, and above all Babette and Héloïse. He had made up his mind that he would behave well with Héloïse. It was up to her whom she talked to, or spent her time with, and she was a young woman who could be expected to have her likes and dislikes, even her fancies. If he could accept that with Gaëlle, he should with Héloïse, who was not so much younger. He also expected that Babette would have other objects for her affections now instead of him, which was as it should be. All in all, he was satisfied with his greater maturity, which partly came from being in a town such as Auray, and learning as much about the world as he had. They might well be impressed with him at Kergohan.

It was dusk by the time he led his horse into the stables, and Daniel came out to help him, expressing surprise and holding him tight. Because it was summer, they were dining late, and there were cries as he came through the door. Gilles made a point of conquering his emotions, as one who was now older and wiser should do. He did not cry when Babette did, he shook Héloïse by the hand, to her complete astonishment, and he gave a little bow to the others at the table — two men who might be familiar and a woman who was not. Amidst the banter and compliments, he saw Babette slipping the woman some quick glances, but she herself did not react. The food was good, the butter even better, and now he was able to drink cider, which must have been brought in recently.

Héloïse was quiet, and Gilles was determined not to stare at her. This meant that he hardly looked at her at all, which did not escape Héloïse. Daniel began to tease him about all the knowledge he must have now about the land and crops, and one of the men smiled and said that might not do him much good when he had the weight of a scythe in his hand tomorrow. They were going to reap and stack the rye once any dew had dried, since the weather boded well. The woman kept glancing at him and then away. She was older but somehow attractive, and he felt flattered that he had made a favourable impression. Héloïse noticed it all. She saw that he was beginning to preen, and she found herself becoming furious at his vanity and his foolishness.

CHAPTER XIX: EUGÈNE FINDS HIS WAY

Caroline North was writing a letter to Justin Wentworth, sitting at a small and rather neat desk that was furnished with suitable materials. She was so far distraught as to have forgotten her normally impeccable manners, sweeping away to leave Eugène standing in the hallway with the street door still open, where he had the shocking news conveyed to him by Mrs Claydon. Caroline heard a tap at the door of the drawing room. Martha opened it and, in a broken voice, she announced Mr Picaud into the room, which she then left.

There was a terrible silence. Eugène began to feel the early symptoms of panic, his mind racing fruitlessly. He stood still and breathed deeply and quietly, partly out of deference to Caroline. Despite the initial impression of activity she gave, she was actually motionless, with her pen in hand.

Eugène gave a cough. 'Madam? Miss North?' He could detect no movement from her at all. He clasped his hands behind his back, unable to wait any longer. 'Miss North!'

'Mr Picaud, Mrs Claydon will no doubt have told you our distressing news. There is no helping it. You are a friend of the family, and indeed of… We are at our wits' end. I have no one here, none at all, whom I can consult, merely a worthless maid and a landlady of good sense but no particular breeding, and absolutely no powers of invention. Oh, if only Dawson…'

'Dawson, madam?'

'My woman, Dawson. Why did I permit her this month's furlough? I must have been out of my senses. Then there was Amelia's fever…'

'Fever? What fever, pray?'

'Never mind, it is all past. Oh dear, forgive me, I am forgetting myself completely. We must have Mrs Claydon bring you some refreshment. That maid is all to pieces…'

Eugène stepped forward as Caroline arose from her chair at the desk. 'Miss North, we must pass by any thought of refreshment for me, if not for yourself. If I may invite you to be seated, and that looks to be a comfortable chair, you will permit me to stand. I think better and more lucidly when I can move around, if you will indulge that licence.'

'No, neither tea nor Madeira will bring me relief from my forebodings. You must turn away if I dab my eyes, Mr Picaud, and make due allowance for a woman's feelings of remorse.'

'Miss North, what you say distresses me greatly, as indeed does what I have already heard. But I remain as yet…'

Caroline North had settled for the chair. She gathered her skirts around her, set her eyes on the far wall, and exercised some control over her countenance. 'As you have gathered, sir, Miss Amelia went missing yesterday morning. She did not return from her habitual walk. We were patient, since by now she is familiar with the local surroundings, and — God forgive me! — I did not wish for her sake to create a stir, even amongst the household here.' She broke off, took a small handkerchief from her sleeve, and dabbed at her eyes.

Eugène looked around the room, saw a decanter of water and a glass, poured Caroline a drink and brought it over to her. She thanked him, sipped at it, and then held it between her hands.

'So I went out myself. I knew where she walked, and I ventured as far as I might onto the heath, which is well populated with gentlefolk at most times of the day, as well as with a few of … the other sort. I could think of no better place. I then returned and took a dish of tea here in the house, to give out an air of normality. I brushed off an enquiry from Mrs Claydon, and then thought of our friend, Mrs Barbauld, who lives across near the church. So, for the sake of appearances, I told Mrs Claydon and the maid that Miss Amelia might well be with her. I then turned out again by myself, and walked through the village.'

'Did you speak to anyone on your walks, madam?'

'No, sir, I did not, nor have I since. There is a reputation to consider here, and I shall not be the cause…'

'No, no, of course not.' Eugène began to feel a little sick at what he feared was emerging, but he kept his silence. Caroline also remained silent, and the atmosphere in the room was oppressive.

'The evening was terrible. Eventually I had to call in Mrs Claydon and the maid, and say that I was profoundly worried, but I urged discretion on them. It was quite likely that Miss Amelia had taken herself to town to visit an acquaintance on an impulse, and in the absence of her maid had been unable to communicate that to us. No doubt a note would be with us in the morning.'

'But it wasn't.'

'No, sir, it wasn't. We had hoped that perhaps you might be bringing it. But that was not to be.'

'You are writing, Miss North?'

'Yes, I came straight in from the hall and started to write, but my heart was so heavy I could not furnish more than the opening inscription. It was to be to her brother, who is your lifelong friend, I believe. I offer you my apologies for such rudeness, but I knew that without any note coming from Amelia I had to seek help, and at least contact her nearest relations. I cannot delay it any longer. I dare not contact my brother, or at least not yet. Mr Wentworth must be the first, hard though it is. I had never thought to be writing such a thing. I am so distressed I hardly know what I am doing.'

Eugène was lost in thought. In an almost absent-minded way, he pulled over a light chair and sat down to one side of Caroline North, his elbows on his knees.

'Yes, you must write to him. Miss North, I must ask you something which I find very difficult. Since Miss Amelia took up residence here in Hampstead, or perhaps even before... Are you aware of... Have there been visitors? Is there any possibility...?'

'Of an attachment? You are speaking here of an elopement, I believe, perhaps one contrived for when Miss Amelia was away from Devon, or a sudden infatuation leading to impulsive conduct?' She sighed heavily. 'There have been such things. I must not simply defend her reputation, but actually believe in its integrity. Yet she is not herself. That much is certain. But to go so far... I believe it to be impossible.'

Had Caroline been observing him, she would have seen palpable signs of relief in Eugène's bearing and countenance, but these were swiftly replaced by profound anxiety. He feared that if anything, the alternative might be worse, if he could only conceive what it might be. An idea occurred to him.

'Might we call in the maid, Miss North? Or rather, is there a room in which I may speak to her alone?'

'Alone? Why would you speak to the chit? I am intensely displeased with her. Had she not so thoughtlessly stubbed her toe and sought permission to come back to the house, Miss

Amelia would never have been on her own. Why, I can hardly think of it without...'

'Ah, I see. That had been my next question, but it is answered. Miss North, with your permission I shall leave you to write to Justin, while I seek an audience with...'

'Martha. I shall send her in to you. I will take my letter upstairs to my room, where I may have better fortune with it.' Caroline rose from her chair, picked up the sheet of paper and left the room.

Eugène stood up, looked at the arrangement of the seating, and placed the light chair opposite the armchair in which Caroline had been sitting. There was a knock on the door.

'Come in!' he called. When the door opened, he went on, 'Ah, Martha, I believe? Please be seated.'

With evident trepidation, the maid came over and sat in the upholstered armchair, sinking a little into its soft cushioning.

Eugène spoke gently to her. 'Now, Martha, I am a friend of the family, of Miss Amelia and her brother, Mr Wentworth. So you may place confidence in me, as indeed we are placing it in you, in your discretion in this unfortunate situation.'

Martha was mute, but her eyes were wide and her face was flushed.

'Let me say how I do hope that your foot is on the mend. A nasty knock, Miss North informs me.'

Martha nodded.

'And you were on your accustomed walk, I gather. Which is down to the heath?'

'Yes, sir, past the gardens and what they call the Pump Room. We go on to the heath, and after a few steps Miss then says she will come back. She is easily spent since her fever, sir.'

Eugène decided that he would now sit down opposite the maid, and he looked directly at her as he asked his next question, smiling all the while. 'Tell me, Martha, and think carefully, have you ever seen anyone strange looking over at you since you arrived here? On those walks, or perhaps in the village? A man, most probably, or men? Has anyone come up to you, addressed you unexpectedly?'

Martha looked sharply across at him, and then away. A tear formed at the corner of her eye and rolled slowly down her cheek. She dabbed at it with a handkerchief, but made an effort to defend herself. 'No, why should they? I… Oh, Lord, I never thought it would do any harm — a lass must have…' She sobbed. 'I'm worried sick after Miss Amelia, sir. I've been up all night crying…'

Eugène became alert, but he made a great effort to remain composed. 'So, let me imagine it, Martha: there were times when you were relieved of your duties, and the ladies were out visiting without you. A pretty girl like you cannot help it if a young man passes the time of day, and maybe he chooses to give you a present or two, such as that handkerchief you have there, with your initial embroidered on it. A very respectable fellow, I'll be bound — in service, I should think.'

There was silence. Martha thought about thrusting the handkerchief out of sight, but decided the damage was done and wiped her eyes.

'Did he ask any questions, Martha? Did you see him yesterday? Have you arranged to see him again?'

Martha shook her head. She knew he had had nothing to do with it, but gentlefolk would never believe that anyone could be interested in the likes of her just for her own sake. 'He dressed nicely. Always. He had a brown suit off an apothecary, so he said. Dare say I won't see him again now. Lord, what will become of us?' The tears were flowing without restraint now, and her eyes were swollen.

'We shall take dinner quietly, Martha, and you will help the housekeeper as you usually do. Do not distress yourself further, but go to your room and wash your face. That will make you feel better.'

Eugène wondered where he got those words from, and wished privately that the mere act of washing his face would calm his own turbulent feelings. To add to it all, he doubted that Martha's ill-advised liaison could remain hidden from Caroline North for long, in which case the maid's days in the household could well be limited, although the need for discretion might argue in favour of leniency.

Caroline's letter to Justin had finally been written and sent to the post, and breakfast had been taken slowly, with not much appetite being shown either by guest or host. They both knew what was to happen: Eugène Picaud would pursue his enquiries, which he assured Caroline would not involve any disclosure. This shocking event had the hallmark of an elopement, whatever he might want to believe. What little he had heard about Amelia's illness here — how the fever had taken her and how her constitution had been weakened — could only match his own previous impressions of the troubled state of her senses. In that condition, who knew what might have occurred to her? Yet despite the gnawing conviction of a crisis, Eugène knew he had to wait. He had discovered the time of day that Amelia took her walk, which had been remarkably regular, and the route. He was determined to trace her steps and see what he could find.

He began his inspection not knowing what he was looking for, and the scale of the endeavour began to daunt him. In his imagination he could hear her crying out for him. He stared with hostility at the men that were strolling in the area of the

Wells, but then he wondered if it had been a woman who had drawn Amelia away. Who was that friend of whom she had spoken? An actress, he remembered, who had evoked her pity — the source, in fact, of the disturbance that had so affected her composure.

Sunk in those thoughts he reached the border of the heath, a lane that ran roughly north and south as he calculated, probably therefore giving out further down the hill onto the London road. If you were planning an elopement, this might be the place to choose, rather than the centre of the village. Here one was not overlooked, and while people passed by and across into the heath, there were few of them. He looked down the lane. There was a single horseman proceeding at a leisurely pace, a gentleman. Nothing to be found there, nor indeed asked. There were also thin tracks leading onto the heath. He followed one in, and reflected as he did so on the greatest horror: it brought him to a standstill. But why would Amelia be lying dead? No footpad would harm her, not here. Yet the trail stopped here, that was certain. If there was no body, then suspicion must surely turn to a vehicle? Not a horse — Amelia was no great horsewoman. A vehicle it would have to be, and by the side of the heath there was a quiet lane, leading away.

A young man walked past, bidding him good day. Eugène heard the gentleman's mount pass by, still at the same pace. A hoverfly aimed to distract him, darting away and back. It was far too dry and dusty to think of tracking, even if he were Justin, although the fellow would surely find a broken twig or some revealing sign. And there on the lane was a pretty young woman. She was on his side of the road, and instantly he remembered the milkmaid. Martha had told him only this morning that they had often encountered her on their morning walks, going back down the hill with her empty pails, and that

Amelia had sometimes talked to her. Eugène pushed out into the open, saw the yoke on the woman's shoulder, and raced after her.

'I see I am too late,' he greeted her.

The milkmaid stopped and put down her pails. Maybe she was used to attention, to being hailed. She said nothing as he came close, and he had the feeling that she was weighing him up. She had full cheeks, a good figure, and a fair complexion, with a few small pock-marks on her cheekbones and forehead.

'Be you jumping out on a lass? I'd say that wasn't kindly, sir. I might be frightened.' Which she did not look, with that mischievous smile.

'It's Molly, isn't it?'

'Why, I don't see how I can be any other person, sir. I've been Molly since the day I was born.'

'And I am sure we are all the luckier for it. You pass here every day about this time, do you not, Molly?'

Molly looked puzzled, and not a little suspicious. The smile faded. 'And why would you be asking that?'

'I have a good reason. Think back, Molly, to two days ago. You were here then?'

'I might have been.'

Eugène reached in his waistcoat pocket and pulled out a coin. 'If you had milk, I'd buy it. So here's a coin for you anyway.'

Her hand came out, and she put it quickly into her pocket, which hung off her apron. There was a slight jingle. 'What of it?' Then her face cleared. 'You're a friend of Miss Amelia?'

Eugène's heart skipped. 'Yes. You met her, didn't you? You often do. You spoke. You went on as usual. Where did she go, Molly?'

Molly bit the end of her thumb and looked along the lane. 'There was a gentleman that came as I stood by. He showed her a paper. I saw that. And a coach, just along here. She got in. There was a woman besides. Will that do? I'd best be getting on.'

Picaud reached out and held her arm in his excitement. Molly looked down at his hand, as if she had been there before.

'You'll take your hand off me before I cry out. I'll give you three. One...'

'No, Molly, I'm sorry. I mean you no harm. Think carefully. Was that gentleman wearing brown?'

'Ay, that he was, brown all over. Now...'

'Molly, this is important. Miss Amelia may be in danger, real danger. Was there anything else you remember? The coach — fancy or plain?'

'I don't know about that. They are all the same to me, since I don't go in them. This one had red wheels, I remember that — queer marks on the door too.'

Eugène held his breath. 'What kind of marks, Molly?'

'How should I know? I only walked on past it. Now, you step aside and let me get on.' She picked up her pails and gave Eugène an unfriendly look. 'Gingham. That's what the marks looked like. The missus has it at home. On the door of that coach — gingham. Or something like that. Good day to you.'

Eugène had told Caroline North that he would in all circumstances report back to her, which he had just done. He said that he should be back at New End before Justin arrived or sent word, and that they should do no more at present until they were both far more certain, for the sake of reputation. Caroline had agreed, with an expressionless face. Eugène rapidly decided that it was no good waiting for the right coachman to come up to Hampstead; it might never happen again. So he took himself and his bag off in a hackney carriage right away, impatient and tense. There must be a trail to be found, he was sure.

The coachman from the stand in the high street took Eugène right down to Holborn, but he resisted the temptation to start searching immediately and instead set off for a small court in Farringdon, dingy and with nothing to show for itself. Behind a dull door, you could find any length of steel that you wanted, with no questions asked, and the sooner you were gone the better. He weighed one or two in his hands, turned down a naval dirk, and took a short hunting knife instead. It was French, and it would go well in his boot, which was where it had to go. He wrapped a piece of cloth around the point and hoped it would protect his foot; there was no sheath.

He wondered whether hackney drivers would suffer people asking questions. His guess was that they would not, but they would not like someone sneaking about either, looking at their carriages rather than asking for a ride. He slung his bag over his shoulder and began by asking around at Holborn for a Hampstead stand. There was one just down the road, and he strolled over. There was nothing there that matched what he was looking for. Coaches were bound to come and go, and so he crossed to the inn opposite and lounged by the door, occasionally chatting without appearing too curious. He saw faded feathers, what might once have been a bear on carriage doors, many other signs painted right over, and too many of those red wheels that obviously could tell him nothing. He ate a pie, drank an ale, went to relieve himself, and walked across the street again. The sun had moved to its zenith and was glaring, so he screwed up his eyes in the hope of seeing the right coach come in.

It was behind him, of course. Justin would have laughed at him: never let them get behind you, or you will never live to learn. It had been painted over roughly, enough to obscure much of it, but the crimson still poked through in places. He had not known what gingham was, but Mrs Claydon knew, and had showed him too: a check pattern, printed on cotton, often crimson and white. Some lord's chequered coat of arms back in the day, no doubt, the carriage supplanted by what the duke or duchess had wanted in the way of a smarter style. It was standing by a trough, the horses warm; maybe it was a regular for the journey up the hill to Hampstead. The driver came to see his nags, gave their ears a rub, checked the harness, and looked around for a fare.

Eugène approached casually; his shabby bag helped. 'Yours looks in good trim. I warm to a man who cares for his animals.'

The driver paid little attention; there had been no mention of money.

Eugène edged forward to peer into the carriage. 'Yes, in very good trim. No damp in there. You do the run regularly, don't you?'

The driver spat on the ground. 'What would you be after … sir?'

Eugène appeared hesitant, or he hoped that he did. He beckoned to the driver. 'A word in your ear, if you please.'

'I ain't got all day…' But this looked like business, so it was worth a try. The driver sidled up to Eugène, sizing up his clothes and the worn bag.

'By any chance, did you take a fare from Hampstead the other morning? Two days ago now? Let me tell you: it would have been a young woman from polite society, and a man, who may have been wearing a brown suit.'

The coachman looked suspicious. He had wondered about that piece of rum business at the time, but the fare had weighed up as it should, and that was good enough. That money was safely stowed away in his tin box, and there might be more now keen on following it. 'I might have done. Can't bring them all to mind. What's it to do with you, anyway?'

'Stay a while. Let's just say that you took this fare, and let's just say that you thought to yourself, being a man who sees the world, that this meeting … looked like a private affair. Now, let's also say that a crown gets a nod to that, no more needed, just a nod.'

The coachman looked Eugène in the eye, looked down at the crown coin in his hand, shrugged and pocketed it. He gave a nod.

'Now, let's just say that, for two more to follow that one, that I'll tell you that young woman is my relation. I am come up from Taunton in Somerset to find her, and that fellow is a gold-digging scoundrel who would stop at nothing. Do you hear me?'

Eugène hoped that he had not overplayed the anger and indignation. They fell a long way short of the feelings he was keeping in check. It was a tense moment. The coachman had listened, and he looked about him, tapping his foot.

'You said two more, mister. A relation, you said. You don't look like her brother, but that's your affair. Hop up and I'll take you there, but I ain't staying, not for all the tea in China.'

CHAPTER XX: THE KISS

The morning dawned brightly, and a slight breeze had taken away any moisture there had been. The fields were inspected. *Père* Guillaume had been down after Mass yesterday at Daniel's invitation to bless the crop before it was harvested, since it was the first grown there for quite some years. There were more men from the village, and several from outlying hamlets, like the two of the night before who had seemed familiar to Gilles, and who had slept over. The woman, however, was gone. Babette had found old clothes for Gilles, and Héloïse felt easier with him dressed like that and holding a scythe. She had one too, which was slightly shorter in the handle than many others, and Gilles risked a joke with her about it being the little sister of his own, thinking back to how she had described them both. She took that quite well and watched as he strolled out to look at the ears of rye. He came back to her and said it was good, and that the straw was long and strong, and she said she was pleased to hear it.

When they started in, it was quite cool, but as they moved in a line up the field it became, inevitably, hot work, and to her annoyance Héloïse found again that she was developing blisters. She went to join Babette and some of the women from the village, who had come down with their menfolk. They were raking behind the scything to bring the crop together to load onto the cart. Daniel decided to work with them, and took up a pitchfork to heave it on. The sun was hot, but they were making good progress when Babette hit the iron ring they had suspended from the cart, and the mowers downed their tools and came over for the cider and onions.

Gilles had stripped to the waist, with his chemise hanging down. Babette came up to him with a pitcher and placed it on the ground. They looked out over the field.

'Not bad,' she said.

'It's a good crop,' he replied.

'There's something I should tell you,' she added. 'Now's as good a time as any.' Her tone was serious. 'The woman last night. I saw you looking at her.'

Gilles felt embarrassed. 'It was nothing; think nothing of it. She was giving me the eye, and so I gave her as good as I got.'

Babette offered him more from the pitcher, but he declined. He was convinced that Héloïse was watching him.

'Well, that woman is your aunt. Your mother's sister. It was sheer chance that she was there last night, but I thought you should know. I'm sorry it had to be like that.'

Gilles bit his lower lip and stared straight ahead. 'What is her name?' he asked quietly.

'Jeanne.'

He felt anger rising in him. 'And where has she been all these years? And why…?'

Babette put her hand on his arm. 'I'm sorry. I should have told you before. But she left and never came back.'

Gilles strode away from her, picked up his scythe, and went into the standing crop, sweeping the blade round. But he stopped after three long arcs, and began to sharpen it.

They had said nothing more about Jeanne since they had finished scything. Babette was aching to tell Gilles all she knew, but he needed more time. Even Babette did not understand why Jeanne had chosen to return now, to seek them out when she had shunned them for so long. But Daniel and Babette had told Gilles about Grosjean, and he had said firmly that he wanted to visit him. It was agreed that he would, and that Héloïse would take him there. Babette felt that it would do him good to be able to talk to her, and after seeing Grosjean and his injuries a week or so ago, Héloïse had insisted on taking an ointment which her mother had given her. She had no idea whether it still had its powers, but her mother had used it for healing wounds. When her daughter had asked for some, she had set aside a small pot for her, which Héloïse had kept as one of her precious things.

They set off early the following morning, because Gilles could not stay for much longer at Kergohan. When they arrived at the charcoal-burners' shelter, Grosjean leant forward and pulled Gilles down to him in an iron grip, knocking him off his feet. He showed them his wounds. The piece of shot had proved not to be deep, and once it was out Daniel had cauterised the opening. It was an ugly sight, but it did not appear to be inflamed, cleaned as it had been by a mixture of brandy and vinegar. Gilles flinched at the sight of the sabre cut. Daniel had sewn it up, and Grosjean mimed screaming with pain, and seized a bit of wood to show how he had bitten into it. They could see after the fooling around that he was exhausted. The wound had been cleaned, a poultice had been applied, and now it was just a matter of time, with the aid of Mary and the saints. Héloïse wanted to apply some of the ointment she had brought, but the big man had rapidly become tired and irritable, and he waved her away.

They left the small pot with the charcoal burners, who nodded. They would do it. She told them to use a little at a time, not in the wound, but round it.

It was still relatively early in the morning. Gilles was impressed that Héloïse knew the way.

'Do you think that only a man can do that?' she demanded. 'The girls from the village can find their way around. I met some of them, not far from here.'

'Why?'

'They had come to teach me a lesson — that it was somehow my fault when a boy chose to hang around me.'

Gilles stopped. 'Yannic,' was all he said. His jaw clenched with anger.

'Well, I thank you for your concern for my safety. It was Yaelle who got me out of it, with Babette, of course. Her sister Erell was the ringleader.'

Gilles tried to remain calm. There were other things to fret about, which cut just as deeply. They walked on, in sun and shade. The smell of the woodsmoke had faded. Héloïse was aware that he was preoccupied, and she believed she could guess what would be troubling him most.

'I think you should admit how much it hurts you,' she said. She held his arm, just as Babette had done the day before. 'I lost my mother too. But there was my aunt, and above all my uncle Daniel.'

'And your father.' Gilles tore the leaves off a stem.

'He died,' Héloïse said simply, although there was a wealth of feeling she might have brought to that. Now was not the time.

'At least you had one!' Gilles shouted, not at her, but at the trees, the air, the sunlight. He dropped his voice. 'I still do not know who he is, or was. No one will tell me.' His voice began to rise again. 'And now this aunt — no one told me about her. Why not? Why this secrecy? Where has she been? Am I not to be told anything, ever?'

He had turned his face to her. It was clear that he would have to meet his aunt, but for the time being Héloïse could do nothing. She reached into the pocket that hung under her summer dress and took out a small bottle with a tiny cork. Maybe this would distract him.

'Here,' she said, 'look at this. Have you ever seen anything like it? What do you think it is?'

Gilles looked without interest. 'Why should I care?'

'Do you know what's in it? Can you guess?'

'Spirits? Laudanum? How should I know?'

Héloïse laughed. 'So you think I come up to the forest to get drunk? No, my mother gave me this as well. I found it when I was looking for the ointment. It's perfume, her own perfume. My father had it sent for from France. She put a little of it in a bottle for me. Now, turn around.'

Gilles looked completely puzzled, so she took his arms and swung him away from her. She took out the cork and dabbed a drop on her finger, and then wiped it under the lobes of her ears. She put the cork back and slipped the bottle into her pocket.

'Now, turn around. Go on, turn around.'

He did, captivated by the strangeness of it all. Héloïse stood close, with one arm on her hip, and with the other hand she stroked her hair back, light and laughter in her eyes. The fragrance drifted from her, and he leant forward to find its source. Her hands came towards his shoulders, and her lips parted slightly. As his own touched hers, and they pressed hard against each other in the shadow of the rocks, he was intoxicated by her warm neck and overwhelmed by the scent of flowers, and the summer sang sweetly in their veins.

CHAPTER XXI: ARABELLA GOES TO HELP

The country routine had a familiarity to it, although Arabella now found the visits of their acquaintances at Chittesleigh slightly irksome. She was conscious that they were really part of Justin and Sempronie's circle, established over many years, into which she had appeared as a relative newcomer. At times, she was tempted to question if she was temperamentally suited to being a wife and a mother. She even wondered, in her darker moments, if she might have been at greater ease in a more relaxed arrangement with the man she undoubtedly loved. But she realised how shocking such an idea would be to him, which made her laugh and shake off her low spirits.

It was sunny, so Arabella took her weekly stroll down to the village. In recent weeks, the journey had been prompted by the confinement of Jenny Mudge, and then to the delight of all by the birth of Robert's and her second son. It was rather grand to call it a confinement, because Jenny had been abed for a day or two but would not hear of resting much over that. The new mother knew that domestic harmony depended on her being up and about as soon as possible, and much calm could be restored even if she was doing little more than sitting on the settle with the babe in her arms.

The air was light and not oppressive at this hour of the morning. Justin was away early to call on tenants in advance of rent-day, encountering by this means any claims against payment on repairs, and taking account of cases of hardship with the evidence before his eyes. This offered Arabella great relief, since she was free from his constant concern. It was a delight to walk on with Grace down the level path to the south gate, passing the new rose plantings that were her addition to the immediate surroundings of the manor, and the charmingly unassuming arbour that Will Cholwick from the village had made on her request, with its plain wooden seating. Twenty or so steps beyond it, Arabella started and turned to Grace, who was just behind her.

'Grace, the Banbury cake! Look in the basket, pray do. I believe we have forgotten it.'

This was quickly done, and Grace tutted. 'And there I was setting it aside to take, with cook having made it specially, but then being occupied with the custard for Billy. It's my fault, madam...'

'Grace, I cannot bear it when you call me "madam". I have informed you of this, and please refrain from it, if you will.'

'My apologies, ma... Mrs Wentworth.'

Arabella looked quite sternly at her. 'I have said, Grace, that when we are together and not in company you may address me as Miss Arabella, as you always did. I do wish you would oblige me in this.'

At this correction, Grace looked quite chastened and became rather flustered after the error with the Banbury cake.

'We must return for it,' said Arabella. 'We are not too far advanced on our journey. Come...'

'I shall not hear of it, Miss Arabella, madam. It is my mistake, and in my charge alone to set it to rights. There is seating just behind us, and the weather is not too hot as yet. If you will allow me to leave the basket with you, perhaps to be placed on the seat, I shall return forthwith.'

Grace did not wait to hear any objection. Placing the basket carefully down on the arbour seating, she returned along the path to the manor.

Arabella watched her deposit the basket, thought briefly about sitting next to it, and then dismissed the idea. She had no occasion to be fatigued. Instead, she decided that she would stroll further along the path towards the location that her father had proposed for the rotunda, which he had insisted he would build for his beloved daughter and her husband as a wedding gift. It was no matter that she protested that this was the taste and fashion of a previous age, and that she would have none of it. For her part, she would have preferred a remodelling of the stables, but that was a step too far for her menfolk. She was cheered to discover that her knee was distinctly less stiff, and her hip less painful than it had been, apart from a few mild twinges.

She looked around her, but she could not recall where her father had planned his ridiculous landskip pimple, the dear man. Perhaps it was over there? She stopped abruptly. That was surely a figure she had just seen? Just the head and shoulders, gone now, behind a slight dip in the land. Perhaps the gamekeeper — but gamekeepers did not wear coloured scarves. Arabella turned slowly, taking care not to wrench her injured knee. And there again was the same figure, plainly a woman, standing at the gate and looking towards her. The woman seemed distraught. She beckoned to Arabella and then collapsed on the ground. Curiosity and concern conquered her, and sensing some distress she hurried down to the gate.

CHAPTER XXII: MRS FITCHETT

Mrs Fitchett was a fine-looking woman of middle years and a healthy disposition, which she said came from a frugal and abstemious way of life, her only indulgences being candied fruits and brandy. Her residence in the Pool brought these items to her table and into her locker with considerable ease, accompanied by men with good manners. Not that her clientele was always of the first rank, nor even some ranks below that. But a woman had to make a living, and there were young women enough who would be on their uppers had she not given them the chance to keep clean and off the street. They thanked her for it when they learned what was best for them.

There was money to be made, and it came from across the road where the ships discharged their cargoes and their crew. Mrs Fitchett had her barkers who would bring the sailors right over to the house before they had a chance to spend their pay elsewhere. She could give them a passable wine, because she had her arrangements, and her speciality was a Dutch cheese which many seemed to like, except the Chinese mariners whom she sent round the back, where such treats were not on offer.

She would rent out vacant rooms in the side house, clean and tidy because that was her way; it was a byword in the main house too that any young woman that was slovenly would soon have to mend her ways. You never knew what a patron might want with a set of rooms, for a day or for a week, and it paid not to ask questions, and to send women through if that was what was wanted. Her man Jencks would pull in business of that kind from time to time, set it all up and give her a cut. The rest of the time he kept the barkers in order, who were an idle lot, given the chance. She had big Artur to sort out any rough stuff, because some thought they could knock a woman around for the same price as treating her nicely, and Mrs Fitchett would have no truck with that. Property was sacred, and damaged goods were a liability until they were healed. The men knew what they were in for as soon as they saw Artur, but by then it was often too late for them, and Jencks would have to whistle him off once they had got the message.

Sal wasn't a bad sort, and she kept it close with Jencks on whatever they were up to, which could be anything that kept them fed and housed. Sal wouldn't let him live near the women, which was understandable, but she and Jencks always had a lodging nearby, and Mrs Fitchett could send a boy to fetch him day or night if he wasn't out on business. Jencks was a sly one, but Sal could handle him, and tear him off a strip if he strayed from his obligations; so Mrs Fitchett took care to keep her sweet, putting sugar in her tea when Dolly forgot, and having a laugh with her. But Sal was always tight-lipped with her, and that's how it was now: not a word so far about who was in the inner room there, or what they would be waiting for. It could be up to a week, Jencks had said.

The little parlour was furnished simply but well, with a neat rug accompanying a small oak table and a set of three cane-bottom chairs, which the late Mr Fitchett had had bequeathed to him by a benevolent aunt in Faversham. Mrs Fitchett and Sal were now comfortably placed on two of them, contemplating the tea set: the Derby teapot with only a small chip on the spout, and the Worcester cups, with the design only slightly faded. The sugar was in an old pewter bowl, but the engraved sugar tongs were of the finest quality.

'Now, Sal, should we be inviting your guest to join us? It's good pekoe in the pot. I will have only the best. There are three cups.'

Sal sipped at her own, in what she hoped was a polite manner, and shook her head. 'With respect, Mrs Fitchett, that's not how Mister Jencks has laid it out, pardoning your presence, which I take as a compliment to us both. But...'

The inner door gave a slight creak, and there in the frame was Amelia. Her countenance was pale, but her voice was firm. 'Oh, your pardon. May I ask if there is news of Miss Farley?'

'There is none, ma'am.' Sal turned in her chair, aiming to convey a relaxed air. 'No, Mister Jencks has gone to fetch her, milady. Let me bring you a dish of tea while we are waiting. Please be seated, and I shall be with you forthwith.'

Amelia paused, as if about to add more, but then went back into her room and closed the door. Mrs Fitchett observed that it had an old sliding bolt on the side that faced into the parlour. Sal got to her feet, poured tea into the third cup, and took a small corked bottle from a pocket under her petticoat. She poured two drops from it into the cup, tapped lightly on the door, disappeared through the doorway, and came back into the parlour a minute later.

Mrs Fitchett rose from her chair and smiled graciously at her companion. 'Well, I had best be going. I shall send Dolly up for the china when she is finished in the kitchen. I don't know what your game is, Sal, and I'm not asking. But I'll wager a sovereign that your "Miss Farley" will prove to have a stout set of shoulders on him.'

Sal's face glowed with sudden anger, and her voice tightened. 'What do your mean by that, eh?'

'Now, don't take offence where none was meant. Business is business. But just tell Jencks for me that when the game's all done, Little Miss Peaches in there might find herself a good situation in life. Their families never take them back, and seeing as how they don't know how to manage things, they're better off with me. I'll wish you good afternoon.'

Eugène's driver was as good as his word. They passed Saint Paul's and the Tower of London but cut across well above the Pool. Eugène glimpsed fields on both sides, and the sun was still to the right above the river. It was a long, straight ride, with Eugène trying to work out what he was going to do. The further they went, the more his suspicions grew. What would Amelia have to do with the eastern part of London? He could easily recall the short conversations they had had about the actress she had rescued, and that woman might be found at work in the theatres, if she had recovered from her injuries. But what was the connection with docks and warehouses? London was completely new to Amelia. Yet if she had taken off, it would surely be out of concern for someone. And, just as surely, she must have believed it to be urgent. No maid, no baggage, no notice given.

The carriage swung to the right and ran down to the riverside. Eugène saw ships, barges and watermen, but as they jolted left into a narrow street, much that was on the far side of the river — seen in glimpses down the alleys above the water stairs — was now open land. This could not be considered a fashionable quarter by any standards. Buildings were high on either side and there were warehouses in front of the wharves. There was much heaving and carting, and bustling crowds — mostly men, but also some women who knew where they were going. He noticed coal spilling out of sacks, hogsheads rolled along, and chests stacked, probably full of tea. The driver pulled up abruptly, although they had not yet left the main street. There was no helping it, so Eugène opened the door and climbed down.

'Surely it was not here, driver?' he said.

The man looked at his horses' heads. 'It's as far as I go.' The carriage was standing next to a public house, which the board declared to be The Anchor.

Eugène put his hand on the footplate of the box. 'Well, where? My crowns get me better than this. He won't come after you, man. Why would he do that? Come now, out with it, and let's get on, the both of us.'

One of the nags shook its head, and the other nudged it. There was some sweat round the harnesses after a long run, but the coachman looked after them, and their necks were not low. 'It's up there a way. You see that building with a hoist sticking out of it, up above? Hops, it is, for beer. You can smell them as you go past. Take a left there. It's up there.'

'Is that all? Come on, now.'

The coachman picked up his reins. 'There's gentlemen go up there. Fitchett's, it is. That's all I know. Rooms and … you'll see. Just mind your purse, and mind your back. That's all I'll say, sir.' He slackened and shook out the reins.

'Hold on.' Eugène looked around and reached again into his pockets, balancing some more coins in his palm. 'I'm giving you two more if you wait for me. Make it an hour, and if I don't show, then take off.'

The coachman sniffed and rubbed a rough, strong hand over his stubble. 'An hour, you say? How do I get what an hour is, sir? I ain't got no pocket watch. Besides, there's no stand here for carriages.'

'Take the alley here at the side of The Anchor. Stand the carriage there. Have an ale in the house.' The coachman still looked uncertain. 'Go by the bells, man. The church bells. They must have them round here.'

The driver took the coins and clicked his tongue to his horses. 'Bells,' he muttered. 'You're lucky it's the afternoon.' The carriage pulled slowly round the side of the building.

Eugène crossed over the busy street and walked into an alley. He then climbed to the top of some waterfront stairs, looking out over the river. With a full view, he could now see all kinds of ships moored there. The prospect made him feel unwell. It would be the work of a moment to sweep a weakened young woman down those stairs and have her rowed to a ship. The turn of the tide, and she would be gone. But why should he imagine the worst? Well, it was not the worst, and that might be why. Fitchett's establishment sounded both sordid and dangerous, and there could be no good motive for taking Amelia there.

The breeze blew across his face. A lighter pulled up at the foot of the stairs, full of cargo, and Eugène retraced his steps before he was swept aside by the porters. In a doorway at the head of the alley, he took the few valuables from his bag and stowed them in his garments. He bent down and loosened the dagger slightly, then slipped across the main road between the carts and stood at the top of the side-street. It was a dead end. There might be a way through to the fields beyond, but he could not see it. He took a deep breath. He was a gentleman and looked like a gentleman; he could be persuasive, and fortunately he had coins. That might be enough, but he doubted it. Above all, he feared what he might have to do: bloodshed in civil life was a heavy charge.

There was a fellow in an old white hat hovering nearby, and as he raised his eyes the man came up to him.

'You might be in need of a little company, good sir. Some good cheer, perhaps. Would I be on the right track? It is between gentlemen, of course.' The man had his thumbs in his waistcoat and a decent shirt collar. His breeches were shiny.

Eugène decided to play along. He feigned innocence and confusion. 'I … must confess… Just stepped ashore, sir. A long time, on the crossing. Need to gather my thoughts before I… You are of these parts, sir?'

'Indeed I am, sir, indeed I am. Man and boy. Your name, sir, if I may?'

'Crabbe.' A good choice. He might need their speed and ability to move sideways.

'Dunston, sir, at your disposal. After a good morning of business, I am requiring a small diversion myself, yes, I am. I know I am. We might make a pair, sir? What do you say?'

Eugène picked up his bag. 'I like your tone, sir. I am happy with it. You are, I trust, thinking of an establishment somewhere near at hand? If so, do you lead on.'

They strolled down together towards the dead end. The man Dunston asked after his trade, and Eugène could only think of knives, steel and cutlery. It would have to do. They swung quickly into a small court, and then were at the door. Dunston knocked lightly but walked straight in. He passed a painted lady to whom he raised his hat, and in jest he ducked under the outstretched arm of the largest man Eugène had ever seen, who regarded him with a hostile stare. He had straw hair, startling blue eyes and a face half-hidden by a bristling beard.

'Never you mind Artur here, Mr Crabbe. He'll be all over you, you'll see, second time around,' said Dunston. 'Now, here we shall find Mrs Fitchett herself, unless I'm much mistaken.'

Eugène felt his shoulders relax — he was in the right place. Their hostess apparently resided up a short flight of stairs, behind a nondescript door with a small brass handle.

Dunston swept in and greeted her. 'Mrs Fitchett, always a pleasure, and how do I find you?'

The lady was at her bureau in a tidy room, with a window to her left that showed the corner of a field with fruit trees in it, a neat little fireplace, and red velvet upholstery for the chairs and the divan. The air was pleasantly scented. Eugène was concentrating; he hoped it made him look diffident.

'Dunston, how often must I tell you… Oh, I see we have a gentleman visitor. My dear sir, how pleased we are to see you here at Fitchett's. You will find everything here suited to your comfort, to which I shall attend personally. You may leave us, Mr Dunston. Dolly will provide you with your perquisites, since Mr Jencks is not in the house. Thank you, Dunston. Now, Mr…?'

'Crabbe, Mr Crabbe.' Eugène followed this up with a bow. 'Happily returned to these shores, madam, after occupation in trade, oh, yes, most successfully occupied, I may say. Yes, thank you.'

'Mr Crabbe, in that case let there be no more ado. I am sure you are a man who makes up his mind. I shall offer you then a very good glass, and we have a fine cut of roast beef, which you must have missed, I'll be bound, in those foreign parts. Now, with your permission, I shall send for one of my young ladies…'

Eugène coughed slightly and then looked obligingly at the bawd, for that was what she was, despite the bureau and the fine cut of beef.

'Mr Crabbe? Do I detect that you have … shall we say, some particular requirements? The late Mr Fitchett used to say…'

'It is a long time… I had a young wife, Mrs Fitchett, who sadly passed away. We were in the early bloom of a marriage when tragedy came upon us. So I…'

Mrs Fitchett was all sympathy. She laid a hand gently on his arm. 'You must say no more, Mr Crabbe. We have many gentlemen who come to us in a dreadful state of bereavement, with tales to tell that would sadden any heart, let alone one as soft as mine. We look after them, Mr Crabbe. We look after them as best we may.'

Eugène swallowed. Diffidence was evidently a good card to play. He was unexpectedly cool about the fiction he was presenting. 'I … well, indeed I thank you. You are most understanding.'

Mrs Fitchett withdrew her hand and went across to the door. 'Shall we say "fresh", Mr Crabbe? Will you let me say it for you? A man in your state perhaps needs to be taken in hand.'

'Yes, fresh has it, Mrs Fitchett. Surprisingly close. But … more than a mere slip of a girl. That would not be it at all. Perhaps… No, it would not be a reasonable demand. You may not…'

Mrs Fitchett paused at the door. 'Mr Crabbe, I am waiting on your pleasure, believe me. A man with your signal successes in business should be attended.'

Eugène took the plunge. 'Tender, Mrs Fitchett. I have a yearning for something tender. Newly taken in, perhaps?'

Mrs Fitchett appeared grave. Her tongue momentarily pushed out her cheek. Eugène's confidence misgave him. Had he played too open…?

'You made me think there, sir, I have to say. Such good young ladies we have here. Newly in? I do have that request from time to time, but... Now, fresh might be easier to answer. You just come with me, if you will, sir, and let me show you to one of our best rooms. Someone to your refined taste will bring you refreshment. We can do overnight, sir, as you will see, and my sheets are always clean.'

CHAPTER XXIII: GUÈVREMONT RECEIVES LEROUX

Leroux had taken great care over his appearance. His boots were shining, his uniform was spotless, the hilt and guard of his sword had been cleaned, and the scabbard had been polished. From being clean-shaven he had begun to sport a small moustache, as some of the officers did, which he believed Joséphine admired. It required particular attention, and he got his barber to trim it carefully and wax it lightly, and to keep his cropped hair in good order. Nothing of that sort ever escaped Lieutenant Vernier, of course, but Leroux surprised himself by retorting that if Vernier wished to spy on vanity, he should merely look in the glass. Because this reply was so out of character, Vernier was stunned into silence.

Leroux decided to carry his hat all the way, thinking that this would give him one less thing to think about when he got to the front door. He vowed to have confidence in his appearance and not to take one last look at himself in the mirror in the hall of the Guèvremont house, as he tended to do. The morning was overcast and hot, and he began to rehearse what he would say as he walked the short distance through the town. There were his prospects, his recent success in finding and dispersing the rebel band of Jean Rohu, how he had been viewed favourably by General Hoche, and then the matter of how he was also viewed favourably by Guèvremont's daughter herself. He was not sure how this would go down with her father, but he felt it ought to be considered important. In fact, dwelling on her evident affection for him made him feel proud, until he

188

came round to what she had warned might be the impending issue of that affection. He dismissed that for the moment: he could not afford to become unnerved.

Bernard opened the door to him with a slight bow, and Leroux strode up the hallway as he might on the parade ground, his boots sounding rather heavily on the resonant oak flooring. He stood aside as Bernard came up behind him to tap on the study door, in the familiar ritual of this household. Then, to his consternation, he saw the door of the salon down the hall open a crack, revealing the tense face of Joséphine, who gave him a wan smile and raised her hand to her lips to waft him a kiss, just as Bernard was tapping.

If Leroux had expected Guèvremont to come towards the study door to meet him with an outstretched hand, he was immediately disappointed. Joséphine's father sat behind his desk, preoccupied with papers, and barely looked up as Leroux was announced. Guèvremont waved vaguely to direct him into a chair, and carried on reading and shuffling.

'Make yourself comfortable, Leroux. I shall be with you shortly. Pressing business here. If only people would do what one told them to do, no more and no less.'

'I am at your disposal, sir.' Leroux stared at the brass mantle-clock. Maybe he should get a clock. It was a sign of civil life. As things were, in the military, his hours were kept for him.

'Now, Leroux, what can I do for you? You have not come to warn me of more disturbances?'

Leroux was conscious of trying to pitch his voice evenly. 'Not at all, Citizen Guèvremont. The region is thoroughly pacified, the last disturbance cleared up by myself just the other day, up in what the peasants call the *landes*, near Grand-Champ.'

'Have you arrested them?'

'No, none were arrested. We wounded a few, sent them running back to their hovels. We may well find them.' He paused for a moment. 'I have been commended for the action.' There was a silence while each waited for the other to speak.

'Is that all, Leroux? I believe the uniforms are now almost all in place at the dyeing works, and some are indeed being moved on. You are aware that everything is most satisfactory, after trial and improvement rather than error? The black walnut is highly effective.'

'Yes, of course.' Leroux found himself hesitating and seized on another topic. 'We have not yet found Picaud.'

'Do not let that trouble you. If that is what you came to tell me, you need not have been concerned. We shall not see him again, I'll be bound.'

'It is your daughter, sir.' There, he had blurted it out. 'Your daughter, *Mademoiselle* Joséphine Guèvremont.'

'What of my daughter, Captain?' Guèvremont's tone was unaccommodating.

Leroux moved the hat from his knees to his lap, where he held it tightly. He seized on some of his prepared phrases. 'Over time I have come to admire your daughter *Mademoiselle* Guèvremont greatly, *Monsieur* Guèvremont. She brings together in her person all that one might wish of elegance and charm, and, indeed, represents to the world a collection of all the virtues and graces…'

'Captain Leroux, may I stop you there? I understand that you admire my daughter, who is indeed well worthy of admiration, and if we were not busy men we might spend a pleasant hour enumerating her virtues. But what is it in particular that you wish to say to me?'

There was nothing for it. Leroux stood up and only just managed to avoid saluting to the man behind the desk. 'With due respect, sir, I am asking for the honour of paying my addresses to your daughter.'

For an instant, it was as if Guèvremont regarded the young officer with compassion. But after that moment, he clasped his hands together on the desk in front of him and spoke quietly. 'Captain Leroux, you are asking something of me that I cannot grant. Now, you are a young man, and young men take things hard, so do you wish to leave it at that, or do you wish to hear what I would have to say in explanation?'

Leroux stayed stiffly standing in front of the desk. His manner was now military. 'I shall hear what you say, sir, with your permission.'

Guèvremont spoke to him flatly, and without preamble. 'I do not wish my daughter to marry a young military man. It has become something of a commonplace in society, Leroux, that young military men in the new regime are self-made men, and that they have nothing in the way of property or income behind them. You are aware of that commonplace?'

'I am, sir.'

'You yourself, as I understand it, have no expectations, and indeed no background to speak of. An officer's stipend, a barely-furnished billet, and an admittedly fine horse, but we are aware of the loan that secured it — it will not do, Leroux. You must see that yourself.'

Leroux could think of nothing to say.

'Now, with your indulgence, I have an important engagement at the hour of eleven, for which I should prepare myself. I am sorry, Leroux, but it may be that fortune will bring you advancement in the years that lie ahead, and with advancement may come the standing in society that you deserve, and at present sadly lack. The new Republic presents us with a world of opportunity, does it not? Now, as I say, if you will forgive me...'

Leroux bowed to him and marched across to the door.

'And, Leroux, a word of personal advice, if I may presume so much: get rid of that dreadful moustache. It makes you look like a sergeant of the local *gendarmerie*.'

Outside, it was beginning to rain, great summer drops that left a scent on the paving as they fell. Leroux went into a haberdashery nearby that he had visited with Joséphine, and asked the proprietor for a piece of paper and a pencil. He stood at one end of the counter and scribbled a few words, and then folded the paper and wrote a 'J' on the front of it. He thanked the woman, who took pleasure in the presence of an officer on her premises, and walked back to the house. He ran up the steps and found the door opening in front of him. Leroux held out the piece of paper and Bernard took it, without asking for an explanation, and closed the door quietly.

CHAPTER XXIV: A REPUGNANT PROPOSITION

Arabella made good progress down the path towards the gate. She had not been hurrying much of late, but she was relieved to feel her limbs coping with a little urgency. She had always run around whenever she could when she was a child, risking the displeasure of her father. She had been pleased to hear that Amelia had shared her love of climbing trees, which Amelia's father had regarded with amused tolerance, while her own had strictly forbidden anything of the kind. Forbidding made anything seem more attractive, and she felt at this moment that Justin would not approve of what she was doing, so she quickened her step. The woman remained collapsed by the gate, and as Arabella drew close, she could hear her sobbing. There was blood on her face.

'Stay still, I shall help you,' said Arabella. 'You must tell me whatever is the matter.'

She swore mildly as she realised this had been a mistake, and that she had scared her, because at her first words the woman looked up, got to her feet, and stumbled off through the gateway, sobbing and seemingly waving her away. Arabella pulled up the skirts of her dress and almost broke into a run, as the woman turned sharply into the undergrowth to the side of the lane just beyond the gate.

'No, please wait. I ... shall have a sixpence for you. I must know what is the matter.'

The woman stopped ahead of her on the path. As she turned, Arabella could see she had quite a young face, and there was indeed blood smeared down one cheek. She held out her hand towards Arabella, who was aware that she had lied, since all she had was halfpennies for the children. Unexpectedly the woman smiled, and Arabella suddenly felt rather weak after the unaccustomed exertion and excitement: she must bring the woman back onto the lane, where Grace could join them. She hardly noticed the crack of a twig behind her, although she did see the woman's glance drift over her shoulder. Before she could speak again, a wet cloth was thrust in her mouth and her arms were pinioned from behind, her hands quickly tied. Another moment and she was pushed forwards along the path, the man behind her rudely insistent and far too strong for her. He was also close enough for her to hear his breathing, and if she wanted to avoid having him pressing up against her, she thought she had best do what he prompted, despite her surging anger.

Her mind was racing, too, as the grotesque procession stumbled through the undergrowth. This sudden and dreadful outrage was incomprehensible and very painful. Her shoulders felt twisted, her wrists were already suffering from what might become lacerations, and the rag made her inclined to choke, although the water in it prevented that, as no doubt it was meant to do. This abduction had been prepared in some way, of that there could be no doubt, and it was certain that the woman had been set to lure her into a trap. In that case, she might wager that the blood was contrived, and it might be that the woman's costume was too. None of this helped in working out what was to be done. The brambles caught at her dress, and more than once the woman came back to free her, the man pushing her on again immediately. She might pretend to twist her ankle, but she could guess that he would then carry her on forcibly himself, a prospect that her dignity would not countenance. No, resistance would have to wait.

The path led through the woods and out into a field. The man put his hand on her arm and brought her to a standstill, while the woman came up to her, took off her own colourful scarf, and wrapped it around Arabella's head. She went forward blindfolded. She had quickly taken the opportunity to look around; there was an old barn in the field, with a track leading to a gate. It was just possible that she recognised it from her walks with Grace into the village. Crossing the field proved to be far less thorny than walking through the woodland, but there were ruts, and the woman took her arm, much to Arabella's indignation, to make sure she did not fall. They were still in a hurry, and the day had become much warmer, so she was by now hot, trussed as she was and not in control of her own movements.

She could smell the barn as they got closer to it, and then she was sure that she could hear the movements of horses and the jangle of harnesses. It was cooler here, the stable-like smells familiar, and she was brought to a halt without a word being spoken. She heard a slight creak, and then another, and the man moved her forward and placed her right foot on a step. So, it was a carriage. He then had the effrontery to lift her upwards, while smaller hands took hold of hers and pulled her in. The door was closed, and she could sense the woman sitting next to her. Still, nothing was said. Arabella began to feel very strange indeed, unwell and then sickly, as the carriage rolled out of the barn. She was just about conscious when the wheels came onto the harder surface of the lane, but she could hold out no longer after that, and she fainted away.

There was an unpleasant taste in Arabella's mouth, and her lips were bruised. She struggled to recover her senses, but the room was a blur, and her wrists hurt abominably. She brought one hand up to her face, and the other followed to rub the sore part. There was something wrong with the room. The window was far too small, and the bed was a couch. She moved about on it, propping her head up. The far wall was too close, and the room was a strange shape, with sides that pressed in upon her. She sat up, determined that this was a dream. She needed to splash her face with a little water, and she spied a jug and basin on a small side table. As she arose, she was in danger of falling, and so she sat back down on the edge of the tattered couch.

The door creaked open, and a young woman dressed respectably entered. 'Ah,' she said.

Arabella was enough herself to challenge her, although her voice cracked as she spoke. 'And who may you be, pray?'

'Never you mind about that, miss. It's you we must get on your feet, now. Here, let me bring you…'

'Get out!' Arabella was relieved to hear her voice more at its usual strength. The young woman hesitated. Arabella decided that she must stand to lend more force to her command, and did so commendably. 'I wish you to leave me alone. Now, get out, and send my own woman to me immediately. Do you hear me?'

To Arabella's chagrin, the woman stood her ground, put her hands on her hips, and looked at her with a mocking smile. 'My, oh, my, aren't you the mistress, then? And I suppose you'll be saying you don't want to see him, then? I like your game, miss, I do.'

With that, the woman spun out of the door behind her, which Arabella heard being locked. All was silent. She thought about sitting back down, but instead walked over to the jug and basin, poured out some water, and patted it on her cheeks and forehead. She looked round the room and began to tremble.

A key turned in the lock, and a man's voice came from the shadows in the doorway. 'Ah, we meet again. The last time I saw you, which I believe must have been back in Plymouth, you were calling yourself Mrs Fitzhugh. I may hardly exaggerate if I claim that, for the moment at least, the pleasure might appear to be all mine.'

Arabella wondered again about her dream. She had heard about people whose minds wandered, and who saw visions, or walked in their sleep. Was this…?

'May I come in?'

The figure spread his arms to encourage a response. There was none. Arabella saw that he was a relatively young man, much her own age, with a face that was somehow familiar. He was dressed elegantly, his hair in a Brutus crop.

'Well, I shall take that for a "yes". I have brought us refreshment.' He was carrying a bottle and two glasses. 'Let us not stand on ceremony. You may take the couch, and I shall take this small chair. There. What is formality between old acquaintances?'

Arabella had not sat down. She was searching to identify that familiarity in his features, but her head ached. Indignation surged as the man settled into the chair and put the glasses on the floor, pouring a deep red wine into them. He corked the bottle carefully.

'I do not believe I am acquainted with you, sir, nor would I wish to be so,' Arabella said fiercely. 'Now, you will inform me of the measures you will now take to…'

'Oh, my dear Mrs Fitzhugh, how can it be that your memory fails you? You were quite confident of who I was only months ago. A quaint little room in Plymouth, and there I was imagining at first that you had come for an assignation with my ever-so-charming self. Dear, oh dear.' His face suddenly took on an expression of exaggerated concern. 'Good Lord, are you by chance subject to such lapses of memory? Perhaps that is an unwanted consequence of your present condition, which is tolerably well advanced, I see. Quite an added attraction for some, amongst whom, now that I consider it, I might find myself to be happily numbered.' The man raised his glass to his lips, swirled the wine gently, held it to his nose in an insolent gesture, and then replaced it on the floor.

Arabella's memory was indeed suffering. Her head was throbbing, and her face was flushed. But she should deny this man familiarity in any circumstance. 'It is plain, sir, that you have mistaken me for another, in a manner that has led to grossly improper conduct — nay, an outrage. You will see to it immediately...'

'Oh, but I shall be seeing to it, Miss Wollaston, or should I say Mrs Wentworth? Now, cease this pretence and take a glass. You may be needing a little Dutch courage to hear what I have to say.' So saying he poured out a glass, came across to her, and held it out.

Arabella breathed in deeply: her eyes were smarting and her legs felt shamefully weak, but the fog had lifted, and the truth now confronted her. She could be in no doubt: the man facing her was none other than Lieutenant Tregothen, the brute who had set his sights on Amelia and then assaulted the actress Miss Farley. But she could not grasp how he could possibly be here in England. Justin had said that he was sent away, disgraced, in the expectation that he would never return from the West Indies. She recognised her dreadful state of weakness, but she had to say something. 'You will step back, sir, and allow me to sit here. A gentleman would fetch me water.'

'Mayhap he would.' His tone was now hard. 'Make yourself comfortable. I have a proposition for you, my estimable Mrs Wentworth, and you would do well to listen carefully.'

She was for the moment too exhausted and bewildered to say any more.

'I shall pass over any explanation of how it is that I come to be returned. I have a score to settle with you. I am here to satisfy a desire, and we shall not part until you have provided me with … how shall we put it, full reparation.'

Arabella was dumb. Her body felt nerveless. The baby moved in her womb.

'You say nothing. I recall you were not always so lost for words, when you thought you could threaten me, and when your family attempted my ruin. A man does not forget those who betray him, Mrs Wentworth. Now, listen. You have a short time. Your reputation is at stake. You may either choose to yield to me willingly, in which case I shall return you swiftly to your home, or I shall force you nonetheless. Do you understand me? That is my proposition.'

Arabella's hands moved on her lap, her eyes flitting about the room. Tregothen was convinced that she understood, and felt a deep sense of satisfaction.

'I can see you comprehend me. If you return home soon, your reputation will remain intact, your husband will see to that, whatever you choose to tell him. But should you refuse me, you will face the consequences, and you and he will hear it rumoured abroad that you were abducted willingly to conceal an amour. Think on it, my dear Mrs Wentworth, and relish your choice.' With that, Tregothen picked up his glass and raised it. 'I shall give you time to reflect. The woman will bring you some water to drink. I shall leave you the bottle in case you choose to rely on Bacchus, as many do.'

The door closed. Arabella sat in disbelief and stared at the bottle of wine. Something so ordinary and yet so foul, contaminated by his touch and his abominable suggestions. She flinched as the door opened. The young woman appeared, holding a carafe of water and a glass goblet.

'Thirsty, are you? Ay, it is thirsty work.'

'Are you mad, woman?' Arabella demanded. 'I am with child. Do you not see?'

'It is a good cover, as they say.' The woman poured out some water and offered it to Arabella, who shook her head. The woman placed it on the small table.

'Now, listen, you may forget about this disgusting nonsense about a game,' Arabella insisted. 'Did he tell you that? There is no game. Did he tell you we were tricking my husband? Is that it?'

The woman looked uncertain. The sun flickered outside the window as it filtered through the branches of a small tree.

'Where are we?' Arabella continued. 'I am not here willingly. This is an outrage. Do you not understand me?' Her voice had risen, and the woman had become anxious. That was a mistake.

'The water's there. Help yourself to it, then. I must be going.' The lock clicked behind her.

The hours passed, or so it seemed to Arabella, who alternately sat or paced about the small room. It was hexagonal, and one side at least faced in a westerly direction, since the sun had moved from one window to the next. These were truly worthless observations, but the planting and hedging prevented further views, notably from the leaded window to the side of the small door. Her headache had peaked and then receded, and her hunger had become acute, but the young woman had not come back.

Arabella would not contemplate the prospect of violation, and the idea of submitting to Tregothen's will was vile and abhorrent. Yet his calculations were ineluctable. The mere circumstances of an unexplained absence from her husband could be construed as dishonourable, with pernicious help from certain scurrilous voices. She had no doubt that Tregothen had such voices to do his bidding. It might be possible to hide an awful truth from her husband: many a wife had done that in the face of a husband who would barely trouble to conceal his own mistresses. But was she such a woman, or her husband such a man? Could she bear him a child while she carried such trauma?

She sobbed and gasped for air, and her foot lashed out and sent the goblet flying across the room. The glass shattered against the table leg. The sharp noise brought an abrupt end to her grief. She stared witlessly at the glass, and then at the bottle, which had miraculously escaped the sweep of her foot.

She crossed to the basin, and once again washed her face. She looked down at the broken glass and bent to pick it up. *One should not leave a mess*, she thought hopelessly.

CHAPTER XXV: A QUESTION OF PATERNITY

Laurent Guèvremont held his cane in his left hand, at a diagonal across his body, so its shining ebony was visible, along with the silverwork of the eagle's head with which it was crowned. His breeches were a charcoal-grey, his coat of brown velvet. Beneath it he wore a striking crimson waistcoat, topped by a white silk necktie. A round hat set off the ensemble, its brims turned up in what he had been told was the latest fashion. Auray was not Rennes, but there were those like him who tried to set a standard.

He walked past the marketplace and then down towards the bridge. He tipped his hat occasionally to ladies. By chance, he happened on *Madame* du Plessis, walking with her maid, and he recalled while he was talking that he had promised to visit her some months ago. She did not mention it, which was hardly surprising, and he realised that with all that was happening around him, he had avoided contemplating a commitment of any kind.

La du Plessis undoubtedly had her charms and had been well provided for by her late husband, who had been Guèvremont's banker until he had chosen to divide his assets between other houses in Pontivy and Vannes. *Madame* du Plessis had reproached Guèvremont for this act of pecuniary disloyalty light-heartedly at a salon he had mistakenly attended, tutting at him and tapping him with an ivory fan. At the time, he had pondered whether the look she had given him was about rather more than money. She had to be past child-bearing age by now, and that could be an attractive feature, since she had retained her figure and was an emblem of elegance throughout the town.

He began to stroll across the bridge and into Saint Goustan. It was a good time of day to come, because the early-morning bustle was over and more respectable people had taken to going about their business. In making the arrangement, he had spoken about the far end of the bridge, leading into the Place Saint Sauveur, and for recognition had mentioned his cane. He believed it was distinctive and so crossed the bridge with confidence, stopping to gaze down the river, which glittered in the morning sun.

'*Bonjour.* I believe I may have the pleasure of greeting *Monsieur* Laurent Guèvremont. You must forgive me if I am by any chance mistaken.'

The speaker was an older man, with fine grey hair and a neatly trimmed beard, the hair longer than was fashionable. He was dressed in a short jacket of a buff colour, a waistcoat of a darker brown that buttoned to the side, and plain breeches and an incongruous pair of black shoes. His voice was low, but soft and melodious.

'My pleasure, sir.' Guèvremont bowed slightly, so as not to occasion much notice, and invited the older man to walk with him along the quay. The older man was wearing a broad-brimmed, flat hat which Guèvremont recognised as belonging to a Breton. He was sure of his man, but politeness demanded confirmation. 'And you, sir, will be Mael Sarzou — a name well known to me over the years. You gave years of service as the steward of the manor of Kergohan, when it was owned by the de Guèrinec family. I regret that it is so long since we last met. And when we did, I was no more than a foolish lad.'

'I remember your features well. It is indeed many years now since the children of the *baronne* were playing in the grounds, and you, sir, with them at times, but not often if my memory serves me well.'

'No, from time to time. It did depend on where my father had his residence.'

Guèvremont noticed that Sarzou spoke French as if it was an effort, and he was unable to make up his mind whether this was a typical Breton affectation, or simply that he had not been speaking the language much recently. Their path lay along the narrow quay, past the few larger boats that were moored there, with one or two porters still crossing from them to small warehouses. It was quiet, which suited Guèvremont's purpose.

'It is good of you to arrange to meet me. I am informed that you have come a long way, at my request, and I am inviting you to call on my banker when you are next in Vannes to defray any expenses. Now…'

'I do not go to Vannes, *Monsieur* Guèvremont, and there have been no expenses, at least none to take note of. It is the bank of du Plessis here in Auray that the family used. I believe it is still in operation. I became well-acquainted with *Monsieur* du Plessis during my time as steward. But this is not to the purpose. You must speak on.'

Guèvremont felt apprehensive suddenly, and out of instinct he directed their steps up a small lane leading off the quay. There was no one here, and it was a little cooler, with what he took to be some vegetables just visible over a low wall.

'*Monsieur* Sarzou, I shall come directly to the point.' Guèvremont lowered his voice. 'I have, in recent months, taken charge of a boy. I am informed that he is the son of a young woman who died soon after his birth, some seventeen years ago. The young woman concerned was in service at

Kergohan. For reasons that need not concern you, I recently met his aunt, who had been estranged from him from the time of her sister's death, if not before. Now, it has become imperative to find out who the father of this boy might be. I have some reason to believe that you may be able to help me.'

Mael Sarzou was looking over the low wall at the vegetables as Guèvremont spoke. He gave no sign of a reaction to what he had just heard, but his voice was low, out of deference to the subject. 'What is it that you are hoping to hear from me, *Monsieur* Guèvremont?'

'I am not sure I am hoping for anything in particular. But it will be plain to you, after your involvement in the management of the estate at Kergohan, that if by any chance a member of the de Guèrinec family were somehow involved, this might have had implications for inheritance. I know I speak even then of a remote possibility…'

'So you are expecting me to know more of this?'

'The young woman was abandoned by her family. She was nominally in your charge, or at least that of your wife, who managed the household but not, I believe, without consultation with you.'

'My wife is dead.'

Guèvremont was beginning to get irritated by what he sensed might be typical Breton obstruction in the face of questions by outsiders. Not that his own family did not have a Breton pedigree, but Sarzou might not see him as a true de Guèrinec, despite his mother's blood.

'You have my sympathy, Sarzou, and I know the young woman's passing was regretted at Kergohan. You will forgive me, but my estimate is that the girl may have seen you as a parent, as a kindly father who did not condemn her out of hand. You did not, did you?'

'I did not. She was a poor little chit who did not know what she was doing; she had her head turned by where she was. We should have seen it earlier and removed her, for her own sake.'

'But did she share confidences with you? Did you ask her to name the father of her child? We cannot ask the priest, because he is bound by the secrecy of the confessional. But you...'

'She would not tell anyone, *Monsieur* Guèvremont. She would not speak about it, for shame. She stayed on at the manor, all through. And then when the boy was little — only just weaned, my wife said — she fell ill, and you have never seen anyone so sorrowful. I would not wish to see that again.'

'But did she reveal the father's name to you before she died, Sarzou? When she knew she was dying?' Guèvremont was agitated.

'The good Lord forgive me, I did make a choice to repeat the question as she was dying. I must have been out of my senses, but like you I was thinking of the things of this world when her soul was preoccupied with those of the next. God forgive me.' Mael crossed himself at the memory of that sunken face, and the thin, wasted body.

'Did she say anything, Sarzou?' Guèvremont's voice was almost a whisper.

'All she was willing to say to me was that it had not been young Wentworth. At least, I asked her if the boy had been loose with her, and she shook her head. He had been struck with her, I already knew that.'

'So he had never touched her? This is important, Sarzou.' Guèvremont's knuckles were white as he held his cane. 'Did she say who it was?'

'She never said anything. She would not. I would not know if she spoke a name to the priest. He came to give her the last rites, and she was desperate for absolution. Her family was religious and unforgiving. I expect she took the knowledge to the grave.'

A silence fell between the two men. Guèvremont reached out his hand and Mael took it, after an almost imperceptible moment of reluctance.

'You will not have far to go today, I am told.'

Mael shook his head. 'No, I have a lodging in the town. Our sister Anne is there — Bernard's and mine. I have not seen her in a long year, living out on the farm with Father as I do now. We in the Sarzou family go our own ways, too much so, it may be.'

'I'll wish you a good day then, Mael, if you will allow me. I am pleased that we have met again.'

By an unspoken agreement, born perhaps of the sorrowful story they had just retold, they chose to leave by opposite ends of the short lane. But Mael halted while Guèvremont was still staring at the wall, lost in thought.

'I saw the boy, once or twice, up at the village there,' Mael told him. 'Striking fair hair, he had. Some have it young, and then go darker.' He shook his head. 'Never seen him since, though others did. Better for him, I thought. Yes, it were an odd thing to see fair hair in these parts. Good day to you, *Monsieur* Guèvremont.'

CHAPTER XXVI: A DAGGER IN ONE HAND

Eugène found himself in the back of Mrs Fitchett's house, which was a warren of a building. The room was plainly furnished, but the simple bed had clean linen and more than one pillow. There was a small window high up on one wall, so the light was poor. It was hot and airless, since the day had progressed and he was several floors above the ground, perhaps under the tiles. Had he been staying — and indulging in the sport that this good lady had in mind for him — he would have found it warm work.

The roast beef lay untouched on a pedestal table of good workmanship. The wine too, although he had been tempted. The deepest disappointment had been that of the young woman who had brought it to him. She was pretty, but she was not Amelia: her hair was red, her face freckled, and she had a gap in her teeth. His gamble had come to nothing. The redhead could not miss the look on his face, and he could not disguise it, although he was profuse in his thanks, allowing her to pour out a glass for him. But he had to raise his hand when she came towards him, at which she turned away with an angry flounce. So he asked her name, and she said she was called Polly. Then Eugène tried to exercise his charm while keeping her at a distance. This situation had persisted awkwardly until he realised that he must get out of the room if he was to search at all. In desperation, he sought her indulgence in letting him rest and returning, if she would, as evening was falling, because they might then make good use of the whole night. Polly seemed satisfied with that — although she still looked at him oddly — and she left in a better mood.

Eugène sat disconsolately on the bed. He could hardly bring himself to believe that Amelia was here, but he could not reject the proposition, because he had nothing with which to replace it. Amelia was not a distressed young woman, sadly in disgrace through a misdemeanour or the callousness of a seducer. She was an amiable and respectable gentlewoman, and whatever one might say about Mrs Fitchett, that lady was not a fool: the coercion of gentlewomen would not for one moment be contemplated by her. It was impossible.

But what else was he to believe? The coachman knew his streets. Amelia had been conveyed here, and estimating the extent of this warren, Eugène was convinced that it occupied most of this cul-de-sac. But to what purpose? There was only one obvious advantage to this location, and that was its proximity to the river, and to ships. The thought of this was so appalling that he did not wish to dwell on it. Yet the idea proved insistent. Amelia might have been brought here to be taken on to some unknown destination abroad.

He wiped his hand across his forehead. If he did not take action, then Polly would be back. He loosened the knife in his boot and got to his feet, opened the door quietly, and listened. There was very little noise up here; it might be a back or side house, something joined onto the main house in a rickety kind of way. There was a door just across from his own. He tapped lightly on it, and hearing nothing he looked in. It was empty. He stood there for a moment. He could just hear voices from the floor below. He had to be barefaced, get into these rooms before declaring it all a lost cause. God knew what he would do then. The stairwell was cramped, dropping down at the far end of the corridor. He slipped lightly down it. One door stood directly in front of him. This time, he did not knock but heaved the door open. A young man with his waistcoat and breeches cast aside turned his head in protest, as an older woman with him covered her bosom and spat some foul words. It was a Hogarthian vision, but he cut it short and slammed the door with an elaborate oath that he hoped would dramatically convey his mistake. He listened for a while. Their indignation found voice for a few moments, but their footsteps did not come close to the door.

Eugène flicked the perspiration from one eye and tiptoed along the adjoining passage. He saw another stairwell at the far end, so he must have passed this corridor on his way up. An ear to the door halfway along it told him nothing, except that by his calculation this must be the room from which he had dimly heard voices rising through the floor. He waited, hearing nothing but his own breathing. A slight movement. There was someone in there. A small sound, and that must be china. No conversation. But a woman, presumably? Would Amelia be drinking tea? He had to go in. He could pretend to have mistaken his own room, and be consumed in polite apology. He stepped in after a perfunctory knock. A woman was sitting on a chair next to a table with a teapot and cups placed on it, holding a pair of sugar tongs with a broken piece of sugar in them above her open mouth. She stared at Eugène in disbelief.

'And who the hell are you? Get out of here sharpish before I call for Artur, or you'll be sorry.' With that, she let the sugar drop and sucked on it.

Eugène stared at her and put on his most winning smile. He closed the door behind him. She might be a lady of the trade, but instinct told him not. If not, what was she doing here? It was a small room, a kind of parlour. He noticed on the far side of it a door with a bolt: it was shot. A clandestine liaison, guarded by this profane and sweet-toothed gatekeeper? His pulse began to throb in his ears.

'And why would I be in a hurry to leave, my dear?' he said. 'You have no company, and I am sure we can settle on something satisfactory between us.'

He had eased his way to her side. But Sal was not new to this game, and although he was a good-looking young lad who might be up for the sport, she had Jencks to think about, and that devil behind him. Still, she stood up to face the intruder, and her posture was not hostile.

'Now, look here…'

Eugène took his opportunity, pressing his mouth tightly on hers, and clasping her arms while he eased her backwards to the door in the wall. He slipped back the bolt, pulled her towards him again, and heaved them both into the far room.

The air was stale in there. Eugène let her go abruptly as he glanced around. Sal was puzzled and amused, but she went back to him with a passion.

'My, have you got fire in your belly! But not here, mister, not here,' she said.

Eugène could now see a figure on the bed. His heart began to thump, but he kept up his act. 'Well, my dear, who have we here, then? You can get rid of her, surely.' He strode over to the bedside, and his senses threatened to overwhelm him. It was Amelia.

'No, leave her be. Come over here with me. I've had it up against a wall before now, and they weren't as pretty as you. Her in the bed won't trouble us.'

Sal began to hoist up her petticoat and unlace her bodice, and made a mess of both. Eugène tore himself away from the bed and strolled casually towards her. He noticed a small bottle on the table, and a porcelain cup. His cheeks were now flushed with anger, but he reached surreptitiously for the handkerchief in his pocket. He came close to Sal and let his lips hover over hers: his voice was a whisper.

'Laudanum, is it?'

His hand quickly thrust the balled handkerchief into her mouth. She struggled as he held her wrists. He looked around for something to tie her hands, then remembered the cloth in which he had wrapped his dagger. He marched Sal over to the bed and reached down for the dagger. When she saw it, Sal's eyes went wide. She shook her head violently from side to side, and then tried to kick him. But he unrolled the cloth with a spin, letting the dagger fall on the floorboards, and bound her hands behind her back. She was wearing fashionable short boots; he tied her laces together, now he had both hands free, to stop her kicking. He then left her on the end of the bed.

Amelia had stirred. She was still dressed, with her shoes just visible on the floor beneath the bed. She raised her head and leaned on one elbow uncomprehendingly, but sank back again, murmuring. So, she was conscious at least, one small mercy. Eugène hardly dared to draw near to her, but he could not risk any delay. She would have to get up, and he would have to support her all the way down the stairs and outside. One arm would be around her, with the dagger held in his other hand. There would be no room for clever manoeuvres.

The woman was still struggling, but could move very little. Eugène thrust her under the bedclothes. He then called up his courage and wrapped his arms around Amelia, lifting her upright and swinging her legs around so she was sitting on the edge of the bed. He placed her shoes on her feet and spoke to her softly.

'Amelia, it is I, Eugène. Your friend, Eugène.' Her eyelids were heavy, but she lifted her eyes to him. He risked a bit more. 'We have to go downstairs. You must lean on me. Try to walk.' He took up the dagger, put his arm round her and persuaded her to stand. They then moved awkwardly to the door. Amelia looked round towards the bed, but Eugène shook his head and took her into the next room. He slammed the bolt home — that would keep the gatekeeper in her own prison for a while; with luck, he would not see her again. They crossed to the door that led into the corridor. In her current state, Amelia could pass for tipsy if not drunk, and that might be enough to get by. The light was beginning to fade just a little, and it was much darker in the stairwell.

Eugène chose the staircase that gave his right hand the freedom to strike with his dagger, with the stairs bending round to the left. A small thing, but it might be decisive. The weight of Amelia on his left arm was bound to hamper him. The stairs creaked, but there was very little noise coming from the rooms that they passed. A door slammed off to their left, and voices came up from below as feet pounded up the stairs on the far side. Silence again. There was now very little light, and he could just see that Amelia was feeling her way with her hand and her feet, since the treads were extremely narrow.

They reached the bottom. The dust had given way to the smell of damp, and it was much darker. To their left there was a glimmer of light under a door at the end of the passage, and more daylight to their right above a planked door with a heavy bolt. Eugène's arm was aching, but he placed his hand on Amelia's shoulder and patted it gently. He spoke again.

'We shall go along here.' In the dim light, he could just see her profile.

'Eugène,' she said. Nothing more.

Eugène took her hand as they went towards the door to the left, which he hoped led onto the street, or at least into an alley leading to a street. There was no more than a latch here, but it was not driven through the door, and so opened only from the inside. A night door, perhaps, to let patrons out but not in? It clicked up easily enough, and the door swung back. He pushed it slowly open, and with immense relief he saw the short street down which he had walked earlier. They stepped through into the sharp light of day.

Amelia screamed as she toppled back, and before Eugène could see what had happened he was grabbed by two powerful arms and thrown against the wall. His head and his neck miraculously escaped, but the giant with hair the colour of bleached straw reached down and picked him up by the collars of his coat. The giant lifted him up like a child and threw him down again. This time, his head hit a timber in the wall, but he could do nothing, let alone get to his feet. Though the side of his head was aching, Eugène could dimly pick out the handle of the dagger on the ground beneath the edge of Amelia's dress, as she desperately held on to the wall.

Artur put his hands on his hips and surveyed his work. Eugène painfully clambered to his feet and raised his fists and forearms as he had seen pugilists do: the giant grinned, licked his lips, and mockingly put one hand behind his back. Eugène stepped forward, waved a fist in front of his face, and kicked Artur as hard as he could on the side of his knee. The giant's grin faded and was replaced by puzzlement. Without warning, his leg suddenly gave way. He went down heavily on the injured knee and let out what Eugène could only describe as a howl.

Over Artur's shoulder, Eugène spied Amelia holding the dagger out to him. He grasped it and then took Amelia's hand, jerking her towards himself and over the giant's sprawling leg. Artur's hand came up and seized her trailing arm, pulling her back. Eugène leaned swiftly forward and stabbed the dagger into the giant's upper arm. Artur fell back with a cry as he clutched one arm with the other, and Amelia almost fell forwards onto Eugène. There was no more to be done: they ran.

The coachman was bored and sleepy. He had enjoyed the hot sherry, and then refused a second glass, but he felt the effects nonetheless. He had also forgotten to listen out for the church bells, but he cared very little. He lounged in the sun, leaning against the wall, and talked to his nags. They listened, in their way, flapping an ear and tossing their heads. Anyway, enough was enough. He kicked his heel against the wall and climbed back on the box. The noise in Narrow Street behind him had died down slightly as the day had gone on. He had not turned the vehicle, thinking that his horses would be less restless if they faced away from the racket, and he realised now that he would have to back them up on the turn, because there was not enough room in this side-street just to swing round. He tutted to himself for being such a fool and jumped down again. He went to the horses' heads and then stared.

A man and a woman were reeling down the road towards him, as if they were both drunk as lords. He recognised them without a shadow of a doubt. She was the young lady he had picked up in Hampstead, and he was the gentleman who had paid him to chase after her. What they had been doing in the meantime to get into that state was anybody's guess.

The coachman shrugged and carried on backing up his horses. He even opened the door for them to get in quickly. At least he had another fare. He climbed back up and clicked his tongue at his horses.

CHAPTER XXVII: JEANNE'S SORROW

Bernard closed the door of the Guèvremont house behind him with some satisfaction. His normal duty was to open it to others and provide them with a welcome, an office he performed without undue unctuousness or curt incivility, both of which he despised. He found himself on this morning acting as an escort for a young man whom he had begun to like. Unlike his brother Mael and his sister Anne, Bernard Sarzou had no children of his own, a matter that had never troubled him until the last few weeks. Now he and Gilles, who had two hours' leave of absence, were to visit his sister Anne in the town, where Gilles would be able talk in private with his aunt, Jeanne. They had been parted almost since Gilles had been born to Jeanne's sister, seventeen years ago in a small room in the manor at Kergohan. The wife of Bernard's brother Mael had been in attendance, with the *gwreg* who was the best midwife south of the *landes*. So much Bernard knew from what Jeanne had told him; the rest was hidden from him.

He felt a liveliness that he realised had been lacking for many years. He and Jeanne had spoken not so much about the boy as about themselves. She had married Henri the farmer, who had been devout and had had good land, as her parents wished, before she had known her own mind or Bernard had had enough behind him to ask their permission to address her. He had not realised how much he cared about her until she was lost to him. He had been a young man with hot blood in his veins, and she was all beauty to him, so he knew what desire was and how fiercely it could burn. But she had kept him at arm's length, hiding behind her parents' love of the

Church. Bernard had not relished being made into the devil's child, and he had hated Henri with a vengeance.

So he had left Brandivy and had gone to seek his fortune in the town, serving in one or two houses and finding he could manage well. That was the kind of thing that Guèvremont noticed, and when the old butler had died, suddenly Bernard had found himself being asked to step into his shoes. He had never looked back. He was respected and diligent, and he made it his principle to treat all who came his way considerately. When what they called the Republic had broken into their lives with fury, he found in his heart that he respected the calls for equality, humanity and fraternity. He had detested the Church for as long as he could remember, his one weakness when it came to tolerance. But that call for humanity was sorely tested by the bitter struggles all over the region. There were also reports of savagery and the appalling executions down on the marshes near Auray. So Bernard settled back into his own life in the household, and kept his thoughts to himself.

He and Gilles walked on together in silence. Each had his own reasons for being abstracted, and the natural good feeling they had for each other made up for the lack of conversation. For his part, Gilles was unsure whether to indulge his anger or his curiosity in relation to his aunt, but he was certain that he wanted to know about his mother. From what Bernard had let drop, Jeanne would not be able to tell him who his father was. They reached the Rue des Tonneaux, with the smell of the stripped oak for the barrels hanging in the air, and Bernard knocked on a weather-beaten door in a poor frame.

The woman who came to answer, wiping her hands on a cloth, looked strikingly like her brother, with beautiful black hair and smooth, dark skin. She stood aside for Gilles, and

Bernard shared a word or two with his sister before he strode off.

'An hour,' he said over his shoulder to Gilles as he left. He was aware that the boy would not hear much from Jeanne that would make him happy, so it might be best to keep it short. But although the encounter and the memories it was bound to provoke would pain her, it would have to be faced. He himself had much to lay at the door of Jeanne's parents, yet there could be no doubt that the daughters had suffered most. He might now have an opportunity to repair some of that harm, but he could not yet presume to guess how Jeanne felt about him.

He noted the cooper in passing with approval. The man and his trade were known to him, but he had had little occasion to think about them until now. The lane gave out into a wider street, where one or two people greeted him, and a friend in service at another house barred his way briefly to tell him a humorous story. At another time he might have appreciated it more, but he was looking for the far end of town, above the port. He almost ran along to his destination, made his way through the ground floor and scuttled down the steps into the cellar, where the vintner was setting wedges under a barrel.

'Bernard! Devil on your tail, man?'

'No more than usual, Gwilherm. Do you have a moment?'

'Not many, but I can find one. A glass?'

'A taste, Gwilherm, and just that. *Yec'hed mat.*'

'*Yec'hed mat.* What will it be? A barrel delivered shortly, or do you want me to roll out something particular for you? You have a fine nose and palate on you. No, it's for Guèvremont, isn't it? He likes a bottle...'

Bernard held up his hand and put down his pot. 'I am not here for Guèvremont this morning, Gwilherm. Tell me, are you still fixed on that building in Vannes? The warehouse with the shop beneath? We spoke about it.'

Gwilherm rolled his eyes. 'I would be. I have been there to talk to them, more than once, but who will purchase a business or a premises here without being a cousin or knowing a cousin or being wedded to a cousin, and my cousins…'

'Are all in Saint Brieuc. I might be interested, Gwilherm.'

'In my business or the premises?'

'Both, I think.'

'*Ma Doue*! We should talk then, Bernard. Not here, but…'

Bernard stood up. 'And not now. But I shall be back to you shortly, if all goes as I hope it may.'

The two men shook hands. Bernard skipped up the steps and was out of the door, leaving Gwilherm to scratch his head in puzzlement. But being a practical man, he got to his feet and began to tap in the remaining wedges.

Gilles felt thoroughly alone in this strange house. Bernard's sister Anne led him down a dim corridor to a parlour, where there were chairs and a chest. His aunt was already there, sitting on the chest. Now he could look at her, he saw she had chestnut hair and a fair complexion, with light freckles on her pale face and forearms. He was not sure whether she was beautiful, but she was attractive.

Anne stood at the threshold, and said, 'I'll leave you to it, then.'

Gilles sat down on one of the chairs, since his aunt had taken the chest, which would have been his choice. 'So, you're Jeanne, aren't you?' He could not help it; the anger came out, and he had slipped right away into behaving like a bully. She looked across at him, and he could see the anguish in her eyes.

'Gilles, I can understand that you are angry with me. If it is any comfort, I am angry with myself. I have been a fool for too much of my life, and if I thought you could possibly understand I would tell you how. I loved your mother, who was my younger sister, and I was mercilessly hard on her when she needed me most. How can I ever forgive myself?'

Her eyes sought his face, and Gilles began to cry. There was nothing he could do to stop himself. His aunt came over, pulled him up gently, and held him in her arms, wracked by her awareness that she had nothing like this lovely boy. Thank God he was alive.

'Thank you,' he said quietly. He wiped his eyes with his sleeve and sat down again. 'Is there anything you can tell me?'

Jeanne sat down too. 'In your heart, you must know most of it. She was a young woman in the household of gentry, where she had been placed by my parents. They thought she would be able to rise in the world while leading a godly life. They were like many. But … young men always look at pretty young women, and if they are close, every day, and the women wish to please them because they are servants… It is not that those in charge at the manor did not do what they could to insist on decency and propriety. They did.'

'What you say I could recognise. Is there more?'

'Sadly, too much more, but you know a large part of it. She became pregnant, the household and the family at the manor did not punish her or reject her, and the result was you. The birth was fine, or so I was told, and you were healthy. It was only later…'

'Why were you not with her?'

'It was a sin. She had sinned. My parents disowned her for conceiving a child out of wedlock. And, God forgive me, I followed in their footsteps. They would not have her name mentioned, although I think that they prayed for her. I prayed for her.'

Gilles buried his face in his hands.

'She would never say who the father was. I am so sorry, Gilles, I do not know, and I do not think there is anyone who does. No one came forward. But Mael...'

Gilles lifted his head. 'Mael?'

'Yes, you remember, he was the steward at Kergohan for many years. His wife kept house there, at the manor. They looked after your mother, and so did the family there. Mael has told Bernard and me that ... oh, my God ... when she was dying...' She could not continue.

He decided to help her. 'Why Bernard? How is it that Bernard is involved?'

'Because Bernard is Mael's younger brother. The woman whose house this is, Anne, is their sister.'

'You spoke of when my mother was dying. This was some time after I was born. Babette has told me that. What was it...?'

Jeanne summoned the will to revisit that terrible scene. 'She was on her deathbed, and Mael says that she told him that it was not the young Wentworth boy. That is all I know. She would say no more. She was given the last rites by the priest after confession. But I do not believe she would have told the priest.'

Gilles breathed deeply. Something in him would not let her leave it there. 'Where were you? Why Mael and the priest? She was dying. She was your sister. I...'

'I did come to her, but only at the end. And you may damn me to hellfire that all I said to her was to seek forgiveness for her sin. To the end, it was all that I said, and God and Jesus Christ and all the saints...'

Gilles stood up. 'You could not save her. Forgiveness would not have saved her.'

'You must hear this, Gilles. I should have tended to you. You were my blood. But my mind was corrupted, and I was bitter. You see, I loved her, and for all that I sought forgiveness for her, it was you I blamed for her loss. I could not forgive you, a child. And the Lord said, "Suffer the little children…" and I was deaf to those words.'

Gilles spoke quietly; he pitied Jeanne. 'Fortunately, there was one who did suffer them. I must go back to her.'

'Yes, Babette was an angel sent from heaven, and the Lord bless her! She gave her youth to you. God is merciful, and if only I had known, I too would have shown mercy, so help me.' And, like Gilles before her, she was overcome with grief.

The door opened, and Mael stood there with Anne, who went over and comforted Jeanne. Mael came forward to grasp Gilles by the hand.

'I will say nothing of this now. But search in your heart to see if you can find some words of kindness to speak to her at some other time. She has punished herself enough.'

There was a knock at the door, and Gilles stepped through to let in Bernard.

CHAPTER XXVIII: ESCAPE FROM THE LODGE

Grace was already flustered. There was a crow on the ground near the arbour, but the basket still had its cloth over it, safe and sound, so that was a relief. She would now need to find her mistress, which was hardly a surprise: it was a lovely morning, and waiting had never suited Arabella's brisk temperament. Grace picked up the basket and walked on hurriedly, but there was no sign of her. She arrived at the gate at the end of the path and went a little way forward on to the road. Nothing. She retraced her steps as far as the arbour and walked up the slope in the grounds, looking at the edge of the woods. She then returned to the arbour and walked down the other way. There was the sound of a gunshot, but then its echo died away.

She would not walk to the village by herself. It was inconceivable that Miss Arabella would have gone that far ahead alone. She might, however, have taken off in another direction and become distracted. But Grace was now concerned; she stepped quickly back towards the manor, forming her resolve as she went. She had to go to the housekeeper, and if she knew her business the housekeeper would refer to the butler, Thomas Paddon.

Mrs Willan was forbearing: she sat in her office, and thought to herself that the new mistress might get herself in a pickle a little too often. She had been in service to the old Mr Wentworth and later his good lady, and then the young squire himself, and this new mistress had her own ways, and so did her maid. That was as it might be. So now the mistress was missing, and there was nothing to be done but to be discreet and to go along the corridor to the butler Thomas, who was at present more charged with the outdoors than she was.

Thomas decided that Mr Wentworth should be sent for immediately, and since the steward had fallen ill some months back, he himself knew where his master would be at that hour. Jem would be sent post-haste for him, and in the meantime a search would be made around the grounds. Arabella's groom Andrew would be taken from the stables to accompany Grace in one circuit and he, Thomas, would go with Mrs Willan in the opposite direction, starting from the back entrance to the kitchen. All those involved could be relied upon to exercise great discretion, to avoid setting the house into a commotion.

What Thomas planned was executed in due form. There had been no satisfactory result to the search, but when he rode in Justin thanked Thomas for his prompt action and locked himself in his study with Grace. She came out of the study looking tearful and went upstairs to her room without a further word, while Justin summoned Andrew to him. The two men left the house by the front door to walk briskly down the path. Justin stopped at the arbour, found nothing there, and continued to the south gate. The ground was largely dry, but he bent down to look in the grass to the side. He then walked carefully through the gate, his eyes on the ground. At the edge of the wood he observed something that attracted him and began to stroll down the path, looking on the ground and to the side. In the shade of some larger trees, he paused again: there was softer ground here. His face became sterner.

'Have you a weapon, Andrew?'

In his haste, he had forgotten to add that precaution. Andrew shook his head, but out of a deep pocket he drew the whip-end that he now carried as a matter of course.

Justin nodded. 'We must go on.'

The path led them into the field with the old barn sitting at some distance. It was clear that the grass and the crop had been trodden recently, and both men began to run across the field, with Andrew breaking away to go round the back of the building, and Justin edging towards the front. He stopped to listen, and then stepped into the broken-down entrance. A bucket of water stood in the shadows with a net of hay, mostly eaten. There was a crust of bread in a corner, and the dust revealed clear traces of the wheels of a vehicle. Justin called out, and the groom appeared at the entrance.

'Andrew, what I say to you must go no further. Your mistress deserves your utmost discretion. I shall require your aid. Her predicament is grave. There is good reason to believe that she has been trapped and taken away.'

Andrew's face looked like stone. He had never come across anything of this kind, although he was aware of such as highwaymen and robbers.

'Andrew, you will hasten back to the house, and take Black Diamond and your mistress's chestnut out of the stalls. My own mount may be too weary from this morning. Meet me at the gate to the lane that you see at the end of this field. I shall look a little more carefully down by the road. Please bring charged pistols, and ask Thomas to find my short sword and pass it to you in private.'

Justin came out of the barn and followed the track towards the gate. Shortly afterwards, Andrew disappeared into the woods, back along the path they had traced.

While their horses enjoyed the long grass by the gate on the lane, the two men debated briefly. There could be no doubt that a four-wheeled carriage had been standing in the barn, and that a pair in harness had drawn it to the lane. They had no hope of tracking it on the roads. But if it had been hired for this purpose, then they had to hope that it was taken from a local stable. They were both persuaded that they might make enquiries at Hatherleigh. Justin could at least declare that the carriage had turned out of the field in that direction, and there was a possibility that it had been noticed in the town this morning, even if it had not been hired from there.

They rode off, taking one pistol each. Their destination was The George Inn on the market square, host to the mail coach from Exeter and the stagecoaches from Plymouth. Andrew had passed the time of day with the ostler, Tom Metherell, amicably enough over the last months since residing at Chittesleigh, and Justin knew the innkeeper to greet at least. They rode up the street in the town quietly, and went through the arch into the yard of The George. It was hot and quiet in there, with only the shuffling of post-horses in the stalls and a whistling from the hayloft. The ostler poked his head out from the loft.

'Good day to you, sirs. What might I do for you?'

'If you'd step down, Tom, squire here would like a word.'

Tom took hold of a beam and swung to the ground in front of them. 'It's quicker than the steps,' he said with a grin. He dusted off his hands. 'Now, what can I do for you, sir?'

Justin had been looking behind some barn doors. 'You keep a carriage for hire, then, Tom, am I right? Would it take just a pair, or am I mistaken?'

'Ay, Mister Wentworth, sir, you're right on that. Right pair of nags, and the coach ain't much. It sits in there doing nought most often, but this gentleman — from upcountry, he was — and his man took it off not so long back.'

'It has a nick in the front right tire, Tom, the one that's narrower than the other,' said Justin. 'Am I right? You would have seen those things.'

Tom looked at him shrewdly. 'Yes, it happens I did, Mister Wentworth. But...'

'Never mind how I know. Have you seen the gentleman again, Tom?'

'No, I have not. But, well, it is strange; his man was in again just now, wanting a stirrup leather for the gentleman's horse. Horse is standing in the stall — a bay, it is. By my reckoning, he's one of old Tremlett's in Okey, better than most, true, but still a hack. Trust old Tremlett's harness to be worn through and rickety.'

'If the horse is here, Tom, where is the man, would you say?' asked Andrew.

Tom snorted. 'He'll be over at the New Inn, on the other side of square. He'll catch it when he goes back.' Tom shot a glance at the squire. 'If you're wanting him for something, Mister Wentworth, Kit's his name and he has an old green coat with buttons, sir, and a wart on his cheek. Got a hair sticking out of it, and all. Cornishman, I'll be bound. Now, with respect, sir, a coach from Bideford will be in shortish...'

He need not have troubled himself. Justin was out of the yard, leaving the horses tied up at the side, with Andrew close behind him.

When it came to it, Justin strode in through the front door of the New Inn, giving Andrew time to work his way round the back. The man looked up as Justin walked towards him, pushed his jug away, and thrust a leg past his companion on the bench. As he slid round the end of the bench, Andrew put his arm through his and propelled him onto a settle against the wall. The man tried to rise, but Andrew pushed him back and lifted the whip-end into sight from his deep pocket. The fellow began to protest, but Justin leant forward and spoke quietly into his face.

'Transportation for you, my man, or worse if there is any harm done, and God help you then, besides. So you had better spill it now, and quickly, or the constable will have my leave to thrash it out of you. Any lies and we'll take you round the back here ourselves. I'll give you five minutes to tell it all.'

A little longer than that and the constable had walked him down, taking a back street to avoid the gossips, and put him under lock and key. The Plymouth stagecoach, hot from the twisting road from Bideford and Torrington, was trailing up the hill at Hatherleigh as two horses swung out of The George and passed it on the way down to the river and the Exeter Road. The man had said Jacobstowe, and that there would be a lane leading to a half-built hunting lodge and an odd-shaped gatehouse fronting it. Once down the hill and by the river, their horses were urged into a canter, the dust partly concealing them as they rode on.

Arabella heard the footsteps approaching. She also heard the lock turning and indiscernible words, muttered by a male voice. The door opened inwards, but he stopped on the threshold.

She had placed the low, faded screen opposite to the door, and hung her gown loosely from it, in what she hoped was a careless way.

'Well, well, I'll be damned! Better than a moll! When they fall, they roll — it is an old saying. Come out, come out! I'll see you now, strumpet...'

She could smell the alcohol on Tregothen's breath from behind the door. As he stepped into the room, she raised the bottle and hit him with all her strength on what she hoped would be the top of his head. She held the smashed drinking glass by its stem in her other hand, as a last resort. He collapsed onto the floor. The bottle was unbroken, its ruby-red contents flowing out over the boards. She could see the spreading bruise on his temple. He might be dead. She stepped over him and ran out of the door, into the sunlight.

Her instinct was to keep running. She had no idea where, and she was dressed solely in her petticoat. Her shoes, at least, were robust, since she had been walking. How far would running take her? The broken glass slipped from her hand as she looked around. To her left, the carriageway led from what must surely be a gatehouse — she had dimly perceived it as a tollhouse before — up to a building which had scaffolding attached to one end and a light portico at the front, reached by steps. That much she could see immediately. To the right, there was a lane, only a few paces away. If she could find a horse... A hand touched her arm. She swung round violently, but the young woman caught her raised arm and lowered it before releasing her.

'Follow me,' she said in a quiet voice. She beckoned, raising a finger to her lips. 'Quick, before he comes round.' She led Arabella towards the house, which was only half-finished. 'The master's man, Kit, is still in the town. He should have been back, but he ain't. I ain't got a dress I can give you, but you can have his coat to wrap round. Best for you to hide or skip off. He'll be the devil when he wakes.'

Arabella stood by the steps of the portico, stunned. So she asked the only question that came into her mind. 'A horse? Is there a horse?'

'Dick has the horse. That's the only one, besides the ones that pull the coach.'

'A pair, or four in harness?' asked Arabella. The woman hesitated. Arabella's tone became shrill with anxiety. 'Two or four, woman? It's important.'

'Just two.'

'Where? Where are they, for heaven's sake?'

'Here, I'll show you.' They walked quickly around the side of the house, and there at the rear was a newly built stable, haunting Arabella grotesquely with a glimpse of what she had wanted for Chittesleigh. Her vision swam briefly, and the woman put out a hand to her.

'You all right, miss? He said it were a game, and you were tricking... If I'd a thought...'

'I do not care what you thought. And do not dare to talk about me. Help me get the horses out. Why did he leave them in harness? A mad man.'

The horses shuffled forwards, and the carriage creaked. There was no saddle. She would have to take the carriage. God help her if she put it in the ditch. She had only driven her father's phaeton, which was far lighter.

'Now, get me that coat. It will have to do. Run, woman!'

Arabella stood at the horses' heads and began to tremble. At any moment, he might come round the corner. She looked around. A pitchfork, leaning against the wall. On a block, a hoof-pick. The woman came back, red in the face.

'Here it is. It ain't nothing much...'

'Hold their heads. Just hold the leather, there, on the side of their head. They won't bite.' Arabella put on the man's coat, which was long on her. The rest would have to do. The hoof-pick went into a pocket of the coat. She climbed onto the box and took up the reins, wrapping her hands into them.

'Which way is the village? Stand off from the horses and answer me! Which way? Right or left?'

'I don't know. It's right out of here, that's for sure.'

Arabella clenched her jaw and tried to fight down the terror that had come over her at the prospect of driving the carriage past the gatehouse and on to the lane. 'Now, listen to me,' she said to the woman. 'You had best leave. Go out the back of this hell house and away. I hope I never see you again.'

Arabella never knew how she had driven past the room in which she believed Tregothen was still lying injured or even dead, and turned out onto the road and steered the vehicle past the ditches on either side of the country lane. Nor did she recall why she had chosen one direction over another at the end of the lane, or if she had seen the church that she now realised would have been visible at Jacobstowe, a possible marker to her. She remembered feeling both hot and cold, waves of sickness passing through her as she made the long journey through the trees overhanging the road.

She slowed as she saw two riders ahead of her in the distance, and her heart threatened to burst out of her body as she saw them spur. Panic took hold as she pulled the carriage over to the side, tumbled down from the box and ran headlong into the woods. She stumbled and fell, tearing her leg on brambles, stood up and ran again.

Justin saw the carriage first, and he and Andrew urged on their horses. The figure on the box was wearing a greatcoat but no hat, presumably because it was still hot even in the shade of the woods. Justin could see that whoever it was had seen them and was pulling the coach over to one side of the road. He motioned to Andrew to slow the pace while they watched. The coachman suddenly climbed down, and Andrew looked at Justin as the figure ran off into the woods. A word only, and they dug their heels in and broke into a gallop. They swung in alongside the carriage, Andrew bending down to pull open the door while Justin sat back, levelling the barrel of his pistol at the darker interior. It was empty.

Justin took a moment to picture the running figure, and a strange kind of sadness crept across his features. He swung down from Arabella's horse, threw the reins to Andrew, went to the edge of the wood and listened. He could hear the figure crashing through the woods, coming round to his right. He ran back along the road and headed into the wood further along, down a narrow animal trail.

It was matter of moments. They came face to face along a broader track, and Justin saw Arabella with blood on her face and scratches on her arm, in a torn dress. If there had been a coat, she was wearing it no longer. Her eyes were feverishly bright. He stepped slowly towards her, letting his arms hang down by his sides and turning his palms outwards, in that age-old gesture of harmlessness. For an instant, peacefulness spread over her face; but then her mouth drew tight, and she raised her right hand. She was holding something that looked like a knife.

A wave of pity and anger swept through him as her eyes searched his. Slowly, she loosened her grip, and the ring of the hoof-pick hung on one finger and then fell on the ground.

Justin reached out a hand, and after hesitating, Arabella's fingers traced a pattern on his palm. He took her other hand gently in his and moved closer. He could feel the warmth of her breath, and watched as her eyes flitted across his face in recognition.

'I am yours still,' she said.

'My dearest, my darling.' His voice was a whisper as they clung together.

CHAPTER XXIX: Guèvremont HOLDS THE CARDS

Fourrier had released him a little early for his meeting with the *bourgeois*, but after looking outside Gilles had ducked back in, since it was raining heavily, and he had nowhere in particular that he wanted to go. So he sat in the kitchen, chatting to Bernard when he was available, coming and going as he did. With the cook's permission, he took some of the lemonade that was standing in a covered jug in the pantry. Gaëlle dallied briefly at the back door, taking the basket from her young man from the bakery, and ribbing him that some of the pastries had got a little damp. But after no more than a minute or two the cook ran off a few choice words to Gaëlle that had her shutting the door and putting an end to the cooing, which Gilles had studiously tried to ignore.

Bernard came back in again and tipped him the wink about upstairs, and he got up and made his way towards the study. He was sure he could hear voices, so he stood back, staring absent-mindedly at the intricate pattern on one of the large and totally useless vases in the hallway, about which he had shared a joke with Leroux once while they were waiting. They agreed that objects of that kind were put there solely to get knocked over and cause an almighty fuss. Leroux was not such a bad sort, and Gilles did not forget that he had put paid to some *connards* from Saint-Domingue who had come after Héloïse. There were times when Gilles ached for her, although he knew it was wrong and could only lead one way.

He put his ear to the study door. He must have been mistaken about the sound of voices, because it was silent now. He tapped. Nothing. He gently opened the door and peered in. The desk where Guèvremont usually sat was empty. Then the voices came again, so he tip-toed out and across the passage, and put his ear to the door of the salon. He heard the rapid footsteps only just in time, and fell back for Guèvremont's daughter to come swirling past him, a blur of pink and yellow, her face flushed. She glared at him, but then sobbed and swept to the staircase, pushing past poor Marguerite, her maid. As usual, Marguerite was too meek to do anything but follow her.

This did not bode well. Now he remembered, the *bourgeois* had said it would be a meeting in the salon, not the study, so there was nothing for it but to push the door back, disregard the perfume, and face whatever was coming. His distant hope was that it would be banishment to Kergohan for life.

Laurent Guèvremont was standing by the window, his hand resting limply on one of the ties that held back the long curtains.

Gilles took a deep breath. 'I believe you wanted to see me, sir?'

Guèvremont tapped the toe of his right shoe on the floor, put both hands behind his back, and swung round to face the awkward young man. He looked him up and down, then his eyes came to rest on his face. Gilles could have sworn that the *bourgeois* was looking at his hair again: it made him extremely tense, but there was nothing he could do about it.

'Ah, yes, Gilles, do come in. Come in, and be good enough to close the door behind you — there's a good fellow.'

It did not bode well. But Gilles did as he was told, since it had proved to be the surest way to keep out of trouble for as long as possible.

'Now, come and sit down with me, Gilles. The rain has brought us a cooler spell of weather, and the room is comfortable. I thought we should be more relaxed here than in the study.'

The salon was indeed more comfortable, although it seemed to have failed to soothe Joséphine, who had clearly been distressed when she had passed Gilles in the hall.

'That's right, make yourself at home in here. We shall have to add a card table. You do like card-play, I presume? Mind you, I shall have it only for sous. The young women of respectable backgrounds like an innocent game. Yes, move that aside. Gaëlle can clear it in a moment.'

Gilles had knocked his shin against the small side-table.

'Yes, that will do. Leave it now, Gilles. We must concentrate.'

Guèvremont leant back in his chair and put on his most serious face, one that he often used to slip in something that was not to the listener's advantage. Sitting quietly through boring discussions let you observe such things; but Gilles recognised that you only really noticed when it was someone else who was being duped. He determined to miss nothing.

'My boy, I appreciate that this has been a difficult period for you.' Guèvremont now smiled sympathetically. 'A great deal has finally emerged, at my instigation, about what we can only call the mystery of your origins. Again, at my instigation, you have heard from those who were closest to … the events of that time, and have yourself been able to ask questions. Sadly, we remain no clearer about many things, and you can be assured of my sincerity when I say that you have my full sympathy. We have lost your mother, and we have failed to find your father. But it has not been for want of concern or effort. I can safely say that all of us are distressed by the past. But...'

Gilles had his own suspicions about a number of things, although he was far from being able to substantiate them. He waited.

'...we must now look to the future, and take firm steps to establish you in the eyes of the world.'

Here Guèvremont came to a halt, as he had done in his previous interview with his daughter at a crucial moment. Even with his hardened experience of negotiation, he tensed for a reaction. There was none. In fact, Gilles had the nerve to raise an eyebrow in inquiry. Guèvremont swallowed involuntarily at this unexpected and unnerving vision of what might well be himself as a younger man.

'It is my intention to make you my ward. I have undertaken as much to my cousin, *Madame* Sempronie Wentworth — who now lives in England — to act in your interest on behalf of our family. This wardship will be until you come of age. It is then very likely that you will be granted possession of the Manor of Kergohan, as my cousin wishes, at a time when you may have property in your own name. Until then, you may receive some charge of it from me. To that end, as you are aware, I have been preparing you slowly, and Fourrier gives me a heartening report on your progress.'

Well, good for him, thought Gilles. All that time spent on mouthing religious platitudes in his presence had been well spent. Yet it was true that he had learnt a great deal from Fourrier, although much of it had little to do with the lived reality of soil, crops and livestock, mixed in with rain and shine. But that could come, and there was Daniel, and the others who knew the ground at Kergohan over a long time.

Guèvremont cleared his throat. 'I can see that you are impressed, and probably satisfied. You will be my *pupille de tutelage*, and with your indulgence we shall walk now into the town to visit the notary who will begin to draw up the appropriate documents, and explain such matters to you as you may need to know. My daughter has been informed.' He cleared his throat again. 'I must make it clear to you that being a ward is not a form of legal adoption. I believe that my daughter was not completely clear about this. I may make over a land-title to you as a gift, but it is not an inheritance. I resolutely intend that, one way or another, my daughter will be the beneficiary of the greater part of my estate, in the fullness of time.'

The *bourgeois* had nothing more to say. Gilles felt an enormous sense of relief. If that was all, then it would hardly keep him awake at night.

Guèvremont stood up. 'Come, then. We shall pay a visit to my tailor. Your present attire will not do for the occasions I have in mind, and for your introduction into society, here and at Pontivy. We must present you well. Here, take my hand.'

Gilles promptly got to his feet and took Guèvremont's outstretched hand. Guèvremont was pleased with the firm grip, but nonetheless found himself unnerved as he looked into the boy's blue eyes, so reminiscent of his own.

'And, of course, we must think of finding you a suitable spouse. We can dismiss thoughts of the titled families now. But there are sound *bourgeois* households, and several of my friends and acquaintances have attractive young daughters. I shall introduce you to them, and I flatter myself that with my standing and reputation you will find that you may take your pick. It is men of our status in society who will be forming the most influential voice in the new France. You will be part of that, my boy — a small part, no doubt, but as an eligible bachelor for a short time and then a married man, you will be influential and respected.'

Gilles was stunned. He had not anticipated this: Kergohan without Héloïse. It was unthinkable.

Guèvremont patted him on the shoulder. 'There, it is all very new and overwhelming. I completely understand. Given time, you will get used to it.'

Gilles did not know what to say. He could imagine Héloïse's beautiful eyes glaring at him.

Joséphine mumbled something to her maid about devotions, and she raised her hand in prohibition when Marguerite offered to step out with her, insisting on privacy. The Église Saint-Gildas was only a short distance away, and time was now pressing. She had not expected the interview with her father, nor the bitter announcements that had been made, with little consideration for her feelings.

She ran down the stairs to the hallway. It was as if her father had ignored all that she had said to him about her hopes and desires, and now that little rat was being placed in front of her. Tears stung her eyes again. What difference did it make for him to be called a ward if he was given Kergohan in front of her? She had been so dutiful to her father and had tried to compensate for the absence of her mother. It was all for nothing. No doubt her father was disappointed that she was a woman, and so the usurper was preferable, favoured as a man. He would no doubt displace her totally in time. It was insufferable, and she could only fear the worst about Nicolas Leroux's application to her father to pay court to her. The harsh truth would emerge this morning, no doubt, to add to her pain. She reached the front door to the house and wrestled with it before Bernard came up behind her and opened it effortlessly.

The rain had stopped. There was something almost indiscreet about walking through the streets alone, even if she had chosen a sombre riding-coat dress topped by a black beaver hat, hardly her usual choice of summer garb. One or two of the older men looked at her, and she caught a pair of them leaning their heads together to exchange a word. Joséphine hurried past. There seemed to be humiliation in everything she did at present, with every possibility of happiness closing down in front of her. It was a relief to reach the church. The clouds had begun to break up and it was growing warm in the summer sun, so the cool of the dark interior was welcome. The acrid smell of guttering candles and the lingering scent of incense was refreshing to her senses, although as she made her way towards the altar she was aware of the onset of a headache. She felt in her reticule for her smelling-bottle, but it had been left behind; there was no more than a handkerchief in the bag.

The pews to the front were empty. Joséphine passed two older women at the rear of the church, one lighting a candle to the image of a saint, the other muttering prayers. Neither had looked at her. A figure came and went in a side chapel; he paused for a moment and then disappeared. A priest, to be expected. She hoped that she was inconspicuous, and that she had the time right. It would be best to bend her head, which indeed suited her mood. She tried to think of appropriate prayers, but her mind was too full of earthly attachments.

She heard his steps. Leroux was a man who could not conceal himself in any setting. For all his humility and occasional shyness, he could never apologise for his presence or his place in the world. Joséphine could hear him approaching from the back of the church, and did not turn round. But like a fool he came into the row of seats behind her, as if that would make their meeting appear casual. This annoyed her in her current state, and she felt a pang that she could not clasp him impulsively, even though he was so close.

'*Mademoiselle*, you are here.' His voice was predictably a whisper, which irritated her even more, as did the emptiness of the statement. She answered more formally than she had intended, and hated herself for it.

'As you see, *monsieur*. I trust that you intend to interrupt my devotions only with the most urgent of matters of importance. The priest will no doubt be attending me soon.'

Which she sincerely hoped he would not. But if Leroux would not sit next to her like a lover should, then the place was left open to others far less desired than he. She could hear those words forming in her head, never to be spoken, but, oh, why was she so resentful?

'Joséphine, I must thank you for affording me this *rendezvous*, for receiving my note to you. It was not as it should have been, but I was constrained. Your man, Bernard, is trustworthy...'

'I do not wish to hear of Bernard. Your choice of the church at least makes our *rendezvous* in some part respectable. Now, if you please, what have you to tell me? And must you sit behind me like some servile acolyte, whispering in my ear?'

There was a rustling noise, and the scraping of wood on the floor, and Leroux edged around to sit next to her. He was wearing his uniform. Was he ever out of it? He placed his hand on hers. 'My darling.'

'But am I yours?' Joséphine withdrew her hand, and then immediately wished she had not done so.

'I spoke to your father. He would have none of my addresses. He would not contemplate an officer for a son-in-law, not of my rank. So…'

'Then there is no future for us. It is over.'

'I am afraid…'

Joséphine inclined her head towards his face and spoke almost inaudibly. 'I am not with child.' She sat back upright and folded her hands in her lap. Her cheeks were flushed. 'You are released from any obligations.'

Leroux was stung into a response, with all the heat of frustration and the terrible uncertainties of their feelings for each other. 'I cannot be free of what rules my heart. You command me…'

She softened. 'But I cannot command my father, Nicolas. We are finished. It has to be so.' The tears were running freely down her cheeks.

Leroux's senses were rioting, the warmth and intoxication of her presence banishing the odours of candlewax and incense into the gloom of the building. With what was almost a delight in the sacrilege, he felt he knew what agony was.

He stood up. His head was throbbing. He had rehearsed the words, yet had clung to the vain hope that he would not need to speak them. His voice was grave, terrible to hear. 'So I had determined. I have applied for, and had accepted by General Hoche, a transfer to the regiments in the north of the country, and on the Rhine. The Republic is sorely pressed there, and in need of able men. I trust I can serve my country well, at the very least. I must take my leave of you, *Mademoiselle*, and wish you all felicity.' But at the end, he could not contain himself. 'I have loved you…!' he burst out, but he corrected himself harshly. 'It has been my great pleasure to have made your acquaintance.'

He could not look at her again. He turned and walked resolutely down the central aisle, and Joséphine heard his footsteps echoing under the portal and then vanishing into the square beyond. She was trembling uncontrollably. She stared up at the large painting of the deposition of Christ, which hung from the reredos above the altar.

CHAPTER XXX: THE SAIL LOFT

A fever had come over Grosjean a week or so into his recovery, and for a while his wound had looked ugly. At times he would shout and lash out, and once in the middle of the night he had got hold of one of the charcoal-burners who was wiping his face, seizing the man in a headlock with a suffocating grip. Fortunately, Grosjean was lying down, so between them the men were able to prise his arm off and get the poor fellow's head out. But Grosjean still muttered and swore, until they managed to cool him down and he fell asleep.

Daniel was summoned from the manor, and he cleaned the wound, talking all the while to Grosjean. He repeated that they should use some of Héloïse's ointment, around it but not in it. After that, Yaelle sat by him day and night, trying to keep him cool and keep his mind straight. Both Babette and Héloïse came up to keep her company, taking it in turns, but also leaving her on her own with him from time to time. It was harrowing to see him in this state, and miserable to fear the worst.

But Grosjean pulled round, miraculously, and they began to joke with him about bringing up the shears to trim his beard. The charcoal-burners brought him down to the village once he was able to walk. Babette sent word to Gilles that Grosjean was coming back, and in her cottage they had had knocked in the keg of cider. He had insisted that he would walk down without support, and indeed he was hardly limping. His right arm was still capable of clasping his friends to him, but for most of the time it was wrapped tightly around Yaelle, who could laugh with him now, although she scolded him about drinking too much. He and Daniel were as thick as thieves, and the men gathered round them both.

Yaelle's sister Erell seemed happy enough. She got a little drunk and came up to Héloïse to kiss her on the cheek, and then in a slurred voice declared, 'We are like sisters now.' She kissed her again several times, and Héloïse saw some of the village girls watching. She thought uncharitably of Judas and the soldiers in the garden at Gethsemane, but then chided herself and left it. She kept hoping to see Gilles appear, but as the hours went by there was still no sign of him. The keg had run dry, and Yaelle wanted to take her husband to their cottage and settle him down before he got himself into a state again.

Ridiculously, Héloïse began to wonder if she had gone too far in the woods with Gilles, with the perfume and the kiss. Perhaps he thought she was thoroughly loose and wanted nothing to do with her. Her mood was not lifted by having Yannic bump up against her, three parts drunk, and she left him quickly and went to find Babette before Erell came looking for her stray. As she sat inside Babette's cottage, Héloïse remembered the day of the two weddings, when Daniel and Babette, and Yaelle and Grosjean had pledged themselves to each other, body and soul. She had held Gilles's hand lightly and told him that they should be like brother and sister, no more than that. She no longer felt that way.

The loft was broad and long, the floor worn smooth from the polishing of rope-shoes and the scrape of canvas. There were eight men and two women, many sitting cross-legged. Coline had a strong wrist, and they had taken her on in the usual kind of way, sink or swim, the master looking severely at her work. After a while he had put her, without explanation, on to sewing up the leech ropes and the cringles, working on the edge of the long canvas. Even with the sailmaker's palm, her hands became sore. She would not stay long at this game. Besides, one of the men was beginning to eye her, and whenever she had that kind of interest it always went badly.

Coline picked up her handkerchief, in which she had her bread and slices of *andouille*, raised her hand to the master, and slipped down the stairs. The quay was heaving with people. There was timber everywhere, the hoists busy and dangerous. The lighters came alongside at the slipways, and there were some women selling, others bending and working on crates. Soldiers lounged and chatted, an idle bunch.

Brest was a narrow port, flanked on its eastern side by the massive bulk of *la bagne*, a monument to imprisonment and forced labour. But ships crowded into the quiet waters, and were de-masted and re-masted, roped and rigged, and provisioned.

The boy Loic came up, swiped a slice of sausage, and sat down next to Coline.

'How's that big canvas smock? Worth all the pain?'

Coline looked at her hands. 'Rough,' she said. 'We should leave. That *connard* I told you about is getting too curious. He may be an agent.'

The boy scoffed. 'What do they know about agents? Still, we don't want him sniffing around.'

'Where is Françoise?'

Loic jerked his thumb up along the quay. 'In and out of the warehouse, fetching and carrying. Rather like me. I doubt if there's many more to come in.'

Coline bit into her bread as she pictured the black-dyed army uniforms that had been unloaded, no doubt in preparation for the French Republic's troops to land abroad. 'No, I doubt it. They're just lying there, stacked up. But they are talking about the end of the year, getting ready by the winter. You can feel it happening.'

Loic nodded. 'Yes, that's what Françoise has heard. She joked to them about mothballs for the uniforms, and they said it wouldn't be that long. The black on them isn't bad.'

The master came to the top of the steps and stared down at them both from a distance.

'God, he's a bastard.' Coline dusted the breadcrumbs from her dress. 'No, that'll have to do. We'll pack up. Tell Françoise. I'll let the English authorities have what we know when we reach Jersey. It's enough. Some of the soldiers have been talking about Ireland, others elsewhere. A regiment in black jackets, landing in the backyard. Sounds mad enough. How many have you counted?'

'About a thousand, Françoise says. Give or take. Winter, eh?'

'A thousand is too small a number for what is going on; there must be more to it than that. Still, I have to get back. Look, Jersey first, and then on to London. All three of us.'

Loic put his head to one side and opened his eyes wide in mock disbelief.

'Don't look at me like that. There is money to be made in London, and where we'll be going all you'll hear around you will be the familiar chatter of the *émigrés*.'

'I thought they were broke...' Loic had to hurl the words after her, because she was off to the sail loft, convinced of everything, as she always was.

CHAPTER XXXI: PICAUD WALKS AWAY

Tregothen had gone by the time Justin and Andrew had ridden back to the gatehouse and the lodge later that day. Justin tossed his wife's gown into the bag he had brought and kicked the stem of the broken glass further into the bushes, but he found nothing else that gave them any help in tracing him.

Eugène and Justin were both convinced that Tregothen was also behind the abduction of Amelia. But when Mrs Fitchett was questioned over the following days about the occupants of the rooms adjoining her own, she denied any knowledge of either of them, let alone any other cove. She kept a respectable house, where young women alone in London might find board and protection, since the world was not to be trusted. As for Artur, his wound needed further attendance. She took the two guineas offered her to defray the costs of the physician, and placed them securely in her own pocket. When all was said and done, his mistake had been an honest one.

After his urgent dash to London, Justin had stayed on at the house at New End for two more days, before returning on the mail coach to be once again by Arabella's side, whom his mother Sempronie was now attending. Eugène took rooms at an inn on the London road in Hampstead village, and it was agreed between them that he would accompany Miss North and Amelia when the latter was considered fit to travel. Poor Amelia was put into the care of Caroline North, and indeed it would have been a bold man or woman who would have denied her that charge. Mrs Claydon brought her daughter down from the other house to help her. With the greatest reluctance, Miss North had agreed to keep Martha on beyond the return from London, since the price of her dismissal might be the spread of unwanted rumours.

Amelia gave cause for worry. Natural though it was for her to sleep deeply through exhaustion after the distressing events, she was also subject to what Mrs Claydon would privately describe as 'fits'. At such times, although awake, her mind was wandering, and there was serious concern until the redoubtable Mr Wilson, the apothecary in whom Mrs Claydon had an almost religious faith, brought reassurance by stating that in his considered opinion, these were the effects of laudanum administered unwisely. Miss North was quick to accept this judgment, not only because it seemed a very likely explanation, but because she did not wish to dwell in front of the apothecary on how that mistake might have come to pass. Mr Wilson recommended broth, rest, and warm bedclothes, to prevent the onset of a fever.

Eugène visited the house at New End frequently but had to content himself with sitting in the drawing room, asking after Amelia's health and receiving answers that made him want to go up to her side. He had been completely astonished to hear from Justin about the appalling abduction of Arabella. Understandably, Justin had glossed over much of the detail. Nonetheless, he could be sure from his friend's manner that a timely intervention had secured his wife from enduring harm, and in the embrace the men exchanged, each could feel the other's profound relief.

It remained essential to maintain a strict confidentiality, especially once all had returned to Devon. Justin soon rode over to his wife's father, Sir Francis Wollaston, and faced his fury over the lack of proper guardianship of his most precious daughter, and in her condition too. Sir Francis had eventually calmed and even taken Justin in his arms, tearful and full of admiration for the tracking of such an execrable scoundrel. He agreed to write to his daughter, and to postpone a visit in person until she was no longer bedridden.

Arabella had confided all that had passed to her husband as he sat next to her, holding her hand. She felt that he deserved to know it all, and even if some part of the account might make him enraged, there was nothing that might make him ashamed. At that statement, he had buried his head in her hair and told her he could never be ashamed of her, and they had embraced with passion. She had eventually pushed him away with tears in her eyes and told him, laughingly, that he should contain himself, for they had all to gain and nothing to lose.

Caroline North and Amelia came back to Devon and to Chittesleigh a week after those dire events, accompanied by Eugène. Caroline was most moved to see Arabella seemingly in such fine spirits. Amelia's mother Sempronie was there to greet her daughter, and it was a tearful occasion, with Grace so overcome that she had to retire to her room to give way to her feelings. A chaise arrived for Miss North, who was to return to her brother in Cornwall and bring him the latest news.

Colonel North would be keen to join himself to the list of visitors in the coming weeks, and not long after Sir Francis. It was assumed that both of these, along with Justin and Eugène, would sit down together to decide what might be done to hunt down Tregothen and bring him to justice, if he were still in the country. Eugène had tentatively shared his suspicion with Justin that Tregothen had been intending an abduction by sea to complete his hell-raking scheme. So it was not beyond possibility that he might have used the same ship lying in the Pool of London to make his escape. The search for him had to be handled with caution and discretion, but they would be relentless about it, notwithstanding.

Eugène found himself secretly cheered to see the state of Amelia's health. But from the day of her arrival, her mother and Arabella monopolised her attention, and with the maids were her constant companions. When secluded, Amelia was full of delight and admiration for Arabella's rounded figure, and placed her hands on it gently, until she was told light-heartedly that if she were so minded, she should look to it herself. Arabella regretted this remark as soon as it had left her lips. Eugène had to make do with polite conversation and occasional games in the drawing room, which he played with a good spirit, if only to take the opportunity to glance at Amelia, and experience once again that urge to protect her that had surged through his veins in London.

Yet there were moments when Amelia fell silent or a distant look came over her features, and her lips trembled. At other times, words would fail her, and she would look about her as if searching for a familiar face, although she was surrounded by them. Eugène wanted to be alone with her, to hold her hand and become that mysterious person whom she was missing. But in this company his heart often misgave him, and he became despondent. He knew he must soon return to London and make an attempt to set his own livelihood in order. That would mean meeting his father, in the busy enclave of the endlessly argumentative French *émigrés* in Marylebone. It was such a drastic change from Devon and Chittesleigh, and he feared that it would, step by step, draw him in and away from Amelia.

The day before he was to leave, he made every effort to find her alone, or to be able to ask her if she would care to take a stroll in the gardens or along the paths. But it was all to no avail. Amelia was with her mother and Justin all morning in the study, and Eugène could hear them laughing from time to time, while he attempted to write a letter to his father. In the afternoon, the whole party decided on a walk through the grounds, since Arabella was determined that they should not be fearful. After dinner, there were card games and the piano, which Arabella played so well, and singing from her and Justin, a talent that Eugène had rarely seen his friend exercise. He himself was so disconcerted by the end of the day that he repeatedly declined invitations to step up to the instrument.

The following morning, after packing the little that he had into a bag and paying some attention to his dress and hair, Eugène went down to breakfast. Justin was lingering over his newspaper and awaiting his wife. The food tasted like ashes to Eugène, and he kept wiping the moisture on his palms onto his napkin. Even the coffee that Thomas came to pour for him failed to raise his spirits. He muttered a word or two to Justin and went in search of Amelia. She was not in the garden, despite the fine weather, and he knew that she did not go far on her own. He looked into the study, but it was empty. As he reached one corner of it, he heard voices coming through the side-door into the drawing room. The female voice was hers, but he did not recognise the man's.

Eugène slipped out of the study, not in his best humour. He had heard no mention of another guest, and this was no farmer or tradesman. It was a young man's voice, cultivated and light in tone. He found it impossible to discipline himself out of a sudden jealousy, and at some risk to his dignity he hid himself just to the side of the staircase, facing the main door into the drawing room. The voices rose and fell, and he heard a little laughter. He could just pick up that there were footsteps coming across to the door, which opened as a young man said,

'No, I shall show myself out, Miss Amelia. I need no ceremony.' The young man turned to face her. 'With your permission, I shall visit you again from Exeter. We may have more news from the Society there. Good day to you, Miss Amelia.' He bowed slightly and walked to the front door of the house, where he let himself out. He was wearing very plain clothes.

Amelia had disappeared from view into the room. Picaud crossed quickly, rapped lightly on the open door, and walked in. Now it came to the point, he did not know what to say. They faced each other at some distance.

'Oh, *Monsieur* Picaud. This is a surprise.' Amelia moved swiftly over to the window and made as if to wave at the receding figure of the young man, but dropped her hand. 'He is not looking.'

Eugène was now completely at a loss, so he said the first thing that came into his head. 'A polite young man.'

'Yes, most polite. And assiduous in his attentions. He will hardly let me sit down without running round to put the chair under me. Still, he is a dear boy.' She spoke to Eugène conspiratorially. 'He would not thank me for that, you know. Calling him a dear boy.'

'Yes. An acquaintance from London, I presume?'

'He is indeed, Eugène —' at last, his personal name — 'Mr Richard Bevington, from the Society of Friends in Lombard Street. He is an abolitionist, you see. As are many Friends, as they call themselves. He has come on a tour to abolitionists and Friends in the meeting houses in Exeter and Plymouth, and he thought to visit me here. It is very kind.'

'And he came unannounced?' Eugène could not help sounding resentful, no doubt a glaring contrast to the mild, peaceful soul who had just had the benefit of Amelia's attention.

'Oh, yes. Quite unannounced.' She came across to him and held one of his hands in both of hers. 'And now, to what do I owe this pleasure?'

'To your adorable self.' Had he said that? The words were on the tip of his tongue. 'I wished to speak with you … before I leave, that is. I am leaving after noon today.'

'Oh, dear.' She seemed suddenly confused and dropped his hand. 'I had foolishly hoped to have your company here for many more days.'

'I am afraid that will not be possible.' Could he be more of a dolt? He saw the precipice in front of him and tumbled straight over the edge. 'I love you. I love and adore you.' He had blurted it out, but then words failed him.

The colour rose in her cheeks, and she hesitated. 'What … what did you say?' Her hand went to her forehead, and he regretted succumbing to that overwhelming impulse. She could not understand, as she was; she had not yet recovered enough. 'I … I know you as my saviour. You were the person who…'

'I have tried to protect you, yes, that is true. I know I am…'

'Forgive me, I am feeling faint.' Amelia placed her hand on the back of one of the armchairs. 'I may not need protecting. But you…'

Eugène was mortified. He had not realised just how inept he was with women. His sympathetic nature carried him so far, but then it deserted him. 'I am so sorry. I shall send your maid in to you. I should not have spoken. I bid you farewell, Amelia, Miss Wentworth.'

Had there been a pit full of venomous snakes in the hall, he would gladly have stepped into it. He could not bear to tear himself away, but he did so. In sweeping up his bag and nursing his aching heart, he managed to forget all about the maid and indeed his good friend and host as he left.

Amelia too had forgotten about the maid. There was minted water in a decanter on the side-table, and she poured it into a glass and drank a little. A thought occurred to her. She went over to the writing table, sat down, and took out a paper and a pen, which she dipped in the inkwell.

She bent her head and carefully wrote 'Eugène' on the paper, placing a dot after it. She thought for a moment, and then added the accent to make him French. That seemed to satisfy her, and she made to lay down the pen, but then a further thought struck her. Pursing her lips, she slowly added beneath his name the words '*Mon Amour*'.

HISTORICAL NOTE

After the failure of the British-backed invasion by a French royalist army at Quiberon in summer 1795 (background to the first book in this series, *The Baron Returns*), the French Republic took a decision to land forces on the coast of the British Isles, aiming particularly to link up with the United Irishmen in a rebellion.

Preparations were made by the French at the Breton seaport of Brest throughout 1796, and involved the strange, seemingly whimsical stratagem of English uniforms that had been captured at Quiberon being dyed from red to black.

The expedition set sail in December 1796, but was blocked and dispersed by adverse winter weather. The main French force was sent, without success, against the coast of south-west Ireland, and returned home. But a small, later landing was made at the Welsh port of Fishguard in February 1797 by members of this bizarre 'Black Legion', clothed in the dyed uniforms.

The invading soldiers and irregulars surrendered to a British commander on the following day.

A NOTE TO THE READER

Dear Reader,

I hope you have enjoyed reading *Lady at the Lodge*, which is the third book in The Wentworth Family Regency Saga Series. If you have come to this novel first, then the previous titles are *The Baron Returns* and *Heir to the Manor*, which are also available through Sapere Books.

Devon and rural Brittany are the settings for the two manors which feature in the saga, and I have great affection for both regions, which are very familiar to me. They are linked in the persons of the Wentworth family, who have the connection with Brittany on the female side, but each manor gathers a range of characters around it who form part of the developing story. In between lies the stretch of ocean that we call the Channel, which so often in history has been an active player in the events that take place either side of it.

Many periods exercise a strong fascination on readers, and most of those then attract fiction to them, as imagination joins itself to curiosity about the large-scale struggles that occupy most of the history books and programmes. The late eighteenth century and the early nineteenth have repeatedly drawn authors to them, largely because of the abilities of one woman, Jane Austen, who wrote not about history but about the world of society as she found it around her. Her choice was to look at personal attraction between the sexes in a kind of detail that had been very rare before, providing the reader with insight into contradictory and turbulent emotions, the constraints imposed by money or the lack of it, and the negotiation of difficulties by wit or with the help of a good dose of luck.

This period is retrospectively known as the Napoleonic Wars, although Napoleon himself is something of a late entrant on that scene, which leads up to the grand finale at Waterloo. My choice has been the earlier part of that time, in which the revolution in France has imposed the Republic and war with Britain has been declared. But the narrative I pursue is one of continuing if fading connections between the two countries, and the legacy of those connections. It is a world in which many players may still speak both French and English, and some of them Breton as well, which is a close relative of Welsh and Cornish. In the background to the saga also lies the conflict between the rural Breton population in some party and the new Republic, which like all civil wars was cruel. Characters in the saga become caught up in it, while others, notably those living in larger towns such as Pontivy and Auray, might continue with their lives and advance themselves and their families.

The French filmmaker Jean Renoir, son of the impressionist painter, coined the phrase '*tout le monde a ses raisons*', and while a novelist may avoid examining the motives that help to create the great events of history, romantic historical fiction will be drawn to those of its warm, living characters. What a saga presents is a relatively broad canvas, on which there are pictured not just intriguing portraits of two lovers but the lives of a number of men and women linked by blood or friendship. This larger cast is often bound together not just by love and longing, but by the overwhelming power of events, duties and responsibilities, and at times hounded by malice and greed.

So, in a saga, while characters return in each narrative, they come into focus at particular times, as their story grows in strength or reaches a crisis — and as they themselves grow, understand their desires better and face the obstacles that lie in their path. What Jean Renoir might also have said, in his insight and wisdom, is that 'nothing is ever the same', and so I have found in writing that characters are as exposed to the failure of plans and expectations as they are to the unpredictability and uncertainties of what happens to themselves or to others.

In the earlier novels of this saga, the action visited not just the rural parts of Devon and Brittany but also the busy port of Plymouth and its naval yards, known as the Dock. In this novel, Amelia and Eugène are caught up in London, in two very different parts: the open spaces and village comforts of Hampstead and its heath in the north, and the busy streets of Holborn and of the Pool of London. As a novelist, I love to tread the same ground as my characters, and there are few locations in the novels that may not still be visited, even if a sighting of the manors of Chittesleigh and Kergohan — as it should — ultimately remains elusive…

Do take a look at my website and blog, if you have a moment: **grahamley.com**. I hope to meet you again there.

If you enjoyed the novel I would be grateful if you could spare a few minutes to post a review on **Amazon** and **Goodreads**.

My mother was the romantic novelist Alice Chetwynd Ley, and her Regency novels may be found at:

saperebooks.com/authors/alice-chetwynd-ley.

Graham Ley

Sapere Books is an exciting new publisher of brilliant fiction and popular history.

To find out more about our latest releases and our monthly bargain books visit our website:
saperebooks.com